Sword
of
The Turul

Based on an Incredible True Story

Catherine Eva Schandl

This book is based on an incredible true story, now told for the first time. What did a "group" led by British intelligence, a church in a cave, and a missing Swedish diplomat all have in common in World War II Hungary – and why did most of the players in this drama disappear? Shocking facts are uncovered about war-torn Budapest, British intelligence, and SMERSH – and how they were all connected.

A 60 year old deception is exposed...

In memory of
my father, Karoly William Schandl,
my grandfather, Karoly Schandl Senior, and
my grandmother, Terezia Schandl.

"Ego Sum Via Veritas Et Vita."

TABLE OF CONTENTS

BOOK TERMINOLOGY

ABWEHR = German intelligence agency from 1921 to 1944.

ARROW CROSS = Hungarian fascist party, Nazi allies.

AVO = *Államvédelmi Osztály*. Hungarian Communist security (secret) police, run by Soviet advisors (1945-1956).

CHEKA = Soviet state security, which evolved into NKVD.

GENDARME = Military police.

I.S. (S.I.S.) = *Secret Intelligence Service/MI6,* U.K.

ISLD = *Inter-Service Liaison Department* (SIS/MI6). U.K. military/secret intelligence.

KGB = agency of Soviet security, intelligence, and secret police from 1954 to 1991.

MAGYAR = Hungarian

NKVD = Soviet secret police, which later evolved into the KGB.

OKH = *Országos Központi Hitelszövetkezet.* Hungarian National Credit Cooperative (dissolved by the Soviets in 1948).

OSS = *Office of Strategic Services.* U.S. intelligence agency which evolved into the CIA in 1947.

RED ARMY = Soviet army/military.

SMERSH = *Death to Spies.* Soviet military counter-intelligence from 1943 to 1946.

WHITEHALL = refers to the administration of the government of the U.K. (United Kingdom).

This is an official document from the Hungarian Defense Department Archives. It proves that the date of Karoly Schandl's official arrest as a "prisoner-of-war" by the Red Army was on **December 8, 1944** and that his imprisonment in the Soviet Union was for 11 years *(from 1950 on, he was held as a "British spy").*

MAGYAR HONVÉDSÉG
KÖZPONTI IRATTÁR

/ .számú példány

Nyt. szám: 331/1323/11/Kné

1994 -08- 31

Canada

Tárgy: Hadifogsági idő
igazolása

A fenti parancsnokság birtokában levő iratok szerint: néhai Dr. Schandl Károly (1912. Menyhárt Teréz) mint főhadnagy

1944.12.08. - 1950.08.01-ig hadifogolyként,
1950.08.02. - 1956.05.18-ig elitéltként tartózkodott a Szovjetunióban.

Budapest, 1994. augusztus 2r -n

A távollévő parancsnok helyett:

/Bíró Géza őrnagy/
parancsnokhelyettes

Készült: 2 példányban
Egy példány: 1 lap
Itsz.: 2104

8

PROLOGUE

Lubyanka Prison, Soviet Union – mid-1940s

"Death to spies – Death to the English spies."

The loudspeaker outside was repeating the same sentences again. He would not know enough Russian until later years, when he would finally realize what those words had meant.

The Soviets had been playing mind games since the beginning. He would never give in. The NKVD, the SMERSH would never break him. They would never find out about the network. The Red Army had already proven themselves to be no more than thugs, arresting him with the Dutchman, without justification. They had all been working with the Allies, not against them. He wondered how many others they had arrested.

And what about his parents and those he had been hiding in Budapest – a Jewish school friend and the British agent, both of whom were disguised as Paulist priests? He had not had enough time to bid anyone farewell, it had all happened so fast. He could not have known that at the time, the Soviets were denying any knowledge of his whereabouts, as well as the whereabouts of the Dutchman, the Diplomat, and others who had met with a similar fate. To the outside world, they had all vanished without a trace.

He leaned against the wall and closed his eyes, exhausted from having been sleep deprived – another one of their sinister tactics. Eventually the door opened and the Dutchman was shoved back inside the tiny, windowless cell. Karoly ignored the monotonous voice on the loudspeaker, which seemed to have grown louder. When the stony-faced guard had once more shut the door, he nodded at the Dutchman, who sat down. "They will have to release us as soon as the war is over."

Unfortunately, such was not his destiny, for he would be doomed to endure the destitute Soviet prison system for the next eleven years, while the Dutchman and the Swedish Diplomat would be even less fortunate …

CHAPTER 1
SECRETS

Canada - January 2005

The museum was relatively quiet as Kati Schandl walked into the front lobby, glancing at the patrons already inside. An elderly couple made their way past her, toward the coat check, and a few employees were engrossed in conversation near the ornate Christmas tree, which had not been taken down. It now served as a showpiece for the museum main floor, which otherwise might have been as somber as the gray clouds outside. A thin middle-aged man seated on one of the benches stood up and nodded in her direction. His suit and demeanor were definitely European. Kati's eyes met his and they each extended a hand at the same time.

"Ms. Schandl, thank you for agreeing to meet me. As I mentioned on the telephone, I am Marcel Lambert of the International War Studies Project. I have come from Geneva, Switzerland."

Kati smiled slightly as he released her hand. "You seem to have recognized me sooner than I recognized you."

"The photographs, of course. I have seen some photographs of your father when he was a younger man and there is a definite resemblance around the eyes. Is there a place here where we might speak privately?"

Kati indicated the bench. "Since it's Friday evening, I don't expect there will be many more visitors." The truth of the matter was, she wasn't at all certain if she should even have agreed to meet with the historian.

"I understand your apprehension." Together they walked toward the dark wooden bench and sat down. He folded his long brown cloth coat and placed it between them.

Kati decided to keep her coat on. She had not been certain what to expect.

"Have you been contacted about your father's wartime activities before?"

"Not really, but he was once misquoted by a Hungarian journalist – after his death. Ironically, in the same article the journalist even got the date of his death wrong."

"I was very sorry to hear that he passed away in 1990, before I had a chance to review his case."

She turned to Lambert and observed him with thoughtful hazel eyes. "Would you mind telling me more about yourself and what kind of research it is that you do?" In their brief telephone conversation the previous day, he had mentioned that he was a Swiss historian who was researching a matter involving her father. He had called her mother's house – where she happened to be staying while her mother was away on a scientific ocean cruise halfway across the world – and she had agreed to meet with him, to further discuss what he referred to as "the case." His angle, however, was still something of a mystery.

"I am the current director of the International War Studies Project based in Geneva, Switzerland and hold a doctorate in history from Oxford University. Our project encourages the sharing of information and sometimes the solving of important 'mysteries.' It is affiliated with the university where I lecture."

"Mysteries?"

Marcel Lambert pursed his thin lips and then explained. "My current … area of research involves former prisoners of the Soviet Union, particularly the high profile ones, hence my interest in your father, Karoly Schandl. We have a file on him, with photographs, significant records, and yet something is missing."

The elderly couple, now wearing their coats, smiled at the pair, and then pushed open the glass doors, disappearing into the dark evening.

Kati watched the doors slowly fall back into place. "He was a lawyer in Hungary who helped Jewish friends during World War II. He was arrested by the Soviets and put in Lubyanka, Lefortovo, and then Vladimir prison. He spent a total of 11 years and 10 months in the Soviet prison system, 4 years of which were in solitary confinement."

"Very tragic, and I am sure it is difficult to think of those times, but did he say anything more? He was high profile and I am trying to determine why. Was it because of something he did or knew?"

"My father was a prisoner of the Soviets who ended up here in Canada, where he became a university professor, got married, and raised a few kids. There's really nothing more to his story than that."

The Swiss historian was adamant. "Ah, but there is. You see, he was given a number and that is how he was known in the jail – as a number. Numbers were only assigned to a few dozen prisoners in the entire Soviet prison system every year and I am wondering what he might have done or known to fall into that category. Prisoners with numbers were kept hidden from the rest of the world. The Soviets assigned them numbers so no one would know their names, and those prisoners simply vanished to the outside world."

She nodded. "I have heard that he was assigned a number in prison before and have no idea why. Maybe it was a mistake."

"Did he ever mention receiving any sort of special training in England prior to or during the Second World War?"

"He did spend some time there as a postgraduate economics research student."

"Where?"

"Cambridge University. John Maynard Keynes was one of his supervisors. He attended his Wednesday seminars."

"That is all you know?"

She looked at him in surprise. "Why would you assume he received any special training?"

"Because, according to their records, the Soviets convicted him of being a British spy, but what he did or knew that so worried them – that I have yet to find out."

Budapest, Hungary - 1928

Fifteen year old Karoly Schandl, a student at the Catholic Piarist High School, cleared his throat and then conjugated the verb "to eat" in Latin. Languages were so easy, he thought – even the dead ones.

The father in charge of the class peered at him for a few seconds. As always, the boy's lesson had been well done. "Good. You may now be seated."

Karoly sat down and the boy in the desk behind him leaned forward to whisper in his ear "We know you like food," he teased.

"You look like you don't get enough," Karoly laughed.

Father Bator took a long, hard look at both boys. "Latin class is not the time for fun and games. Now, Nicholas, you may stand and recite the same verb in the past tense."

Nick pushed back his glasses, which had slid partly down his nose, and eagerly stood up, conjugating the verb with ease.

When classes were over for the day, Karoly and Nick were joined by their two friends, Sam and George. Of course, there were others in the class, but never was there a closer group of boys in all of Hungary than Karoly, George, Nick, and Sam. Karoly and George had a great deal in common – both had a keen desire to become lawyers and travel the world. Nick was still undecided about his future, while Sam had plans to become, as he put it, some sort of leader.

That afternoon, the four boys walked toward the Schandl villa, which was located on Gellert Hill at 16-18 Kelenhegyi Street.

The house, with its large lot and tennis court, was next to the Finnish Embassy. Just behind it stood the Swedish Embassy.

Gellert Hill was on the Buda side of the city. The private homes were grand, the hot springs abundant, and the Independence Bridge at the foot connected it to the rest of the city, via the Danube River, which the Hungarians called the Duna. The winding streets, paths, and stone steps of the historic Gellert Hill were as complex and unpredictable as the outsiders who would later gather there beneath the clouds of war.

Today, however, there were no thoughts or hint of world

wars and intrigues. It was 1928, their world was free, and the boys had their youth.

Karoly had invited his friends over for dessert.

The aroma of freshly baked pastries soon reached their nostrils and they quickened their pace, excitedly conversing.

A car was heard approaching and they turned to look at it as the vehicle came around the corner, pulled up to the Schandl villa, and then stopped.

The driver stepped out and meticulously opened the back door. A solemn man with a dark mustache slowly got out of the back seat, nodded at the now quiet boys, opened the gate, and strode toward the front doors. Karoly Schandl Senior, State Secretary of Agriculture, lifetime Member of the Hungarian Upper House, had just arrived home.

Canada - January 2005

Kati tossed her long leather coat onto an armchair and sat down on the pale blue velvet sofa in her mother's living room, pondering the Swiss historian's words. Had her father really been a British spy with a secret? She remembered him as a university professor correcting term papers and exams while smoking his pipe. She remembered the family vacations, the way he used to come home from the bakery with dozens of donuts, éclairs, and any pastry that happened to be fresh that day.

She then remembered Marcel Lambert's words before she walked away from him only an hour earlier. "In addition to looking through all the papers he may have left behind, think of anything he might have said, anyone you might have met – anything that might help me in my research."

Kati walked toward the fireplace and turned on the switch. She sat before it, watching as the flame engulfed the near perfect log. To begin with, what had he ever said about those war years? It had all been so vague – just bits and pieces of anecdotes with various friends, the story of how a Jewish school friend had been hiding in his apartment, then the arrest of both Karoly and the Dutchman, followed by years of lost youth, surrounded by death in the Soviet prisons. Lubyanka, Lefortovo, and Vladimir. It had never occurred to her before that there might have been a reason he had not been sent to a work camp like thousands of others.

His imprisonment had seemed so definite and unusually long. He had joked about it at dinner parties and the neighbors had listened intently. The evil empire of the Soviet Union had been a world away from the towns and cities of North America, and hearing that he had experienced it first-hand had made people either nervous or intrigued. Then there was that local television interview he'd once been talked into giving. At the beginning, the interviewer had asked him how he'd ended up in a Soviet prison and all of a sudden he had become uncommunicative, as though it had been the wrong question to ask, as though he had not been able to answer it.

Standing up, she coiled her hair into a ponytail and made her way to the mahogany end table beside the sofa. Opening the drawer, she found the small key and then shut the drawer. The key would open the old attic door and that was where she would find the old family boxes, filled with papers, documents, notes, and photographs. Perhaps it was time to look through them.

Starting for the stairs, she was caught off guard by the ringing telephone. It was the house phone, not her cell phone, so it could not have been Lambert. When he had emailed her a few days earlier, she had given him her cell phone number only.

Kati returned to the mahogany table and lifted the receiver, unable to conceal the impatience in her voice.

"Hello?"

There was a pause, followed by a man's deep, slightly accented voice. "This is the Schandl residence?"

"Yes."

"Mrs. Schandl?"

"No," Kati replied. "I'm afraid she's away and will be gone for several months."

"Oh." His disappointment was evident. "Are you the maid?"

"No, there is no maid. I'm her daughter."

"Your name is...?"

"Kati."

"I knew the Schandls back in Hungary. My name is John Riley. That is the anglicized version of my name. We changed it after we left Hungary. I have been looking for your father, Karoly, for years. I heard he had died some years ago but I have been trying to track down anyone related to him. He was a friend of mine."

Kati was perplexed. "Were you his school friend?"

"Actually he was a friend of my parents…"

"Your parents?"

"Yes, my parents attended your mother and father's wedding in the Hungarian church."

She held up the key and examined it against the living room light. Her parents had not been married in a Hungarian church.

"Have you seen the house?" he said suddenly.

"I beg your pardon?"

"The family house on Gellert Hill. Have you ever been there?"

She placed the key in an emerald green Zsolnay bowl on the table before continuing. "No, I'm afraid I've never been to that house."

"Has anyone from the family been there?"

"Not to my knowledge, no."

"Oh. Well, I'd still love to meet and chat with you and also with your mother when she returns. To talk about the old days. The good old days I spent in that house."

"The good old days?"

"It was like my second home back in the 1940s, and I have such nice memories of it."

Kati was baffled. He must have been referring to the period during the Second World War. Nice memories?

"May we get together for a chat?"

"I'm afraid I'm … busy at the moment."

"You work in the city?"

She picked up the key again. "Yes, I'm an instructor at the college."

"What do you teach?"

"English."

"May I leave you my telephone number? In case you have time to arrange a meeting."

Kati reluctantly agreed, grabbed the pen and pad next to the telephone, hastily scribbled the local number he repeated to her, then said her goodbyes, and hung up. Convinced that the odd exchange had been no more than another attempt by Lambert to procure information from her – this time by having one of his contacts call her up, pretending to be an old family friend – she put the matter out of her mind and headed upstairs to the attic, taking two steps at a time.

After reaching the door at the top of the second flight of stairs, she inserted the small key into the lock and turned the doorknob, then pushing the door open. It creaked slightly and she remembered how her father had insisted the door be kept locked at all times, the key hidden in a special place. "Important family papers are in there," he had explained. At the time, it had seemed no more than an old school European's eccentricity that the door should be kept locked.

Kati squinted through the darkness, then reached for the light switch. The lack of window and dark low ceiling accentuated her shadow as she walked toward the stack of boxes. They were piled, one on top of the other, in two rows. The top box was labeled "Photos from Family Vacations."

She removed it and looked at the next one. It was labeled "Other Photos." Eventually there would be time to look through that box – with photographs – but first she would have to know the names of those she was looking for. They would be anyone with whom Karoly Schandl had been associated prior to December 4, 1944 – the day he'd been arrested by the Soviets and taken to Moscow. That was the last day he'd ever seen the soil of the Hungary he knew and the first day of eleven years of Soviet captivity. Eleven years and ten months, as he always used to point out.

The next box was labeled "Important Letters" and she removed the sturdy cover. There were manila envelopes inside – each inscribed with the slightly shaky handwriting of an aging man who'd lived through more than most.

The top envelope consisted mostly of birthday cards, old postcards from overseas. The second, however, was filled with letters, apparently all from the same return address in New York.

Kati pulled one out and proceeded to read.

October 25, 1961.

Dear Karoly,
I trust that you are well.
I think the writer you passed on to me really
wished to write about what happened to you.
You were right not to get involved, though, for
it would have, as you feared, put your parents
in peril before they were able to get out of Hungary.

To make a long story short – after our meeting,
the fellow decided that without names or other
such specifics, he would be unable to write about
our resistance group, for he would need some facts
to back it up. I wish I could have told him about
George, the Dutchman, the Diplomat, Tommy, my
brother, our missing friend Nick, and the Paulist
fathers ....

Sam

Kati folded the letter and placed it back in the envelope. When she met Marcel Lambert again later that week at a restaurant to show the letter to him, she also told him about the mysterious Riley.

His reaction caught her off guard.

"As far as you and I are concerned, the Second World War is still not over. It is possible that someone somewhere who betrayed your father is still alive and has a great deal to lose."

The waitress returned with their drinks and tossed a pair of napkins on the table, placing the glasses on them. When she had walked away from their table, Lambert went on.

"I believe that Karoly was set up to be arrested by the Soviets. Someone close to him somehow tricked him and that is how he, the Dutchman and George wound up in Soviet hands."

Kati was not sure what he meant. She reached into her handbag for the letter, which she then handed to him. "I hope it's helpful. It's all I found so far."

Lambert unfolded the letter and read it despite the dim lighting. After a few moments, he handed it back to her. "I can only tell you with certainty about George and the Dutchman, as I do know who they were and the facts about them. George was the resistance leader from whom Karoly presumably took his orders. He was Hungarian. The Dutchman was the unfortunate young Dutch anti-Nazi resistance member who was arrested with Karoly. The Dutchman did not survive life in the Soviet prison."

She nodded. "I know. He did mention the Dutchman a lot. It troubled him greatly what had happened to him."

He handed the letter back to her. "You need to look for his memoirs. It is all in there, I have no doubt, that he will mention the rest of these names and tell his story."

She slipped the folded letter back in her handbag. "What about George? What happened to him? I remember he said he had a boyhood friend by that name. Maybe that's who he meant."

Lambert frowned. "George was even less fortunate than the Dutchman, I am sorry to say. From what I understand, he was tortured to death in late 1944, by the NKVD, the predecessor to the KGB."

Gellert Hill, Budapest, Hungary – 1939

"My friends, as you know I have been in contact with certain legations in Budapest. To be brief, they will soon need our help."

There was a light knock on the door.

Jack ceased speaking.

All eyes were on the door as Karoly stood up and opened it to one of the servants. He spoke a few words and then she was gone, leaving them in privacy once more.

He sat back down and Jack continued. "The situation in Europe has become impossible. Hitler has already taken half of Poland and the government of Hungary is expected to be more and more pressured by the Germans."

"Szálasi's Arrow Cross party has 31 seats in the Parliament," Karoly said angrily. "We can never let Hungary be overtaken by these fascists!"

"Anti-Semites," Nick muttered.

Karoly looked around the living room of his apartment, at his three best friends, who were presently seated on plush chairs. There was Sam, the tall, dark haired serious one with political aspirations for better times, Nick, the quiet engineer, and George, the young lawyer whose usual smile had vanished from his face. All three were his closest old friends from the Piarist Catholic High School and the Piarist Boy Scouts – and all three were of Jewish origin. He would never let anything happen to them. *Never.*

Jack cleared his throat. "Are you ready for involvement if it is needed? Can we count on you?"

The four friends readily agreed.

George reached for his brandy glass, raising it in a toast. The others followed suit. "A toast, to our beloved Hungary, that she shall remain beautiful and free of Nazis as long as we are alive to do something about it."

Once the brandy glasses were empty, Jack stood up. "Gentlemen, welcome to the future of the anti-Nazi resistance."

They all shook hands.

After Jack had left, the four friends made a pact – they would act as a team for all time, and would never do or say anything if it risked the safety of any member of their group. It was a pact that would never be broken.

Later that evening, Karoly went downstairs to join his parents in their dining room for dinner. The table had been set with white linen and fine china at each place setting. Terezia Schandl was a woman who cared about appearances, yet she was not pretentious. Her husband Karoly Schandl Sr. had been a well known politician, but he was neither an opportunist nor a social climber. While the State Secretary of Agriculture from 1921 until 1928, his interest had always been the plight of the farmers, the small land owners.

When the servants had finished bringing out the assorted dishes, Terezia said grace and the party of three served themselves.

She patted some butter on a fresh slice of bread and sighed. "Karoly, where is your fiancée?"

His father grinned.

Karoly shrugged his shoulders. "I don't have a fiancée, just time for girlfriends right now."

"When will you get married?"

"Eventually."

"Your sister already has a husband and child and you are still resisting marriage."

"I will get married when the war is over."

His father nodded solemnly. "I have heard that the situation in Poland is looking very grim."

"Something must be done to ensure that Hungary is not invaded by the Nazis," Karoly replied.

He did not mention that his Polish friend Jack was now an agent – and he and his friends were going to help him in any way possible when the time came...

Budapest, Hungary - 1940

The Bokreta Women's Retirement Home was abuzz with the news that the Chairwoman of the board, Terezia Schandl, was visiting. She had dropped by to meet with Sister Sara, the new head of the facility.

"It's very good of you to come by." The nun poured her visitor a cup of tea.

Terezia accepted the tea and gracefully placed the floral

cup and saucer on her lap. "I am sorry I was unable to meet you earlier, dear sister, but there were some problems in the other homes that needed immediate attention. How are you finding the home? Is it adequately staffed? If you wish, I can arrange for more helpers."

"We can manage for the time being."

"And how is the cook?"

"He is working out very well but he is worried about his family."

Terezia sipped her tea. "They are having problems?"

Sister Sara stood up and nervously shut the door, then turning around with a look of consternation on her face. "He is worried because they are of Jewish origin, which to the Nazis, makes them Jewish."

Terezia frowned and placed the cup and saucer on the small table next to her.

Sister Sara continued. "There is such terrible news coming from Poland. One of the new helpers in the kitchen, a Polish woman who recently escaped, told us of the horrors the Germans have committed in her homeland."

Terezia stood up and touched the small gold cross she wore around her neck. "Please tell the cook not to worry. If anything happens here, I will take steps to ensure that he and his family are protected. You have my word."

"I will let him know." Sister Sara smiled gratefully as she also stood up. She then escorted her guest to the large drawing room where some elderly women were engrossed in knitting, and others were quietly reading.

Terezia looked around, making a mental note of the spotless, comfortably furnished room with its well stacked bookcase, piano, and the endless number of teacups and saucers behind the glass door of a large buffet. She nodded approvingly and sat down for a chat with the group of women who were busily knitting for the next bazaar.

Canada – January 2005

Traffic had been unusually light so the drive home had been both smooth and fast. Turning onto a dark side street, Kati recalled the exchange that had taken place between herself and Lambert – after he had informed her of the fate of George and she'd gotten over the shock.

"That letter also mentioned Nick and someone who was a diplomat," she had said.

"Both missing, presumed arrested by the Soviets."

"Your father," Lambert had added,"was not a background player. He must have been a very big fish for the Soviets to go to such great lengths to capture him."

"He didn't seem to think so," she'd replied. "I thought he felt it was a mix-up. Maybe he just happened to know these people, that's all."

"Ms. Schandl," the historian had suddenly said. "Are you aware that back in the 1960s, your father reportedly sent a letter to the CIA? In addition to his possible memoirs, I would very much appreciate it if you searched for that letter. It might be significant in this investigation. Here is my mobile phone number. I will be leaving for London in the morning, to request some files from the National Archives. Should there be any developments, do contact me. Also, please be cautious about whomever you speak to about this matter."

That was basically how their conversation had ended – leaving her with more questions than she'd had when it began.

Once back at the house, she walked up the stone steps to the door and was about to unlock it but then noticed, from the corner of her eye, a folded white paper sticking out of the mailbox.

It had been empty before she left for the meeting with Lambert.

She pulled it out, entered the front hall, and turned on the lights. The message had been typed on what must have been an old typewriter, as the letters were thick and dark.

*She poured a cup of social sewage into the
historian's ear. If you stretch the bow too
far it will break. I seek only truth, not
corruption. Lubyanka. If you stretch the
bow too far, it will break.*

A warning but from whom? Clearly, Lambert had been
right – World War II had not ended for their purposes and it
seemed that someone wanted to stop his investigation. But why?
The door was locked, the alarm set, so she would be safe for at
least the time being.

There was much work to do, not enough time for worries.

Climbing the staircase, the warning note still crumpled in
her hand, she eventually reached the attic and went inside to find
the box containing Karoly's memoirs. All Europeans, he had
once said, wrote their memoirs. She would find them and read
them – tonight.

The veiled threat had not succeeded.

Tossing the paper to the floor, she proceeded to read all
the box labels until she found one on which had been written
"The Yagoda Siren." She blinked. He had mentioned writing a
report about the psychological torture he'd endured in the Soviet
prisons. Perhaps it contained his memoirs, as well as all that had
led up to his imprisonment. After all, he might have wished to
avoid using the title "Memoirs," as it would have been too
obvious, too easy to find and destroy.

Even during her childhood, she had heard comments her
father made under his breath now and then about how "the
Russians" were still aware of his actions, his movements. She
hadn't really given it a second thought at the time.

And what about his funeral fifteen years earlier? Who had
been the lone, nervous man with the mustache whom no one
knew? That same man had repeatedly approached his family
members before and after the service, imploring them to tell him
if Karoly had told them "anything." When they had insisted they

had no idea what he was referring to, he had begun to perspire as though had had a great deal to fear "That is not good," he had nervously retorted. "Not good."

After the funeral, it became evident that no one present had known who he was or what he really wanted.

Her attention returned to the box.

"The Yagoda Siren."

Kati removed the slightly yellowed manuscript, which was typed - with her father's hand-made ink corrections - and turned the cover page ...

CHAPTER 2
COVERT OPERATIONS

Budapest, Hungary - March 1944

Europe was at war and Hungary was on the wrong side. While openly supporting the Germans against the Red Army, Prime Minister Kallay, it was rumored, had also made contact with British and American governments – yet nothing had materialized. People in the capital whispered about what they heard was happening. Sadly, the repression of Hungary's Jewish citizens continued.

The anti-Nazi resistance continued, but not without hardship. People in the capital, it seemed, were as complex and unpredictable as the winding pathways of Gellert Hill, which were surrounded by dense foliage. One could never be sure of who to trust and whether or not one was dealing with a real person or someone with an invented or stolen identity. Spies and those with hidden interests permeated Budapest, some with the best intentions, others feeding off their own self-serving agendas.

There were Polish, Dutch and Hungarian groups who worked tirelessly to ensure that the Nazis would not prevail, yet none would prove as relentless as the group, which was officially led by George, now a British intelligence agent. *British intelligence had trained George in Alexandria and Bari to officially lead their group. He continued to report to Jack.*

Karoly stared out at the courtyard/garden of his family villa as Nick examined the small parts of a radio transmitter George had handed him to re-assemble. The group needed the radio transmitter to send and receive messages from Bari, also known as Allied Headquarters. The last such device had been damaged, but not before George had received a transmission of the utmost importance which had led him to request today's meeting.

Sam inhaled his cigarette and came to stand beside Karoly. "We're in the same boat."

"How so?"

"We will both likely be re-activated as Hungarian Army reservists," he said matter-of-factly.

Karoly nodded. "At least as a Second Lieutenant in the Hungarian Reserves, I might have access to certain information. However, I would walk away from any order that compromised my principles, regardless of the consequences."

"You haven't been the same since '42, my friend," Sam remarked. "I still don't understand why Regent Horthy sent the Hungarian army unprepared and unnecessarily to Russia. So many deaths in freezing temperatures and for what?"

Karoly said nothing, but remembered. He remembered walking so that the men in his unit could ride the tank in the bitter cold. He also remembered how it had been hit by mortar and the tank and men inside had been obliterated in a split second. He then remembered seeing the death marches in Poland and remembered vowing to himself that he would somehow do something about the wave of terror when he had the chance …

Both men turned around as Nick dropped the repaired transmitter into the bag at his side.

George removed a piece of paper from his trouser pocket. "Friends, Bari is aware of our efforts and I believe that British intelligence now has files on all of us."

"That could be to our benefit someday," Sam replied. "If any of us ever gets in a bind, the British will come to our aid."

"Churchill," Nick added. "Churchill would save us."

Karoly remained quiet, wondering how he would break the news he had heard earlier on to his group. Darkness would soon descend upon their land, making any kind of movement difficult. They would all be scrutinized like never before and George, being their official leader, as a member of British intelligence, would need to be especially cautious. They functioned as one unit, and that was the key to their success. What had started out as an idealistic undertaking had swiftly evolved into a clandestine operation of immense value to the Allies. Their contacts were many, as was their ability to procure information, and they were always organized about sharing it in a timely manner.

A few moments passed and they all sat down. Nick glanced at his watch, anxious to return to George's secret location so that the fixed transmitter could be tested. Sam finished smoking his cigarette and crossed a foot over his knee. George held up the piece of paper, as though stressing its significance.

"In my last transmission, I received orders for our latest mission. It is to be an ongoing one. We will have to take escaped Allied prisoners-of-war to the southern border, along with monthly reports to the Center."

Sam put his foot back on the floor. "How are these Allied prisoners going to escape?"

George lit a match and held it to the paper, then tossing it into the fireplace. "They are not. We will get them out – with money. We will bribe the guards."

"Where will we take them?" Sam said incredulously. "It sounds sketchy and not without serious logistic problems."

"That I have yet to find out," George explained. "Now that Nick has attended to my transmitter, I expect to be able to receive the details shortly."

"Everything may have changed by then," Karoly informed his friends. "Based on a credible source in the military, word has it that Hitler has just given the order for Hungary to be occupied by the Germans. In the next few days, we will see just how awful that really is. I suggest we reconvene at a safer place exactly one week from now, in order to assess our situation. In the meantime, we should not be seen together. The city is likely crawling with more Nazi spies and informers than ever. "

George, Sam, and Nick fell silent, suddenly aware that now the time had come that their resolve would truly be tested.

The days that followed were like the beginning of a nightmare. The Germans marched into Hungary. Thousands of openly pro-Western political, aristocratic, and intellectual figures were arrested and carted off to concentration camps in Germany. The Hungarian police and gendarmes collaborated with the much dreaded Gestapo in these arrests and others. There was no military resistance. The Prime Minister went into hiding in the Turkish Embassy. Hungarians were divided - many were paralyzed by the vast numbers of the Nazis, while some took the opportunity to express their hatred by joining them.

Karoly would later be mobilized again, but only to perform his administrative duties at Hungarian Air Defense Headquarters. Because of it, he would receive the distinction of having a sign placed on the family villa, that there dwelled a Second Lieutenant of the Hungarian Army. It was a perfect cover, he would later decide, should they need to hide anyone.

The resistance group met frequently on Gellert Hill, sometimes at his apartment, other times in a less conspicuous place.

In 1926, a church and monastery had been built into a limestone cave in a cliff – or rather at the base of an enormous rock on Gellert Hill. The Hungarians called it the *Sziklatemplom.* It was here where the Paulist Order was based. The monastery, with its neo-gothic turrets, lay behind the church and the Paulist friars who dwelled there spent a great deal of time in prayer. The Cave Church was approximately 200 meters down the street from the Schandl villa and the fathers were involved in helping the anti-Nazi resistance.

When the time came for the group's next meeting, the men met at the Cave Church.

Father Horvath ushered them quickly inside lest they be seen by any Nazis or gendarmes.

"It will not be safe to wander through the city streets," he said sagely, "unless you are well disguised. The gendarmes and Gestapo would think nothing of stopping young men." He stepped into a small room off to the side and returned a moment later, carrying a pile of robes. "These are the frocks which our fathers wear. They will serve you well in the cause."

Karoly put his on and tied the sash. His friends quietly followed suit. George then filled them in on the details of their next mission.

A few weeks later, Karoly found himself walking along the dark road which led to the place of POW transfers. It had all been proceeding smoothly; Sam and Nick would pass the payment to the bribed guards, who would help the prisoners fake an escape. In reality, the guards were setting them free, but the Gestapo would have shot the bribed guards had that been known, hence the pretense of an "escape." After Sam handed over the payment and the prisoners were freed, they would be taken by Sam and Nick to the designated meeting place, where Karoly or someone from the group would be waiting. It was ideal – and they were always given forged identification papers.

Part of the key to their success was the teamwork and that no one suspected they would actually be transporting POWs on foot to their escape. If they were stopped, they would all show their fake documents and Karoly would do the talking. However, it never came to that because Karoly knew the area like the back of his hand and could have navigated anywhere from Hungary to Yugoslavia with his eyes closed.

Sam was waiting with two nervous looking men. They were both French this time.

Karoly slowly approached them and waved so that his new charges would not be afraid. They were each presented with false papers, which identified them as Poles. When the older man protested that he could not speak Polish and would therefore be shot on the spot if stopped, Karoly patiently explained.

"Don't worry, I know what roads to take. By the way, you are not carrying any weapons, are you?"

The older POW replied in the negative. *"Non, nous n'avons pas d'armes*. We have no weapons."

A slight whistle came from a few meters away. Sam tossed his half smoked cigarette to the ground and stepped on it.

"It is safe for me to go back now, with Nick. He has seen no one that resembled a Nazi. Good luck and Godspeed." Then he was gone, having noiselessly disappeared behind a patch of dark trees.

Karoly motioned for the two men not to speak and then walked a few steps ahead of them. They followed along the dirt road, still unsure as to where they were being taken. They were already far from Budapest and were now headed south, but to what location?

The air was crisp but at least there was no snow, as it was

no longer winter. Snow and ice would have made it that much more difficult for the escapees to reach their destination. After an hour, Karoly looked back and addressed them in French, a language he spoke fluently and had mastered while studying as a postgraduate student in the École Libre des Sciences Politiques in Paris in the 1930s. *"Vous êtes fatigués?* You are tired?"

The older man shook his head, though the younger Frenchman sighed and quietly complained that his feet were sore, since they had beaten his soles back in the camp, before they had "escaped."

Karoly led the two men for a few minutes more, then veered off to the right, through a lightly wooded area. There was a farmhouse behind a clearing. He approached it from the back and knocked on the door. It opened slightly and he said the password. The door was completely opened and the two Frenchmen walked in, after Karoly. Their host had disappeared into another room so they never saw him clearly. Such precautions were necessary. The small back room looked like some sort of servant's area, where pots and pans were hung from the walls. Inside there was also a long bench. The young Frenchman gratefully sat down, while his superior chose to stand and address their escort.

"Eh bien. Do you do this often?"

Karoly firmly shut the door and bolted it. "It's my mission. I perform it as often as is needed."

"But you are not the Allies."

"We are the Hungarian resistance. We work with the Allies, for they are able to help us in our cause. You will be taken to the Allies, so you have no reason to worry."

The French officer reached forward to shake his hand. "My name is Jean Luc. Thank you for your assistance. No doubt the Nazis would have tortured us to death for information."

Karoly shook hands with the escapee. "Karoly."

"Where exactly are you taking us? The borders are not at all stable, from what I gather."

"South," was the immediate reply. "You will be transferred south, to our contacts there, and then taken by plane to Bari."

"Contacts?"

"Agents. We should continue now." Karoly watched as the younger man stood up, and then unlocked the door. Together the three continued back to the dirt road and resumed their journey. Karoly had no hesitation in his movements, for he knew the area well.

The moon was brighter now and that made it easier to see what was around them. It was therefore with some apprehension that the two Frenchmen realized he was leading them toward a group of men holding guns.

"Move quickly," Karoly instructed.

The stocky leader of the men advanced to greet them, his hand on his weapon. Karoly said the code word. The man looked the two escapees up and down and then said, in clear English, "Please go with my men. They will escort you the rest of the way." He then addressed Karoly. "They are not Poles. Last time you brought out Poles."

"Today was different."

When the two POWs were no longer in earshot, Karoly pulled a large envelope from underneath his coat and handed it to him. The man nodded, said a few words in broken Hungarian, then turned around to rejoin his Serbian group. Karoly watched the party disappear from view.

It was such an ingenious operation, the way these missions were coordinated. First George received the instructions from Bari concerning the next Allied POWs that needed to be smuggled out of the country. Nick then scouted around and did some asking, to find out which guard was in charge and how much it would take to "buy" the prisoners.Then their Polish friends in the network made contact in the prison or camp, to inform the POWs of what was going to take place. Next, Sam would arrive on scene to make the payment to the guards, with Nick in the background. The POWs were sprung in a "daring escape," which was in fact staged so that the bribed guards could save face and avoid execution. Then Karoly met them at the designated place and they began the long journey on foot.

He was an official messenger of the group, responsible for the safe delivery of the escapees to their contacts on the border of

Hungary and Yugoslavia. That was where the Allies had regular planes from Alexandria or Bari bringing supplies to the rebels. The escaped prisoners were the load to be taken back, along with reports to "the Center." The envelope containing the report was something he was careful not to reveal, until he had reached the Serb, who had been educated in Canada. All in all, it was a brilliant operation. No one suspected that the supply planes were taking escaped POWs back to Allied headquarters, along with a report for the Center.

Karoly placed his hands in his pockets and began the long journey back to Budapest.

He did not know that on the same day, Terezia Schandl was meeting with Father Horvath of the Cave Church in the living room of the Schandl villa on Gellert Hill.

"More tea, father? Or a biscuit?"

Father Hovarth accepted a cheese filled biscuit on his Herendy plate. "Thank you. How is Mr. Schandl?"

Terezia absentmindedly readjusted the pearls around her neck. "He is asleep."

The priest nodded.

"He has been very tired lately. I pray his health is all right. It pains him that the Nazis are here. It pains us all."

Father Horvath wondered if she was aware of her son's activities. "There are many who are courageous enough to help the cause of saving the innocent, many who are deeply involved."

"As I would like to be!" she said suddenly. "Father, God willing, I would like to help, to offer my home ..."

"You risk certain arrest if the Nazis hear of it," he quietly warned. "It is dangerous to even speak of such an undertaking."

"I cannot stand idly by and do nothing," she sighed. "It is my responsibility. I can offer my home as a safe house for those who need to escape persecution, in case the Allies do not liberate us quickly and Eichmann starts to carry out his evil intentions against our citizens."

"You are a very brave woman. But what would your husband say?"

"I have already mentioned it to him. He, of course, is in complete agreement for he too loathes the Nazis and their evil ideology."

She paused. "Would it be possible for the Cave Church to assist me in this matter?"

"The Paulist Order does not support the Nazis. Already we have given priest's frocks from the Cave Church to the anti-Nazi resistance, as disguises. How might we be able to assist so devout a parishoner and such a good friend as yourself?"

Terezia smiled. "Bless you for your kindness. I had in mind that the Paulist Order could claim to be renting the upstairs apartment of the villa for priests who were visiting from out of town. That way, no authorities would dare question our reasons for having so many 'guests.'"

"Guests wearing the frocks of Paulist priests," Father Horvath added.

When Karoly finally returned from his mission, the sun was beginning to rise over the horizon. He walked up the stairs to the separate entrance of his upstairs apartment and unlocked the door, surprised to find his mother waiting for him.

He kissed her on each cheek and removed his coat.

"You look tired, my son."

"Tired of Nazis." He removed his heavy shoes and leaned against the wall. "How is father?"

"He is sleeping. I am here because I must tell you about a conversation I had with Father Horvath. I know that the guest you had in your apartment for a few days last week must have been someone who was leaving Budapest in secret."

"Resistance business. It won't happen again, he simply had nowhere else to go."

"It will happen again – and it should." Terezia Schandl took her son's hands in hers and regarded him soberly, her hazel eyes filled with steely determination. She informed him of her conversation with Father Horvath, and how he had agreed to her plan. It did not mean Karoly would have to leave his apartment, only that they would have to pretend that any "guests" from then on were visiting priests of the Paulist Order.

"In addition to being the only safe house on the street, we will be all set with the frocks the good father is now providing,"

Karoly mused.

His mother shook her head. "I should have known that it was your group! Tell me, is that where you were?"

"There was some resistance business, yes."

He could not bring himself to tell her that he had been on a routine mission to deliver POWs to the much feared Tito partisans, along with a secret report, for these were dangerous times indeed – and the less anyone knew about his activities, the better off they surely were.

CHAPTER 3
INTELLIGENCE

Kew, England – January 2005

It was a relatively quiet day at the National Archives. Marcel Lambert had not ordered the documents he was seeking before his visit, for it was in the best interest of his investigation to remain as inconspicuous as possible. The previous afternoon, he had rung Kati Schandl, who had told him of the discovery she had made via her father's memoirs – Karoly Schandl had belonged to a high profile group in the Hungarian resistance, which had been involved with British intelligence. In fact, the leader of the group ended up becoming an official agent of British intelligence and he himself reported to a "British chief." Bari must have known about them back then.

This had led Lambert to venture to the National Archives with something very specific in mind. He simply had to see all records pertaining to any British agents' activities in Hungary during the Second World War. He already knew the name of one, and he had told Kati about it, suggesting she somehow procure a book he had apparently written fifty years later. "Dan," as he was known, had actually stayed in the apartment of Karoly Schandl before Karoly and the Dutchman had been arrested by the Soviets. A Jewish friend of Karoly's had been hiding there at the same time. Lambert, however, hadn't told her as much. He felt it was best to let her continue studying her father's memoirs for the time being, in addition to that book. She had promised to do so and they had then ended their conversation, promising to keep in touch.

What Kati Schandl did not – and could not – know was that Lambert was probing the 60 year old mystery for very specific reasons.

Karoly had been approached by officials in later years,

though something was missing from his story – names. Now Lambert understood. There had been a veil of secrecy around his group because it was involved in British supported resistance, and the Cold War had been ongoing during Schandl's life. Thus, it would have been too risky for him to admit the names of his resistance group participants. The Soviet Union had still occupied Hungary, where he must have had family and friends, and such resistance members of past or present were generally viewed as potentially anti-Soviet elements. It would have been foolhardy to admit to being part of the group, unless he was willing to risk the safety of anyone still left behind the Iron Curtain. That had to have been the reason for Karoly Schandl's guarded testimony.

He had pulled the wool over their eyes the entire time.

It amazed Lambert, as a historian and investigator, that the man had never slipped up over the years. Of course, if he had, he might not have lived until the age of 77.

The KGB back then were not without their own people and "helpers" scattered at various locations throughout the world – and Schandl must have known that he was being watched.

After ordering the file of British agents' activities, Lambert headed to the National Archives restaurant and waited until 1:22 p.m., when a familiar figure in a gray coat joined him at his table, carrying a cup of tea. "Anything to report?"

"I do have a lead."

"And?"

"He was in a resistance group. They were somehow involved with British intelligence. How deeply, I have yet to find out." He did not mention that Schandl's group had actually been led by British intelligence, for that might have resulted in Kati Schandl being questioned and he sensed that she would only cooperate as long as she trusted him.

"You're not holding out on me, are you?" His superior pensively sipped some tea.

Lambert paused. "You've never doubted me before."

"That was different, you had no personal invlovement. I sense you are protective about your new contact."

Lambert shrugged his shoulders. "It won't hinder the investigation. But there is one thing that is troubling me.

Someone else has tried to make contact with her – and I do not believe he was one of ours."

"What was his name?"

"Riley. John Riley."

"An alias, no doubt." His superior stood up, his cup of tea still in hand. "Then we were right. Someone still has cause to worry. I will check on this name John Riley but don't expect much. He wouldn't have left any sort of trail. These types are rarely sloppy. I will be in touch in the next few days – when you are able to fill me in on what you found in the files and what it might mean to us." Then he was gone.

Lambert felt a sense of relief that he hadn't prodded him for more details. Despite being part of the complex organization which, for all practical purposes, prohibited him from acting alone, it was at times best to keep things to oneself – to internalize. He stood up and made his way back to the Archives reception desk, where he inquired about his order. He hoped he would be able to learn more before being told to merely pass on what he knew. After all, in the organization's eyes, he was simply a historian, a researcher.

Ten minutes later, he found himself entering a quiet reading room, with two loose files under his arm. He sat at a table that had no one nearby and opened the first file. It was supposed to contain the names of the British agents in Hungary who had been taking orders from Bari, Allied Headquarters. There was a blank page inside. He shook his head in disbelief. The contents must have been removed, but by whom and when?

The next file was not empty. The cover page of the thick document read "Public Record Office ... The National Archives." It contained summaries that had been given to Prime Minister Churchill in late 1944 and early 1945 about the activities of certain British agents in Europe. At the top lefthand corner of the first page had been typed and underlined TOP SECRET.

There were lists of acts of sabotage against the Nazis, air operations, organized resistance groups, the captures of important persons, the arrests and possible executions of agents, train derailments, unnamed acts of subversion, and awards. Any historical researcher would have been riveted by its contents, for here, in its concise form, was a piece of history – a moment in the governance of a great politician.

The only reason Marcel Lambert was dismayed was that it was supposed to summarize all the activities reported throughout Europe with such agents – and Hungary was notably absent. There was no mention on any page of Hungary. Nations included were Germany and Austria, Poland, Czechoslovakia, Italy, Norway, Holland – but not Hungary. Lambert could scarcely believe his eyes. Either the pages containing what had transpired in Hungary were not yet declassified and perhaps never would be – or no one had reported anything to Churchill about British led operations in Hungary. He shut the files and stood up. Perhaps an old contact would prove more fruitful.

Later that afternoon, he was back in downtown London, walking briskly to a building in an elegant residential neighborhood. He knocked at the door of a flat and was let in by a distinguished older gentleman with very straight posture and a gray moustache – a retired, highly educated military looking type with continental manners. "Do come in."

Lambert entered. His host led him to the tidy living room, where they both sat down.

"May I offer you something – coffee, tea?"

Lambert declined with a shake of the head. "No, but thank you all the same."

His host got straight to the point. "I realized you were disappointed by what you found – or rather did not find – at the National Archives. I think your expectations of finding everything out in the open are a direct result of your being Swiss. Not everything is clear and evident, Marcel."

"I was close and was sure there would be something."

"Yet, as I gathered from your desperate phone call, the actual documented evidence was not available or simply never existed."

Lambert smiled slightly. "Retirement hasn't slowed you down one bit. Your mind is as sharp as ever."

"Thank you, though the cane does slow my movements somewhat, under the guise of helping me get around faster. I see you are impatient. I wonder if that is because they have not changed at all at the organization – still pressuring those involved to meet their deadlines. I cannot say I miss the frantic pace of it. Before you came, dear friend, I was in touch with a former contact of the OSS, which, as we know, became the CIA in 1947. He too is retired but not without certain … resources that led to information that will help you. That group of Hungarians was familiar to him but not for the resaons you think. Not only did they successfully smuggle out from Hungary dozens of foreign POWs who were of great importance to the Allies, but they had a key role in intelligence as well. These young men were the elite and had a number of contacts and resources at their fingertips. As a result, they had significant reports for the Allies, which were smuggled out to Bari via the Tito partisans, always in a sealed envelope, often delivered by Karoly Schandl. He was a messenger."

Hungary – April 1944

No one would have suspected that a British intelligence unit actually had an office in the bedroom of a family estate in Hungary. That was what made it so ingenious. It had been set up at George's family villa, with one of the many spare bedrooms the exact location for radio transmissions to Bari. Anytime communication needed to be made with the Allies, it was readily available, and the radio operator was currently Nick, who was proving to be more and more skillful with electronics. He was a very fast learner

The group sat around in the chairs, waiting for the message from headquarters. Had the two French POWs arrived safely? When the affirmative answer was finally transmitted, they breathed a sigh of relief.

George patted Karoly on the back. "Good job."

"It was just the usual delivery."

Sam watched Nick writing the update in the small notebook. "Did they mention the envelope as well? Did that arrive safely?" He had never concealed his distrust of the Tito partisans. "Thugs masquerading as freedom fighters," he had once called them.

Nick finished and shut the notebook. "The envelope arrived safely, too."

George nodded. "Good."

Sam decided it was a good time to bring up his new contact. "Yesterday I was approached by a fellow from the OSS, otherwise known as Operational Special Services, the American organization. Said his name was Marty Taylor and if we were ever in dire straits, we could go to him. Seemed like a pretty decent fellow. His hideout is an apartment near Andrassy Street."

"An expensive address for an agent," Nick said pensively.

George shook his head. "The Americans haven't been as successful at clandestine operations as the British."

Sam shrugged his shoulders. There had simply been something about Marty Taylor that had impressed him – his sincerity.

Nick once more turned the transmitter on, before their meeting was over, and it began to make a series of beeps. He opened the notebook again and picked up his pencil. "Bari is sending us another message." He scribbled down a few notes and continued until the morse code transmission had stopped.

Karoly stood up. "Is it about the next mission?"

"This one's just for George alone," came the sober reply. "It's something about intelligence agents."

George nodded. "I know they've been trying to drop more British agents into the country, via Yugoslavia, but things haven't been going as neatly as planned."

Nick stood up and handed him the notebook once the message had been interpreted. George read it and frowned.

Karoly, whose hand had been on the doorknob, turned back to his group, the dark circles beneath his eyes evident. It had been another long walk, another long night.

George tossed the notebook back onto the table. "I might have to go into hiding."

"You are in hiding." Nick sat back down at the transmitter and turned it off. "No one would think that your family's estate was where a British intelligence group would be conducting operations from."

"It's because of my Jewish heritage. As the leader of our group, which we all know is being run under the auspices of the British, I am supposed to take certain precautions so as not to compromise the safety of anyone involved."

"We all feel that way," Nick pointed out. "It's part of our creed."

Karoly leaned back against the door, having completely understood the concerns of George's superiors. "They worry that you might talk and give names and radio codes if the Germans torture you."

"Sensitive information about current British and Allied operations," Sam went on. "And because George is of Jewish origin, there is a higher probability of him being caught than other British agents. All it would take is for some opportunistic person to report him."

Nick removed his glasses and rubbed his tired eyes. "But if you leave, then how are we supposed to keep going with our missions? Plus, there are the reports we need to get out to the Allies and you are the one they trust since you're now one of them. They gave you special training in Alexandria and Bari. They need us and we need you and they trained you."

"It just means finding an alias," George stated simply. "I will have to procure false papers and a new identity. Once I hear from Jack, I will ask him to make the necessary arrangements. We will continue everything as before unless something changes."

Unbeknownst to the four friends, that very night would mark the start of the bombing of Budapest's strategic targets.

Periodic explosions filled the night sky.

Canada - January 10, 2005

Someone was banging on the front door so hard, it sounded as if it might break. Kati glanced through the frosty side window, where she beheld a familiar face. She opened the door, unable to conceal her surprise.

"Aren't you going to invite me in? It's freezing out here."

"Come on in." She further opened the door and he walked inside.

Chris Miller, professor of law, hadn't changed since she'd last seen him three months earlier. As usual, he was quietly self-assured and had a way of conveying his state of mind without having to use words. The vibe she was picking up from him today indicated that he was there for a specific reason and she assumed it had to do with the fact that he hadn't heard from her. They had promised to remain friends.

She shut the door and locked it.

"You really don't know why I'm here?"

"It was nice of you to drop by." She smiled and was about to offer him a coffee …

"It's January 10, which means that yesterday it was January 9." He suddenly looked concerned. "Is everything okay with you?"

"I have just been trying to sort through things."

He removed his Italian leather shoes and followed her into the living room, which was strewn with papers and boxes.

"This place looks like it's been hit by a bomb," he muttered.

"I've been looking through my dad's boxes. I brought down the three most important ones because the attic lighting wasn't good enough."

"It must be something pretty important for you to forget that we were supposed to meet yesterday for a friendly lunch."

"Chris, I'm sorry – I completely forgot about it. Maybe we can reschedule. Can I offer you a coffee?"

He crouched down beside her as she started to pile some large envelopes into one of the boxes. "I realize we're not romantically involved anymore but that doesn't mean we can't still be good friends. I'm worried about you. It's not like you to forget an appointment. What gives?"

She sighed and stood up. "The past. Some things have to be resolved about the past."

He stood up and looked at her with his intense blue eyes. "I'll stay for that coffee you just offered – black, no sugar. The usual."

A few minutes later, Kati returned with two mugs of coffee and handed Chris the one containing black coffee. They sat together on the sofa in silence for a moment, her eyes still fixed on the array of papers.

His power of observation was astute. "You haven't been sleeping much."

"I have to find the second part," she said matter-of-factly.

"Of what exactly?"

"Dad's memoirs. I have read the first part but the rest is missing and I know it has to be somewhere. If it's not in the boxes from the attic, I have no idea where to look. He always kept two copies of anything that was significant but they were always in the same place."

"Are you writing a book about him?"

"No, but I wish I had years ago," she said seriously. "That way, everything would have been out in the open sooner."

"You sound like you need a friend on this one, Kati, and I'm pretty trustworthy, so why not let me know everything? You know what they say – two heads are better than one."

She nodded and put her mug on the glass table in front of the sofa. "All right, I will. Maybe you'll be able to help in some way."

For the next hour, she filled him in on what had been transpiring. He listened with interest, interrupting at times to ask for details. When she had finished, he shook his head in disbelief. "Soviet prisons, mysterious phone calls, Swiss historians. So far it's a remarkable story. Have you had Lambert and this Riley person checked out?"

"Not yet. I've been too busy trying to put together the pieces of the puzzle."

Chris stood up. "I have a class in half an hour but I'll be

back after that. I've got a contact who might be able to get a lead on Lambert and the so-called John Riley, whom I believe was using an alias and not, as he said, a changed name. I'll have something soon."

Kati stood up and nodded. "Thanks, I really appreciate it, although I'm sure Lambert's on the up and up. I found his name on the website of the historical association he said he was heading up."

"We also need to find out what his research areas of interest are," he added as an afterthought, "to get a handle on his agenda."

Kati was unable to conceal her surprise. "You think he has an agenda?"

Chris smiled. "Real life isn't like English literature–everybody has an agenda. I'll be in touch as soon as I know more."

"Thanks for your help."

Once he was gone, she returned to the boxes. That was when she noticed that the base of one of them seemed much thicker than the rest. Kneeling down, she emptied the contents of the box and lifted the bottom flaps. There was a yellowing, wrinkled manuscript, with headers on each page. The first page was numbered 33 – where the first part of Karoly's memoirs had left off. She had found part two and would shortly know the rest of his story. The print was faded but she could still make out the first sentence.

"In June 1944, I met my friend Tommy at the Basilica ..."

CHAPTER 4
THE SAFE HOUSE

Budapest, Hungary – Summer 1944

The Germans had installed a Jewish ghetto in Budapest and all citizens whom they considered to be Jews were required to wear the yellow star badge, also known as the Star of David. Hundreds of thousands of men, women, and children were being deported on feight trains.

Tommy Lazar had exactly one day left before he would be shipped out to one of the dreaded camps – and that was what had prompted him to meet his old school friend. He stood alone in front of St. Stephen's Basilica, where they had agreed to meet and, had the circumstances been different, he might have appreciated the fact that it was a sunny day. As it was, he was overcome with a feeling of loss – and that he would never again see the friend he had always thought of as a brother. He remembered how, when he had found out about the resistance group to which Karoly belonged, Karoly had been adamant about his reasons for having kept it a secret. "It was for your own good," he had explained to the young law student, who was years younger. "It's too dangerous to know about or be involved in." He had felt protective toward Tommy the way an older brother felt toward a younger brother and this was what had prompted Tommy to call and ask to see him one last time – he was the only one he could trust to somehow make him feel better.

St. Stephen's Basilica, named after the first king of Hungary, was the city's largest and most imposing Roman Catholic church. The dome was as tall as the Parliament and the view from high up was believed to be the most beautiful in Budapest. No one cared about city views anymore, however, for everywhere there was desperation and terror for anyone who had a drop of Jewish blood.

Karoly walked quickly toward Tommy, across Saint Stephen's Square, his face flushed from walking in the heat while wearing his uniform. These days it was safest to make one's way through the city in the uniform of a Hungarian Second Lieutenant, particularly on the way to meeting a friend who happened to be of Jewish origin. The gendarmes who regularly patrolled the streets would not stop him, there would be no suspicion. He had been mobilized as a technical adjutant at Air Defense Headquarters in May and was months away from being promoted to a captain. No one would have imagined him to be active in underground resistance activities against the Nazis.

Tommy tried to smile but the smile would not come. "I called you here to say goodbye."

Karoly shook his head, opened one of the heavy wooden doors, and motioned for his friend to follow him inside. The Basilica was dim and gave a surrealistic atmosphere to their exchange.

Together they walked around the enormous church, where a few women were immersed in prayers. They stopped next to an empty mahogany confessional.

Karoly lowered his voice "You are leaving?" He had heard it was next to impossible to escape the capital now that the criminal Nazis had enforced the yellow star badge. The group had complained to Bari that they needed help, as the agents who were supposed to be dropped in had not arrived. At present there were simply too many Nazis, too many gendarmes, too many informers.

"They are shipping me out tomorrow."

"What exactly do you mean?"

"The Nazis."

Karoly felt his head spinning. No, it could not be. They could not take away Tommy; he was so good, so young. He stared at him through the semi-darkness.

"Where? Did they say?"

"I think they are taking us to the camp in Auschwitz."

Karoly frowned and his dismay was soon replaced with fury. Fury that the fascist criminals who were rumored to have been condemning people to death in those camps would spread such evil and do it with calculated precision. "You are not going." He reached up with a hand, tore the yellow star off his friend's jacket, and angrily threw it down to the polished stone floor. "You are coming home, with me."

"But ..."

"Don't say a word. If we are stopped, let me do the talking." He then bent down, retrieved the star, and hid it in his pocket.

Tommy nodded. He knew he could count on Karoly. Together they walked out at a brisk pace and headed down the street, looking at no one. Some old women on the corner – also wearing the yellow star – were embracing family members, in an attempt to console them. Karoly's heart became heavy as he had to walk by with his friend. Tommy dared not even glance in their direction as he walked away from the all too familiar wails. The air was heavy with mourning. A few blocks later, they encountered a group of light haired children being given candies by some laughing German soldiers. They saluted Karoly and he nodded, quickening his gait, as though he were on his way to an important meeting.

Once they had reached the Schandl villa, the pair hastily climbed the steps to the second floor apartment. Tommy was trembling. "What now?" he wondered aloud. "Someone may have seen us and they might notice when I don't come out, so the Nazis will be dispatched. I noticed there were guards outside the embassy next door and one of them looked like he was watching as he smoked. How can one be certain that they are trustworthy?"

"Don't worry about the Finnish Embassy guards."

"You are sure?"

"I am sure. Besides, no one will be able to prove you are here." Karoly led him to the bathroom, where there was what appeared to be a panel. He pressed on a certain part of the wood and the panel was then shown to be a door, which opened with ease. "It's a secret large closet," he explained, "and you can lock it from the inside. There will be enough air so you don't have to worry about suffocating. Of course, you only need to hide when the Nazis or anyone else is around. Otherwise, my home is yours. I will bring you food every day."

"How can I thank you, Karoly?"

"Stay alive, Tommy. Just stay alive."

The following weeks, no one at the Schandl villa appeared to notice that Karoly made frequent trips to the kitchen for food, without gaining any extra weight – no one, that is, except his mother, Terezia. She noted the way he hastily departed, often with stuffed sleeves, and wondered to whom he was taking the food. She waited until one day when, after dinner, he stood up and excused himself, a breadroll in hand. She winked at Karoly Senior, who chuckled despite the danger of their situation.

"My son, wait." Terezia stood up, placed a large serving of chicken in paprika sauce with dumplings on a porcelain plate, and handed it to him. "For the guest you are hiding."

Karoly accepted the plate, a look of consternation on his face. "It isn't a woman."

"No." Terezia waved the servants away before continuing. "You are hiding in your apartment a Jewish refugee. I have thought as much for weeks.Why did you not tell us?"

"It puts everyone in grave danger to know. We could all be shot."

Terezia raised her head proudly. "Tell your friend that he is welcome to join us for dinner at any time, provided, for his own safety, that he is wearing the frock of a Paulist priest." She reminded him of the arrangement that had been made with the fathers, for precisely such occasions – they had even supplied a document claiming to have been renting the upstairs apartment for priests who were visiting from out of town.

Karoly kissed his mother on both cheeks and took the plate of food upstairs to his friend. From then on, Tommy would sometimes join the family for dinner in the dining room, dressed as a priest, though from time to time, Terezia had to help him rearrange the sash correctly.

With his friend now safe, Karoly once more focused on the activities of the resistance group. They simply had to do more. When they had their next meeting in the Cave Church, he listened quietly as each man spoke. They were clad in priest's robes, except for Karoly, who had argued that as he lived just up the street, he really needed no disguise.

Father Horvath came in every now and then, without making a sound, to ensure that things were going smoothly. All of the fathers and brothers possessed an almost ethereal quality of being present and yet somehow invisible. *It would serve Father Horvath well in later months, when the Germans themselves would use their dining room for a meeting of their own.*

After George had assured them that Bari was doing everything in their power to send them assistance, Sam spoke up. "I''ve made contact with another resistance group, led entirely by Hungarians. They say they will be able to supply us with machine guns."

Nick seemed skeptical. "If the Germans find anyone with such guns, they will be shot on the spot."

Sam rolled his eyes.

"Armed men will eventually be required to protect the new anti-Nazi Hungarian government," George pointed out. His friends looked at him in surprise and he went on. "There have been meetings taking place behind closed doors, much like this one – meetings that involve well connected friends of our cause. After our work is complete, they will be ready to govern."

"The Allies have to get here first," Karoly pointed out. "The Germans are amassing more troops by the day and before long, every boy will be dragged in to enlist as well. We cannot wait for that to happen. We also cannot stand idly by as Jewish men, women and children are rounded up. They need more protection – protection that we are unable to provide due to our small numbers. How many men do we have to date?"

"A few dozen trustworthy fellows are now part of our resistance umbrella," George replied. "And our network is growing by the day."

"There is also the Diplomat who is excellent at providing papers," Nick interjected. "I heard he has returned to Budapest and there are Dutchmen working alongside him in the cause. Karoly, his embassy is just behind your villa."

Karoly nodded. "He is quite remarkable, though our paths have not yet crossed."

Bokreta Street, Budapest, Hungary

Sister Sara patted the head of the thirteen year old boy, who stared at her with dark, round, very frightened eyes.

"I don't want to die."

"Don't worry, Joseph, everything will be fine. Your parents have left you in good hands."

"Why couldn't I go with them to the house where they are hiding?" he said unhappily, his voice quiet. "I don't take up very much room. I didn't want us to be separated."

"It would have been too risky. They will stay there with others and don't know how long they will be able to remain there. Remember, your father said it was a temporary arrangement. Once they have found a more secure, permanent place, they will send for you."

Terezia rushed into the kitchen of the Bokreta Retirement Home for Working Women, where an elderly lady had told her she would find Sister Sara. The women there called Sara the Angel, not only because of her serene and kind disposition, but also for the way she took such good care of everyone, with sweet determination.

"I hope I am not too late! Where are they?"

"Joseph's father and his wife thought it would be best if they went elsewhere, to one of the safe houses."

Terezia shook her head. "They should have waited. I could have taken them to my home."

"An entire family suddenly appearing at your house would prove too risky." Sister Sara wiped the tears from the boy's face. "Joseph will stay with us for the time being, until his parents can send for him."

Terezia nodded "Very well. Joseph, I am going to give you a new identity."

"I won't be called Joseph anymore?"

"You may remain Joseph if you wish, but your last name must be different. How does Heyes sound?"

"It's all right."

"From now on you are Joseph Heyes, a Transylvanian refugee who recently arrived to Budapest." She went on to tell

51

him the new story of his life, based on the experiences she had heard of recently arrived Transylvanian refugees. Terezia Schandl was a wonderful storyteller, who could combine the realities of various people into a single new one. It had to be believable – that way, if anyone questioned the boy, he would not be suspected of hiding his true identity.

Joseph nodded earnestly when she had finished.

Sister Sara smiled.

"One must somehow outsmart the authorities." Terezia opened her black purse and took out a rosary. She had many. "This will make it even more authentic. Keep it in your pocket, Joseph, and if the Nazis ever question you, tell them it is from your grandmother, who is still in Transylvania."

When she put it in his hand, he examined it with youthful curiosity. "Lots of beads."

Sister Sara and Terezia smiled at his innocence. Then Terezia was serious again. "I will be back in a few days with the papers to back up his new identity."

Sister Sara smiled like an angel and Joseph suddenly felt safe. *Things would be fine here and after a while, he would be able to join his parents.* He shoved the rosary in his pocket. Sister Sara suggested he start cutting onions, which she would help him finish. There were many hungry guests in the home to take care of.

"You start and I will join you in a few minutes," she said softly, walking into the hall with Terezia. Once they were out of earshot, she was serious again. "For now I will try and keep him out of sight. As soon as the papers are ready, perhaps he can work in the guard's booth, to justify why he is staying here. I will insist he is helping me."

"Yes," Terezia agreed. "It would be wise, sister."

Sister Sara then returned to the kitchen - and Joseph.

Terezia turned around and was on the verge of walking outdoors when a tall, elegantly dressed young woman, her auburn hair piled atop her head, walked toward her, seeming to have appeared form the shadows.

"Pardon me, Mrs. Schandl? Might I have a word with you? I was told I might find you here."

She came closer, her steps echoing on the wooden floor, and Terezia noticed she was wearing the yellow Star of David on her coat.

Terezia suddenly realized that the woman looked familiar, but from where did she know her? "I beg your pardon?"

"I am Esther Suto. I work at the hair salon you frequent. I ... I hear that you are helping people ..."

Terezia recognized her and then paused. It was a well known fact that certain tactics were being used in order to entrap those who went against the German's instructions. How could she be sure she was not a plant or an informer? Had Tommy been discovered? Her heart began to pound and she wondered how to respond.

"I need help. I have heard that you are helping people and your son is involved with ..."

"Please do not speak of such things out in the open." She still did not quite know what to make of it, yet was relieved that Tommy's safety had not been compromised. He was such a nice boy – like one of the family.

Esther opened her mouth to speak, but then lost her composure and collapsed to the floor, tears streaming down her cheeks. "I know they are going to send me to the camp. I will die there. You ... were my last hope ... please ... help me. I heard you are a compassionate woman. I have nowehere else to turn. They have already taken my husband."

Terezia looked around to make sure that none of the elderly guests of the home had wandered into the hall. They were alone. She suddenly reached down, yanked the yellow star off Esther's coat and hastily put it in her purse, snapping it shut. *She would later burn it.*

She nodded. "I will help you."

Esther slowly stood up and brushed away her tears.

Terezia took her by the hand. "I will take you home with me. You mustn't cry. With all these deportations, the Germans suspect anyone who weeps in public nowadays. We must give an impression of tranquility, in order to escape detection."

Esther caught her breath in her throat and willed away any tears.

Terezia produced a handkerchief and gently wiped the remaining tears from Esther's face. "Do not worry – I will not let the Nazis take you."

After they had reached the villa, Terezia ushered her guest inside and sat her down in the living room. "You will stay here for now, until I have papers and a more suitable placement."

"Another home?"

"I can find you employment as a helper at a retirement home. Otherwise, there will be too many risks."

Esther appeared perplexed. "But how?"

"You will have a new identity as a recently arrived Transylvanian refugee and will have to memorize everything to the letter. In the meantime, you will stay here but we will have to pretend you are in my employ."

A few minutes later, Terezia summoned her housekeeper and informed her that Esther – a new employee – would be assisting her in household matters.

Esther was then given the dress and apron of a maid to wear, and disappeared with the housekeeper, who was to assign her indoor chores, to make it all appear legitimate.

That was the day Terezia decided that the five charities on whose board she served would be the ideal cover for those in need. She would be able to place scores of men and women as "helpers" and no one would suspect anything. The time had come to make arrangements, for she now needed papers for two refugees in her care - and soon, she did not doubt, there would be many more ...

A few days later, things were in place and Terezia approached the two Hungarian guards outside the Finnish Embassy, who smiled upon seeing her.

"Good afternoon, Mrs. Schandl."

"Good afternoon."

"It was kind of you to have one of your servants bring us cold drinks today," the senior of the two said gratefully. "It was such a hot day."

"One does help as one can," she replied soberly. She then

glanced around, to ensure that no one else was outside, and nodded. The senior guard asked the junior guard to take out the list, which he then gave to Terezia Schandl.

She was pleased to see dozens of names of recently arrived Transylvanians – ethnic Hungarians who had escaped from Romania to Hungary. As per their arrangement, the guards would procure such lists from the local police station and give them to her. That way, she would have a concrete list of names to give the Jewish refugees so that their identities would be as real as possible.Then she would give the list to her new contact, who would, in return, provide her with the forged papers she needed for the Jewish refugees she would be hiding in various places. It was an arrangement that the Nazis would never discover and the guards were never in any danger, for they themselves believed she only wanted the lists to see whether any of her own relatives were among the recent arrivals.

It was the perfect cover.

Terezia thanked the guards, concealed the list in her purse, and hastily returned to her villa next door in time to oversee that day's dinner. It would only take her a few days to have the necessary papers, as the list of possible names was already in her possession.

CHAPTER 5
PARTISAN ORGANIZER

Budapest, Hungary – Autumn 1944

A captured British agent was being held in one of the prisons and he was supposed to be rescued. It wasn't going to be the kind of unrealistic rescue that one read about in stories, for this POW, like all the others who had been "sprung," would simply be bought. The guards liked money and that was something Karoly's group could easily provide. The agent in question - a partisan organizer - had been dropped into Slovakia, crossed into Hungary, and had been arrested when he tried to cross back. Hence his imprisonment.

"Dan," the agent, was to be taken by certain members of the group to a safe location where he would be able to hide as long as he needed to. That location just happened to be the Schandl villa on Gellert Hill, on the Buda side of Budapest. Karoly was away at Headquarters at the time the "escape" was scheduled, so Dan was taken to the Cave Church, where he was provided with a priest's frock. Then he was sent to the villa up the street, but he had to be dressed as a Paulist father for that was the only way Terezia Schandl would accept him.

When the doorbell rang, Esther started for the door but Terezia stopped her. The housekeeper had unwisely suggested that Esther answer the door every time a knock or doorbell ring was heard, not realizing what kind of danger she put herself in by the otherwise trivial act. If anyone happened to recognize her as Esther the hairdresser, they would immediately question why she was now one of the household staff and it would not take them long to put the pieces together.

Thus, after a short time, Terezia quickly procured papers for Esther and arranged for her to be safely transferred to another home.

The doorbell ran again. Terezia opened the door and was greeted by a nervous man who was clad in the frock of the Paulist Order. She knew all of the fathers and brothers, given how close the Schandls were to the Cave Church – both physically and spiritually – yet had never before seen this man. In addition, his sash was incorrectly tied. He might have been connected with her son's underground group – or he might have been a Nazi spy.

"I came from the church, the one down the street," he said in English.

She had to be sure. "Who took you there?"

"Nick and someone called Tibor."

The sun bore down on Terezia's face and she quickly ushered him inside. Tibor was one of the new additions to the British led resistance.

"They told me Karoly will know what to do."

The housekeeper peered curiously around the corner. Terezia took no notice of her, ushered the man inside, and shut and locked the door. It had been a bad night. The Allies had dropped bombs again and a neighbor on the next street had been killed. Everyone was hoping for a speedy end to the war – everyone, that is, except the fascists, hate mongers, and opportunists that pervaded the city.

"Karoly is away for the day. Can you speak Hungarian? If an informer overhears you, you will be carted off by the Germans as soon as they can get a reward for your head." She walked toward him and pointed at his sash. "It is not correctly tied. One must be careful, even among the neighbors." She then showed him how to put on the sash correctly.

"Are you hungry?"

"Starved, madam …"

"Mrs. Schandl."

He nodded and switched to Hungarian. "I'm Dan. I sure am glad to be here."

"We are all happy to help the cause. You seem to speak Hungarian well for an Englishman."

"I was born in Hungary. Your husband is here?"

She took a step back, surveyed the sash, which he had re-tied, and nodded approvingly. "My husband is resting. I have a housekeeper and servants here at all times. My son Karoly is a Second Lieutenant in the Hungarian Reserves. You will be staying in his apartment upstairs … with his other guest. It has a separate entrance. You will be able to hide there, with Tommy." She excused herself for a moment to ask one of the servants to bring their guest some nourishment.

When she returned, Dan appeared to be nervous again. "Is Tommy also a British agent?"

"No, he is not with the English. He is a … friend who is staying with Karoly. He's a Hungarian law student."

Dan seemed relieved.

A few hours later, Karoly arrived at the villa and introduced himself. Dan nodded quietly and the two men shook hands. They then left and walked up the separate entrance to Karoly's apartment. The guards at the embassy next door seemed to make Dan uncomfortable. Once they were inside, Karoly walked toward the wall in the bathroom and tapped on it. A secret door opened and a thin young man walked out.

"This is Tommy, a good friend. He lives here."

Dan stared in awe.

Tommy grinned. "You don't look like a priest."

"Dan is a partisan organizer, an English agent."

An awkward silence filled the room. Dan then mentioned he was extremely tired so Karoly showed him the guest room where he would be sleeping. "But never come down without the Paulist frock on," he warned. "The Germans are increasingly nosy about the goings-on at the house."

"They searched the house a few times while I was hiding in the secret closet and Karoly led them around, as cool as a cucumber!" Tommy boasted.

"Things are not always what they appear," Karoly chuckled.

"I saw the housckeeper talking to a maid earlier but she didn't seem like a maid," Dan remarked.

It didn't surprise Karoly that he had noticed as much. All British agents had received training before being sent to the continent. Part of that training was to be an expert in the art of observation. "She is hiding here for the time being, until her papers are ready. Then she and the others will be transferred to a safe place."

"There are others hiding here, too?"

Karoly shrugged his shoulders. "The villa is busy. People come, people go. It's the nature of a safe house."

Before Dan shut the door, Karoly casually inquired "By the way, what was your mission before you were caught by the Germans?"

Dan hesitated and responded by yawning and explaining that he was sleep deprived as they had scarcely let him shut his eyes in the prison camp.

Karoly turned and walked back to the living room after he had closed the door. Tommy was sitting on the sofa, having donned his priest's frock. "What is for dinner this evening?"

Karoly sat in the armchair across from him. "I forgot to ask."

Tommy gestured toward the shut guest room door. "He sure didn't act like the organizer of anything."

"He was just sprung from the prison by the group today. For all practical pupuses, he was a captured prisoner-of-war, who is now an escapee, someone in hiding."

"You are always pragmatic, Karoly. Will he be staying long?"

"As long as he needs to hide."

"Maybe tomorrow he'll fill us in on what his mission was."

"Tomorrow our group has a meeting."

"Here?"

Karoly stood up. "No, it's getting too risky. It would probably be more advisable to hold the meeting at the Cave Church." He glanced in the direction of the guest room but said nothing more.

Tommy stood up as well and announced that he was looking forward to another family dinner.

That night, Karoly went out, to stay with a lady friend. Tommy slept, as always, in a comfortable bed near the secret closet in case anyone was heard approaching, and Dan was left in the guest room – at least that was what everyone assumed.

The loud bombing the previous night had made the housekeeper too anxious to fall asleep. She was pacing her room when she heard the distinct sounds of movement outside. The wind perhaps? Noisy bats? Everyone else was fast asleep and the family dog was indoors. Had Karoly Junior brought home a friend? Eventually her curiosity got the better of her. She quietly walked to the window and looked out.

In the moonlight, she could see a man who looked like the Schandls' English guest near the bushes, where two figures who appeared to be men were crouching – and they were all discussing something in hushed tones. The housekeeper watched them for a few moments, then deciding to return to bed. She would have an early morning.

Never mind the Englishman and his unknown friends.

The following morning, Karoly returned in time to have an early breakfast with his mother. The British agent was still sleeping.

Terezia sipped her tea slowly, carefully weighing her words. "I know that something is troubling you, my son." She did not wish to pry into his underground activities, yet somehow, these last few days had been different. He no longer exuded optimism.

"The army will promote me in a few months, to the rank of captain. I am to continue in an administrative capacity … if I am present by then."

"Perhaps by then the war will be over and no one will need to think of the horrible Nazis."

Karoly shook his head. "Unfortunately, mother, by then things might be even worse than they already are."

Canada - January 10, 2005

Chris had returned to the house, as promised, with news of the results of his findings on Lambert and the mysterious Riley. He sat down in an armchair next to the fireplace and opened his file. Kati could not help but smile. He had always been organized.

"Lambert is on the up and up. Just an international historian from what I gathered, with all kinds of research interests."

"I guessed as much."

"He is likely just ambitious."

"Anything else?"

"There was no record of a John Riley who had anything to do with anyone in Budapest, Hungary at that time – or so the records indicate. I was unable to find what name it had been changed from. What troubles me, however, is that this so-called Riley person called you from nearby."

"He didn't say it was long distance, and left a local number. It just didn't happen to be a working one," Kati pointed out, carefully placing the yellowing manuscript on the coffee table before her.

"Is that what I think it is?"

"I came across it after you left."

"That would be …"

"The next part of his memoirs. I've been pouring through it all day, going back to old photographs, old documents, the half empty old address book."

Chris shut the file. "My lawyer's instincts tell me there's a story behind that comment about the address book."

"We don't have his original one, the one that had all the names and addresses from all over the world."

"Enlighten me on that."

"The original address book he had was lost."

"How did that happen?"

"He wasn't sure. Dad was carrying it around once when he had Christmas cards to mail. He put it down with some envelopes at the post office but when he picked up his things to leave, it was gone." She reached across the table and tapped on a worn green address book which appeared to be falling apart at the seams. "This is the replacement one. It still has a lot of names and addresses in it, but only those of people who sent him Christmas cards that year. That was how he found some of the addresses again – from the arriving correspondence and greetings."

Chris sighed. "Basically that means that only the addresses of friends are in that book."

"It could also include people he thought were his friends or people who wanted him to think they were his friends – in addition to his regular contacts."

"I see you're getting very good at this sleuthing, though I still have a major concern. First Riley's tall tales about knowing your father, then the threatening note. You are obviously being watched, Kati, and we don't even know why or by whom. I think it would be a good idea for me to move into the house with you for the next while."

CHAPTER 6
THE MISSION

Budapest, Hungary – late November, 1944

The capital had become a nightmare. As of October 16, the Germans had removed the no longer cooperative Hungarian government, handing over power to the much dreaded Arrow Cross fascist Ferenc Szálasi, who had been dubbed the new head of state. The Arrow Cross were allies of the Nazis. Eichmann's sickening "final solution" was to be carried out, and the fascist soldiers of the Arrow Cross, with their German guns, were rounding up anyone of Jewish origin. They had no humanity. Men, women and children were being sent on death marches, thousands dying along the way, and anyone who tried to help risked being shot on the spot. Regent Horthy, after attempting to side with the Allies, had been removed from power by Hitler and was in German "protective custody."

George was just days away from going into hiding and there was considerable strain on the group as they met in the Cave Church for what would be their final meeting, though none at the time would know as much.

Karoly was the first one to speak. "I will no longer stay in the army." He then addressed George. "How are the negotiations going?"

Dan seemed interested all of a sudden. He had casually asked to attend the meeting in order to meet with the main members of the British resistance group, yet had appeared to be less than in tune with their activities and objectives – at least until now. "You have important contacts you are negotiating with?" *He had heard their forte was intelligence and connections ...*

"The anti-Nazi Hungarian government will be ready to govern soon," George announced.

"We need things to happen faster," Nick complained.

"People are being killed every day …"

"The Russians are advancing," Karoly stated. "The Nazis will be defeated eventually."

"That reminds me of another matter." George, who had become progressively thinner in the last few months, withdrew from under his priest's sash a scrap of paper. "Bari says we need to continue delivering the reports as usual, along with the Allied POWs."

Karoly was surprised. "But the Russians are now heavily based in the south, blocking passage to the Tito partisans. How can we deliver anything or anyone to them?"

"It has been difficult," George admitted. "There was a Palestinian sergeant who was unable to get through the designated route just last week."

Karoly frowned. "Then the Dutchman has not been safely returned to the Dutch?"

"No, he has not. He is still here in Budapest, waiting to be safely delivered."

Nick glanced at Dan, whose eyes were suddenly downcast. "You met the Dutchman, didn't you?"

"Of course he did," Karoly replied. "It was the Dutchman who came and took his and Tommy's photographs for their fake IDs. He's very good at it, too. He has made hundreds of those photo IDs, and helped numerous people with documents. He is an admirable fellow."

Sam, whose mind was still on a weapons transaction he had been involved in earlier that day, nodded absentmindedly. "The Swedish Diplomat is lucky to have him."

Dan raised his eyes. "The Dutchman works for the Diplomat? He never said that."

Karoly shrugged his shoulders. "Why should he say it. It's a known fact."

"The Diplomat has been seen in a lot of places in the city," Nick marvelled. "He is not only a great humanitarian, but a brave fellow as well."

"Yes," George agreed, "and I hope he and his driver are careful."

"Budapest is more dangerous by the day," Karoly

complained. "The Arrow Cross are marching up to the villa almost every day now, demanding to do a search of the premises. We have refugees in hiding, and the Swedish Diplomat is hiding 30 Jewish men, women, and children in the Finnish Embassy next door."

Sam frowned. "How are Tommy and the others?"

"They are fine for now."

George tucked the paper under his priest's sash. "I have received orders that we are to take the Dutchman to a place south of Lake Velence, where he is to meet up with the Russians. Karoly, I'd like you to accept the task. That will be your mission. It's all been arranged."

Dan began to fidget uncomfortably. "I hope I am not supposed to go with him."

Sam turned toward him. "I thought a partisan organizer would be ready for action."

Dan said nothing. George tried to smooth things over. "Dan is in a foreign land, and Hungary is a dangerous place, especially for an English agent. One cannot blame him for wanting to be cautious. If he were caught by the Nazis, he would be tortured and executed."

"Like all of us," Sam pointed out.

George did not disagree.

"When will I have more specifics of the mission, like the time?" Karoly inquired.

"I will deliver them to you in a few days," Sam offered, "along with the Dutchman."

"It is to be December 4," George explained. "The Russians will be informed of the special meeting place." He added where the meeting place would be - at an estate.

Father Horvath appeared in the doorway and then slowly walked toward the group. "Some Germans were here earlier," he said quietly. "They were discussing plans they have, strategic plans."

They listened with interest as he went on. "It seems they intend to blow up the bridges of Budapest. I heard them talking about it in the dining room of the monastery. They came in and took over, saying they were having their meeting here. After an hour, they left."

"We will warn Bari about the bridges." George nodded at Nick. "In the next radio transmission."

"So it wasn't a rumor," Sam scoffed. "They really do intend to fight the Russians to the bitter end once they arrive."

"They will lose," Karoly said matter-of-factly.

Dan paled considerably. "Germans were here? Are they coming back?"

Father Horvath shook his head. "No, my son, they are nowhere near the church."

When he had left, they continued discussing their resistance activities. The group which had access to guns was going to provide them in the next few days, the Dutchman would be delivered to the Russians, along with a message, and then the Dutchman would be forwarded to the I.S. (Intelligence Service), and Karoly to the newly formed anti-Nazi Hungarian government. George stated that when the Russians reached Budapest, he would put on his British uniform and go to their headquarters to ask for "food and transportation for all the escapees in hiding."

Meanwhile, Sam would lead a small underground army of armed anti-Nazi Hungarians who would help restore law and order. Nick would continue the transmissions with Bari, so as to maintain contact, and they could continue carrying out their orders as per British intelligence. It would be a joint British and Russian effort that would help the small Hungarian resistance – and the Nazis would be no more. Logistically, the scenario was not without certain problems, but if they worked together and followed the orders from their friends at Allied Headquarters, George was certain they would succeed.

"And then," he finished, "we will have a great reunion."

"What about afterwards?" Everyone appeared puzzled by Dan's question. "Will this group continue its activities after?"

Nick shook his head. The English agent was less than well versed in international politics. "There will be no need when the war is over. There will be free elections and safety for everyone in Hungary."

"Look for the Smallholders party to win," Sam added.

"Their mandate is an excellent one."

"You mean your mandate," Karoly joked. They all chuckled. Sam had made no secret of his political aspirations.

"Our resistance group will cease to exist when things are as they should be." George stood up and bowed slightly. "However, my friends, I will go on."

"As a British agent?" Karoly said incredulously.

"Exactly so. I cannot say what my orders will be or where they will take me, but rest assured, my loyalty will be to you, my best friends from the Piarist Boy Scouts."

Sam stood up and patted his friend on the back. "British intelligence is lucky to have you, George …"

"Albert." Nick rose from his seat. "That's how he's already known in Bari and with the intelligence contacts."

Karoly stared at his friend, his brow creased with apprehension. He knew all to well that once an intelligence agent was assigned a name by which he would then be known, he belonged more to the organization to which he had pledged allegiance than any other earthly entity. "It is to be your career, then?"

They all reached for their guns, which they had placed on the wooden table for the meeting – as an act of good faith for the fathers – and once more concealed them underneath their robes. Karoly was no longer wearing his uniform, and placed his gun in his dark coat pocket.

"Yes, I've agreed to remain in the Intelligence Service indefinitely." Remembering the business at hand, George went on. "When you come in contact with the Russians, Karoly, be sure and say that Albert sent you. That's my code name. Then they will understand that everything is on the up and up."

Karoly nodded. Sam reiterated that he would bring the specific instructions and the Dutchman in the next few days. Nick reminded them that he and George would be going into hiding. There were a few places where they would be able to stay. They would be in touch when things settled down. No one knew how long that would be. The friends then said their goodbyes and went their separate ways into the night. Karoly disappeared behind the Cave Church, up the path. Dan followed closely behind.

They walked up the path to the Schandl villa, which was approximately 200 meters from the Cave Church. It was a cool evening so the embassy guards were standing in the garage. Terezia Schandl gave them permission to come and stand in the garage anytime it was cold. They too often expressed their loathing of the Nazis and Arrow Cross and hoped that the war would be over soon, with the Germans gone. They had families – wives who did not want them to remain at such a dangerous location.

The family dog, a friendly black corgi, bounded toward them and barked. Karoly patted him and let him inside.

In the nights that followed, everyone had to gather downstairs in the bunker to endure the heavy bombing of the Allied planes. It had become a fact of life. Terezia sat next to Karoly Senior, whose hair had whitened and whose eyes had become even more tired. They had been married since she was sixteen years old and her devotion to him was matched only by her faith and her commitment to doing what was right.

Karoly, Dan, and Tommy soon joined them, both Dan and Tommy having donned their priest's frocks. There were a few neighbors and relations as well, yet no children.

The children had been sent to the bunker at the Cave Church, as it was 25 meters underground.

There was an elderly retired nurse who was staying at the villa. That night, she was nowhere to be seen. Dan fidgeted nervously with his sash as the neighbors huddled and prepared for a long, loud night. Somewhere in the distant night sky an explosion was heard and everything vibrated.

Terezia stood up. "Mrs. Kovacs is not here. It is unlike her. Perhaps she was frightened by the loud noise and went to find shelter elscwhere. I am worried. What if she did not make it elsewhere in time?"

Karoly was at her side in an instant. "I will go and find her. Please stay with the others."

There was a whirring, screaming sound and then another explosion – this one so loud that it made everyone's ears ring.

The bombs were getting closer, and the fact that the Schandl villa was between two embassies meant it would continue. The Germans were notorious for occupying foreign embassies and that was what the Allies must therefore have incorrectly assumed. Hence the Allied planes' bombardment of the area.

Terezia insisted on going with her son. She followed him out as the planes roared overhead, and felt her way around in the darkness.

Karoly took her by the hand. "Quickly! They might spot us moving and think we are Germans!"

Together they raced outside, to search for her in the back garden. Mrs Kovacs was not there, though the door leading indoors was slightly ajar. She must have been frightened back indoors. They went back inside toward her room. Her quarters had not been damaged by any bombs and yet some shrapnel must have somehow found its way inside, for Mrs. Kovacs was sitting in a chair, dead. Half of her head had been blown away from her lifeless body. It was a horrifying sight. Brain matter was splattered on the wall.

Terezia gasped and Karoly shook his head. When and how had it happened? Shrapnel? The room had not been destroyed. In fact, nothing else in the room appeared to have been touched.

Together they quietly returned to the bunker, Terezia praying as they went, Karoly wondering what exactly had transpired in that room.

Budapest, Hungary – Monday, December 4, 1944

Karoly opened the door to the young visitor and ushered him inside. The Dutchman had remembered which entrance to take – the separate one which led upstairs to Karoly's private apartment.

"Good day." His face was drawn and he carried his belongings, including his camera, in a small bag. He had the features and bearing of one who came from a privileged background. He was 24 years old.

"I've been expecting you," Karoly said quietly.

Dan and Tommy were downstairs, disguised as priests, helping to repair some of the damage which had been done to the windows in the last air raid, so they were alone.

Sam stepped in after the Dutchman, his hand in his pocket where his gun was concealed. "What a relief that they haven't come for you, Karoly."

Karoly shut and locked the door. "They won't have realized it yet. I was on leave yesterday."

"Indefinitely extended now."

"Nazis are dispicable." Karoly muttered something under his breath in Hungarian.

The Dutchman did not appear to understand so Sam and Karoly switched to German again. They had often wondered if that was the reason their group had been recruited by British intelligence – not only did they all hail from influential families, but also they spoke several languages, with the exception of Russian.

"It's a cool day." Sam handed Karoly the instructions. Karoly read the slip of paper and then tossed it into his living room fireplace.

He watched the flames engulf it until it was gone and only graying dead ashes remained. "So we are to go to the estate in the wine country and wait there for the Russians. That is still to be the meeting place."

Sam nodded. "Nick received confirmation from Allied Headquarters in Bari. It was sent from their radio to George at our group's headquarters – or should I say, Albert. They said the Russians will meet you at the estate at the given time. It is the same plan as what we discussed at our last meeting, in the Cave Church."

"Everything is the same?"

"Yes. They will forward you to the newly formed anti-Nazi Hungarian government, and your guest will be taken to the I.S."

The Dutchman nodded. "I appreciate your assistance, gentlemen."

Karoly put on his coat, after checking that his watch was accurate and well wound. "It will be a very long walk and I will not be able to wear the uniform of a Second Lieutenant of the Hungarian army. We will need to be careful."

The Dutchman did not hesitate to respond. "We have outwitted the Germans already on many occasions."

Sam agreed and made his way to the door. Before leaving, he glanced at Karoly, his dark eyes serious. "Godspeed, my friend." Then he was gone.

Shortly afterwards, two figures quietly made their way out of the apartment, down the stairs, and got in the car that was awaiting them. The plan was that Tibor would drive them part of the way, and the rest would need to be on foot. As Karoly knew the area well, he knew he would succeed in reaching their destination – unlike the Palestinian sergeant before them, who had been unable to get through.

Tibor dropped them off on a road that was lined with leafless trees and sped back toward the capital. Karoly stared at the road ahead, aware of the risks that were involved. The Palestinian sergeant before them had been stopped on the road. He therefore opted to take a less traveled route that would have been unfamiliar to the Gestapo or SS. They would walk through frozen vineyards and terrain, far from the glare of any Nazi patrols. The Dutchman walked with him as they progressed, their boots crunching over the frozen land.

Had the circumstances been different, Karoly would have been happy to tell him about where they were going – that Lake Velence was the region where hundreds of hectares of land were cultivated for wine. In the summer, the vineyards were spectacular. Now, however, the land was frozen, the estates were half empty, and the country was embroiled in the midst of a war. He wished the Dutchman and the Diplomat for whom the Dutchman worked would have been able to see Hungary in a different time.

They continued to walk and the temperature fell – or had they just been walking that long? He knew exactly where they were going. It was to the estate of a friend whose family had been in the wine making business for generations. He motioned to the Dutchman that he would carry the bag for him now, yet the Dutchman shook his head. Thus far, the hardship had not bothered him.

For hours they marched on as Karoly the messenger led the visitor through frozen marsh and back gardens, never stopping, never slowing down. They could see their breath it was so cold and their fingers were starting to feel numb even inside their thick gloves. Finally, by nightfall, they reached their destination, 18 kilometers south of Lake Velence. Karoly nodded knowingly at the Dutchman and they noiselessly approached the front door of the house. Karoly knocked, using the predetermined code.

The door was opened by a servant. He motioned for them to enter, took them to a sitting room, and then disappeared. Karoly would have liked to ask him to bring them some tea but doubted he would return. He removed his gloves and rubbed his hands to warm them. The Dutchman placed his bag on the floor and sat down in a Louis XVI chair. Karoly remained standing.

The Dutchman appeared to be fatigued. "They are not here."

"It is early. We will wait." There was a Swiss clock on the marble mantelpiece. He watched it ticking and his mind began to wander. He had told his parents of his orders to take the Dutchman to the Russians. They had not been happy that he had to leave for the front lines. He had assured them that he would be gone for only a few weeks, yet what if that had been a gross miscalculation on his part? What if the war took even longer to come to an end? He also had the matter of Mrs. Kovacs' death to look into. How long would it be until he could actually do something about it?

All at once there was a loud bang. The Dutchman looked surprised. Karoly frowned. The banging resumed and he realized it was a person – or persons – at the front door. He slid to the window and looked through the white lace curtains, perceiving the outlines of men in uniforms – and those uniforms were not German.

"It's them."

The Dutchman picked up his bag and together they walked to the front door. Karoly opened it. There were five soldiers wearing the uniform of the Red Army. The fact that there were five caught him off guard, as five men were not needed for a simple transfer. Apprehension turned to disbelief when they drew their machine guns and began to yell orders in Russian, a language neither he nor the Dutchman knew. They instinctively raised their hands.

Karoly stared at them through the semi-darkness. "Albert sent us," he explained in Hungarian, then German. "We were sent by Albert, of British intelligence."

The stony-faced soldiers took the Dutchman's bag and relieved them each of their watches, motioning for them to place their hands behind their backs.

"Is this a robbery?" the Dutchman said incredulously.

Karoly shook his head as the soldiers handcuffed them and roughly yanked them out of the doorway. Had it been a robbery, they would have gone inside and looted or at least looked for valuables. They seemed intent on taking prisoners in this case, and nothing else. *There must have been a problem somewhere in the lines of communication.*

Karoly repeated again "Albert sent us. We are with Albert. We are resistance. I am from Albert's group."

Silence.

Karoly said it again.

"Nyet," was the stern reply.

"George."

The soldiers tightened their grip on their guns.

Karoly was exasperated. "It was all arranged by George. I am the messenger. I am delivering the Dutchman to you. He is to be taken to the I.S., the British Intelligence Service, and I am to be forwarded to the newly formed anti-Nazi Hungarian government." He said it in Hungarian and then in German.

A tall figure in a long black coat, the collar flipped up to partially conceal his face, stepped out of the shadows. He was smoking and he watched them for a few moments with a pair of very small, keen eyes before opening his mouth to speak.

"Karoly Schandl, you and your friend are now in the hands of the Red Army." He dropped the cigarette onto the ground and crushed it with his shiny black boot. "You are spies and will be dealt with accordingly."

They were taken to a long black car and shoved inside. The Dutchman appeared dazed but Karoly suddenly understood exactly what was happening. They had just been arrested by the NKVD. It was about to get worse. They were about to be handed over to SMERSH, the brutal counter-intelligence of the Red Army.

Something had gone terribly wrong.

CHAPTER 7
THE SUITCASE

Budapest, Hungary – December 1944

It was Dan and Tommy who placed Mrs. Kovacs's lifeless form in a wooden box, which they then carried to nearby Orlay Street for burial. They buried her in a garden there. Orlay Street was the designated place where the neighbors temporarily buried bodies which would later be properly buried in cemeteries.

Dan was quiet the whole time and then disappeared back into Karoly's apartment without uttering a word to anyone.

Tommy returned with Terezia to the living room and informed her that Karoly had departed the previous day. She touched the cross which hung from the small chain around her neck. She looked worried. The tragedy of Mrs. Kovacs had left her shaken."Where exactly has he gone?"

"To take someone somewhere."

"The Dutchman?"

Tommy wished he knew all the specifics. He could perceive the anxiety on Mrs. Schandl's face and wished he could reassure her. "All I know is that he said he will be gone for a little while. Yes, he had to take the Dutchman."

" The one who works for the Diplomat?"

"Yes. He had to deliver him somewhere safely."

"Where?"

"He did not say."

Terezia dropped her hand and lowered her eyes. "I do not have a good feeling about this. He did tell us about it but he was very vague. He told us that he had to take the Dutchman to the Russians. I hoped he might have told you more. Do you know how long he will be gone?"

"He wasn't sure – anywhere from a few days to a few weeks. He has left the Hungarian army."

All of a sudden the housekeeper darted into the room.

Terezia looked up. "Whatever is the matter?"

"Someone is walking up to the gate!"

Tommy jumped up and headed for the kitchen. Terezia stood up, smoothed down her blue dress and went to the front door. When she opened it, she expected to find the Arrow Cross men who had been bothering her for regular searches for weeks now. She would simply tell them that her husband was asleep, that they would have to return another time. Upon opening the door, however, she was greeted instead by the sight of one of Karoly Schandl Senior's former employees, whose name she recalled was William Kis. Despite the cold, he was sweating and carrying a large suitcase.

"William, you are all right?"

"May I come in?" he gasped.

"Yes, of course." Terezia shut the door after him once he'd stepped inside. She glanced at his suitcase. "You are leaving Budapest?"

"Everything is in shambles but my mother and I will stay until the madness is over." He set the suitcase down and pulled out a handkerchief, dabbing at his temples. "They will probably force me into service like the others, even though I'm not such a young man. It is a death sentence to have to fight alongside the Nazis and the capital will soon be under siege even more, if that's possible!"

Terezia nodded sadly. "There is so much death."

"The death marches of the innocent continue and nearby they say the fighting is intensifying."

"Today we buried an elderly nurse who was staying with us."

"How awful! I understand you are hiding ..."

Terezia's eyes widened and she cut him off. "I do not know what you mean." Mr. Kis was from a respectable family, yet these were trying times. How did she know that William could be trusted? People's lives hung in the balance and she had been helping more and more refugees these past months. As soon as their papers were ready, they were usually forwarded to another location. Still, at any given time, there could be a number of refugees in her house, masquerading as servants and priests. She would not risk their lives, nor the lives of her family members. They would all be shot on the spot were the Arrow Cross or the Germans to get wind of her activities.

He lowered his voice and patted the suitcase. "I heard that you have a special and very safe place for hiding important documents."

"I do," she agreed, her eyes filled with relief. "Is your suitcase very heavy?"

"Almost too heavy for me," he complained. "Would it be possible for me to leave it here for safekeeping?"

"What is in it?"

"Documents. My mother suggested I bring it here and ask you to hide it for safekeeping."

Terezia smiled slightly. "We will look after your suitcase for the duration of the bombing. I can ask someone to help me move it to the hiding place. Give your mother my best and tell her to pray, for that is almost all we can do at present."

William Kis bowed, thanked her profusely, and took his leave. Moments later, Tommy had summoned Dan to help him drag the heavy dark suitcase down to the basement. It must have contained thousands of pages of family documents. When they had reached the bottom, Terezia pointed to a pile of coal. "Under there. We can bury it deep underneath."

It took a long time to dig under the coal, but when they had finally made a deep hole, the suitcase was placed in it and then covered with coal. No one would suspect it was there.

Tommy and Dan then returned to Karoly's apartment. Tommy found it difficult to be there without his friend and hoped he had succeeded in delivering the Dutchman.

After their 2 o'clock lunch, Dan announced to Tommy that he wanted to talk to him. "What do you know about the Diplomat? He has come around the vicinity many times, I've been watching through the window. What can you tell me about him?"

"Which diplomat?"

Dan said his name, with a hint of anger in his voice.

"I have never met the Diplomat." Tommy shrugged his

shoulders and decided to go back downstairs to see if Mrs. Schandl needed any moral support. She had seemed so perturbed about her son's absence. He did not place any importance on Dan's questions, as many were curious about the Diplomat, particularly because the Diplomat had become vital in the anti-Nazi resistance movement - and he himself was not a Hungarian.

CHAPTER 8
SMERSH

South of Budapest, Hungary – mid December, 1944

Karoly lifted his tired head and stared the Russian interrogator in the eye. "I told you my story a dozen times already. I am cooperating fully."

The interrogator impatiently tapped the end of his pencil on the wooden table. The military interpreter seated next to him translated.

"Tell me what you know."

"Albert sent us."

"Why?"

"We are with British intelligence."

"Why did Albert not make the journey himself?"

"It was impossible for anyone to get through."

"You are German spies."

Karoly sighed. "I am with the British led anti-Nazi Hungarian resistance. I take my orders from the British intelligence officer Albert. He gets his instructions from Bari."

"Why do you help the British?"

Karoly shook his head in confusion. One minute he was accused of being a German spy, the next he was all but accused of helping the British and yet the British and Russians were supposed to be Allies! It also did not help matters that he had been sleep deprived for days. On December 8, the Russians had decided to make their arrest official.

The major scoffed. "Why did you help the Americans and the British? Why did you not join forces with the Russians? Why did you not help the Russians?"

"I never came into contact with any Russians in Budapest."

"Have you ever been to Germany?"

"Yes, Germany, Austria, France and England – before the war."

"Were you ever at Cambridge?"

"For a year, from 1936 until 1937, as a postgraduate economics student."

"What did you do there?"

"Research."

"That is all?"

"I also attended the weekly seminars of John Maynard Keynes."

"Who is your father?"

"Karoly Schandl Senior, current president of OKH, the Hungarian Credit Cooperative."

"And before that?"

"He was the State Secretary of Agriculture. He is a lifetime member of the Upper House.

"What languages do you know?"

"Hungarian, German, English, French, Italian." He paused. "And Latin."

"Have you ever been a member of the Communist party?"

"No. Look, I had an important report which was in the envelope that was lost when they first arrested us. I will cooperate and tell you what I know. We are with the Allies."

"Why should I believe anything a German spy says?"

Karoly frowned. There was something very odd going on here. The Russians had been expecting them and it had all been arranged – of that he was certain. Otherwise, they would not have ventured to the estate to find them. They had not walked to the Russians; the Russians had come to them. Just what kind of a game was the major playing? No one could be so ignorant as to assume an ally was an enemy spy. Or were they simply paranoid?

"You do not care about the report one of your men took?"

"No."

A pause was followed by a long, cold stare. "What were you doing with the Dutchman?"

"I was asked to deliver him to you. In fact, I was following orders. Those were my orders."

The major snapped the pencil in half. Clearly he was not

getting the answers he wanted in this game of cat and mouse. "How did you meet the Dutchman?"

Karoly said nothing. Thus far, things were not going as planned so why should he entrust his captors with sensitive information? In addition, he had absolutely no intention of filling them in on the activities and names of the other members in his resistance group – not until he could trust them. Thus far, it did not appear too promising.

"We know about the Dutchman."

Karoly looked the major in the eye. Were the NKVD and SMERSH now aware of the two refugees in his apartment? Would they be arrested as well?

"I was asked to deliver the Dutchman. We were supposed to report to the Russians to be forwarded, transferred. Those were the orders that Albert …"

"You are all German spies." The major stood up.

Today's interrogation was over. Karoly wished they would at least remove his handcuffs and wondered how the Dutchman was faring. They must have been interrogating them separately.

Back in his holding area, he reflected on the events of the last several days, looking for a clue, a logical indication as to why they were being incorrectly categorized as prisoners-of-war. Somewhere along the lines of communication there had been a problem. There had never been a problem before. Was there some sort of problem on the ground then? Had someone misunderstood the instructions or, worse yet, had they forgotten to deliver them properly? No, that was unlikely as well, given how the Russians had arrived at the estate almost on schedule. They had been expecting to find them.

Perhaps the cat and mouse interrogation games would stop once they realized they were mistaken. British intelligence presumably had files on all of them. They would be able to clear things up. As long as they remained in Hungary, there was a chance that the arrest would be discovered to have been a gross mistake.

An hour later, he was led back to the interrogation room and shoved in a chair. The Dutchman was brought in as well and sat down next to him. Neither said a word. Karoly had not seen the Dutchman for days and was relieved that he appeared to be surviving.

This time the major pushed a paper in front of each. "Your interrogation reports."

Karoly blinked. "And?"

"You may read them."

"I cannot read Russian."

The major snickered. "You are both accused by the Red Army of being German spies until you prove otherwise."

Karoly frowned. Had he not given enough indications that they were working with the Allies? The Dutchman tried to stand up but was shoved back down by the guard behind him.

The major lit a cigarette and placed it between his thin lips.

"You will both be moved to Bucharest and from there transported to the Soviet Union, where you are to be held indefinitely as prisoners-of-war."

Karoly shook his head in disbelief.

The major continued. "SMERSH, military counter-intelligence, will continue to be in charge of your case."

CHAPTER 9
BLOOD IN THE DANUBE

Bokreta Street, Budapest, Hungary – December 22, 1944

Sister Sara, Joseph, and all the residents of the Bokreta Retirement Home for Working Women had survived another night of heavy bombing. There had been deafening explosions around them, the sounds of planes and anti-aircraft fire. The bombing had gone on all night. They had begun counting the hits, as if to reassure themselves that they still had some small control over their environment. That night there had been dozens.

Daytime lately was different from the night, though equally terrifying. The next day, as the past several days, they continued to hear shots being fired in the distance. The Allies were said to be closing in and everyone knew that the Nazis had been ordered not to surrender.

No one dared to venture out. In fact, Sister Sara had asked that everyone remain inside and try to be as calm as possible. If they continued as though things were normal, perhaps in some ways they would be. It was a simple philosophy which, in addition to her great faith, enabled her to continue to manage the home despite the war which now raged around them.

She and Joseph had become close in the past months. He loved the way she smiled every time he told a silly joke or story. She had commended him on his kindness toward the elderly ladies in the home and told him that soon, when the war was over, the place would be very empty without him seated at the guard's booth, always ready to lend a helping hand.

He had helped board up the broken windows to shield them from the cold and had ventured out to find firewood when they were running low. Supplies were increasingly hard to come by and everyone hoped and prayed for the best. Water had become something of a luxury.

It was a cold morning and Joseph was wearing a pair of gloves that one of the retired ladies had knitted for him. They called him everyone's child. It was a title which provided him comfort, as scarcely had he been able to receive any news of his parents. At first, there had been a few letters delivered by someone, and then nothing. All he knew was that they were still hiding with others in a safe house in another district of Pest and that it would have been too dangerous for him to go there. Perhaps it was equally dangerous for them to write to him or perhaps they hadn't any paper or pencils available.

Time passed ever so slowly and after a while, his nervousness had vanished. He was not the only Jewish refugee hiding at the Bokreta retirement home – there were others, masquerading as helpers. Terezia Schandl had brought them to the home with their papers, but even the secretary wasn't aware of it. Sister Sara and Terezia had been careful to keep their real identities a secret.

The secretary had stepped away from her office, accompanying the doctor, to attend to an elderly woman with a persistent cough. She was worried that it might be tuberculosis, in which case the woman would have to be quarantined so as not to spread the disease. It was her unattended office that led the messenger to deliver an urgent message, which had been intended for her, instead to the boy in the guard's booth. The messenger, himself a young boy, pulled down his cap and headed back out without saying a word. Joseph unfolded the paper and looked down at the message, which had come without an envelope. It had been hastily written by a nervous hand.

The news was bad. Two safe houses had been cleared out by the Nazis, all the occupants marched toward Austria. They were doomed.

Joseph looked at the familiar address and tears filled his eyes. It was the address of the safe house where his parents had been hiding.

"Mama!" he sobbed uncontrollably. "Mama! Mama!" How else would a boy of thirteen act after learning that his parents had been at one of the raided safe houses?

The boy they called everyone's child buried his face in his

84

hands and continued to cry out for his mother and then his father. So overcome was he with grief that he failed to notice when two Arrow Cross men marched up to the home and banged on his booth.

He finally raised his reddened eyes and they motioned for him to open the door. He complied and attempted to dry his eyes.

They stared at him with contempt as the taller of the two grabbed the note, all at once understanding. It confirmed what they had long suspected. "You weep for these lost people because you yourself are Jewish."

He did not answer.

"Speak when you are spoken to!"

Silence.

They pulled him out of the chair and shook him by the shoulders. "You lost someone! You lost someone! Admit it!"

Tears streamed down his face. It was answer enough for the hate mongers. They dragged him to the secretary's office, which Sister Sara had just entered from the other door.

"Joseph!" Her eyes filled with dread. "What are you men doing with Joseph!"

"He is a Jew." They tied his hands behind his back and the taller Arrow Cross soldier pulled his gun. "Show me the file of those who serve on the board of this charity or we will start shooting everyone inside."

Sister Sara fumbled with the desk drawer. "It is here. Wait, I will show you, but you are mistaken. Joseph is a Transylvanian refugee who is helping us. We have his papers. I will show you them."

"We have no wish to see your forged documents."

"But we have papers," she calmly insisted.

"All the more reason for us to know the names of those who would give you those false papers," the shorter one sneered. "They are all going to be arrested."

"Give us the file, damn you!" the other one shouted. "The file with the names!"

Sister Sara looked down at the file she presently held in hand, which was quickly snatched by the taller one. Her gentle eyes met those of Joseph, who now felt as though he were in a strange dream. Sara looked back at the two young men whose green shirts and ties were without a crease. One would almost have mistaken them for part of an enthusiastic school group had the circumstances been different, had they not been wearing the dreaded Arrow Cross arm band. How could they have given their souls over to such evil? They were well past the point of no return and carried out what was expected of them with menacing precision and zombie-like eyes. She wondered how many innocent people these fascists had already murdered.

"All of the names and addresses are listed here," she said softly. "But they will tell you what I have – that we have no refugees hiding here at the Bokreta home."

"You are hiding Jews."

"Joseph has papers."

"That is a matter of opinion."

"I beg you to see reason."

The tall one pulled out the paper containing the names and addresses of all board members, nodded, and folded it, placing it in his pocket. "They will be dealt with accordingly."

All at once the secretary returned, her face ashen. She opened her mouth to speak but no words came.

Sister Sara made the sign of the cross.

The Arrow Cross soldier was blunt. "We will be rounding up all members who sit on the board of this retirement home. They will all be arrested for falsifying papers and harboring a Jew. Justice will be served."

The secretary gasped and fell back in a chair. She had fainted.

Joseph's thoughts returned to his parents. He hoped they had survived their march. He was not so sure he was going to survive his.

They grabbed Sister Sara by the arm and led her out of the room with Joseph. Some elderly residents who had gathered upon hearing the commotion began to openly weep in the hallway.

"Silence!" the taller Arrow Cross barked, waving his gun.

The old women scattered for cover. His partner tied the nun's hands behind her back. She did not wince in pain but held her head high.

They marched Sister Sara and Joseph outside. It was cold and windy. They marched them to the banks of the Danube and lined them up side by side, as they had already done with hundreds before them. Sister Sara looked at Joseph.

"I cannot swim," he whispered, tears streaming down his young cheeks.

"In Heaven, all is possible, Joseph."

The first shot was to the back of Sister Sara's head, then to the back of the head of the boy they called everyone's child. The two fell into the icy Danube River together, blood gushing all around them, and were carried away by the fast current.

The Arrow Cross man then noticed something red on the ground and bent over to retrieve it. It was a rosary which had fallen from the boy's pocket. He picked it up, tossed it in after them, and walked away.

Sister Sara and Joseph were murdered by the Arrow Cross three days before Christmas in 1944.

CHAPTER 10
SIGNS

Gellert Hill, Budapest, Hungary – December 23, 1944

The previous day, Terezia Schandl had heard from the secretary of the Bokreta Home for Working Women. She was in hysterics. Sister Sara and thirteen year old Joseph had been shot by the Arrow Cross, who had vowed to round up all members of the board. They would likely be executed. Terezia had felt numb upon receiving the news, devastated about what had happened to poor Joseph and Sister Sara.

The Arrow Cross, it had seemed, would soon be at her doorstep. Any ordinary person would have fled, yet Terezia Schandl was no ordinary woman and she had others to consider. She could not abandon the refugees, friends, and family presently hiding in her home, nor could she leave her husband, who was in no condition to attempt an escape.

Thus, she had remained in the villa, quietly overseeing the housekeeper after their light 8 o'clock dinner, until all had disappeared to their rooms. She had not told anyone of the tragedy or what might lie in store for her. She had been tired and terribly saddened, yet she had to go on. Too many people were depending on her.

All night long she had prayed, clutching her rosary, kneeling near the front door so that she would be ready. She had prayed for Sister Sara and Joseph and she had prayed for the future. Eventually daybreak had come and no Arrow Cross men appeared. The knocking on the door she later heard was not strong enough to be that of a man, so she opened it without hesitation.

It was a neighbor. "I have news!" she said. She did not seem to notice that Terezia was subdued.

She invited her in for tea, in spite of the broken windows,

damaged ceiling, and shortage of water. She made the tea herself in the kitchen and apologized for the state of the house. They sat in the living room in privacy, as the few servants had not yet stirred. Terezia continued to clutch the rosary, still feeling the weight of the world on her shoulders.

The neighbor got straight to the point. "There is heavy fighting in Budapest. The Russians are now engaging the Germans in combat in the 10th district in Pest! It seems the Germans and the Arrow Cross will be too busy to venture here anymore. We might have seen the last of them!"

Terezia whispered her thanks to the heavens. For now, their lives had been spared. It was a bittersweet day. Sister Sara and the boy Joseph had not been as fortunate. *If only they had not been discovered.*

She then wondered about her son Karoly. There had been nothing forthcoming from any of his contacts and she was increasingly worried. The city was plagued by the stench of death.

When the neighbor had left, Terezia walked outside and looked over next door, where the Finnish Embassy had been. It was such a terrible thing that had occurred there in recent days. The Arrow Cross had discovered that there were 30 Jews in hiding at the embassy, and had dispatched a youth group to set fire to the building. The blaze had sent people scrambling and in the commotion, an entire Jewish family had been killed by the youth group. Not much was left of the mansion and the guards no longer came. So much misery, so much death.

Would the city ever recover?

She had an uneasy feeling that more hardship was just around the corner. They went through the motions of eating what food they had and rationing the small amount of water available to them. The nights were cold.

On one of those long nights, they all huddled in the bunker. It was a very bad night. One of the explosions was so loud that it shook the ground. A neighbor started to moan that he had lost his hearing in one ear.

The next day, the light revealed what Terezia had already felt. Karoly's upstairs apartment had been almost completely destroyed by the bomb. Where once had been life now dwelled only remnants of the past, in the form of a broken ceiling, shattered windows, piles of rubble and dust where heavy furniture had stood. Tommy had tried to talk her out of going up there. She did not listen. She was searching for signs of what once was, searching for something to indicate that the foundation of her son's life had not been obliterated. *Terezia Schandl, as many other times in her life, was looking for a sign from God.*

When she came down the stairs, she was holding the only thing which had survived – a Herendy statue of the Virgin Mary which she had given Karoly as a Christmas gift when he had first moved to the upstairs apartment. There was a small chip in Mary's halo, but it was otherwise intact. The Virgin Mary was still holding the baby Jesus, her face serene. Terezia held the statue up for all to see.

She now knew that Karoly was alive.

Gellert Hill, Budapest, Hungary – Christmas 1944

The Hungarian army was retreating. Most of the men had been forced to fight in the name of their German occupiers. They retreated like tired old men who knew that life would have nothing decent to offer them in the future. They were weak and tired. The Schandls were ordered to give up their villa to them, except for two rooms. It was a difficult time. On Christmas day, Terezia had to give food to twenty-five men.

As news of the advancing Russians spread, the soldiers dispersed, not wanting to be captured. When they had all gone, Tommy made a startling discovery in one of the rooms - a pile of antique guns. No one knew where they had come from.

Terezia, her husband, and Dan followed Tommy into the room to investigate. It had been badly damaged by the bombing and the gun collection had been placed in the corner, under some debris, with a blanket thrown over.

Tommy shook his head. "If the Russians find us with these guns, we will all be shot. We simply have to hide them somewhere."

Terezia agreed and then added, "Any ideas?"

Dan mentioned the large crater which a bomb had made in front of what was left of the Finnish Embassy. "We should bury them there."

It took a while, but Tommy, Dan, and Mr. Schandl finally buried the antique guns in that crater. It was quite a sight – the pair of men wearing priest's frocks, shoveling dirt in front of the remains of the foreign embassy, accompanied by a renowned statesman and economist. Fortunately, their part of the street was relatively secluded so no one noticed what they had been doing that night.

Only Terezia, Karoly Sr.,Tommy, and Dan knew about those guns.

The next morning, there was the sound of barking German shepherds. A group of Russian soldiers had approached the front of the Finnish Embassy with sniffing dogs. Shortly afterwards, the hidden guns were retrieved and the soldiers left with them.

It seemed odd how they had gone directly to the crater the next day, as if they already knew there were guns hidden there...

Terezia later made her way down to the bottom of Gellert Hill, anxious about the fathers. Arriving at the Cave Church, she was relieved to find that it had not been destroyed. The church had been well protected by the solid rock.

Father Horvath was subdued upon hearing the tragic fate of Sister Sara and Joseph. He suggested they pray for them, and all the others who had been lost. Terezia knelt and bowed her head in worship as Father Horvath did the same, his outline contrasting against the dimness like a beacon of hope.They had their faith to guide them. When Terezia later turned toward Father Horvath, what she beheld shocked her, for the priest's white frock was covered with blood. She closed her eyes for a moment. When she opened them again, she looked at Father Horvath, who continued to pray.

The blood was gone.

Budapest, Hungary - January 1945

Sam had known for a long time that he was being followed. It had started when he'd returned from taking the Dutchman to Karoly's apartment. Then it had just been a feeling. He soon spotted two men in suits, whose steps were always behind his, their eyes focused on his every move. The two men in suits never came up to speak to him and that was beginning to make him uneasy. Originally he had thought they might wish to make contact with the resistance, yet all that had changed today.

He had been returning home from meeting with Tibor when the same two men quickened their pace behind him. For this reason, he did not return to his apartment but went to the apartment of a trusted friend who was also involved, albeit on a smaller scale, in the activities of the group. *By now they had enlisted the aid of a few dozen individuals, though only the original group remained in charge of sensitive matters, such as intelligence and high level negotiations.*

Her name was Eva and her keen eye was matched by her continental beauty. Sam just happened to be engaged to her cousin, who was already safely in Switzerland, waiting for the war to end.

When she opened her door, she was clad in a simple dress, her hand in the pocket where a small revolver was concealed.

"No need for a shootout, it's only me." Sam hastily went inside and shut the door after himself. "Do you have company?"

She shook her head. "What is the matter? Another air raid?"

"I was being followed. Can I stay here for the night?"

"You don't have to ask. There isn't much food but I'll make us a couple of strong coffees and then you can fill me in."

As they drank their espressos, he told her about the two men in suits and added that something else was not right. "We have not received confirmation that one of our men is safe. He went to the Russians to deliver someone."

"Maybe he went somewhere else."

Sam shook his head. "He was the messenger. He would

not have done that. I still have to do some digging, talk to contacts, but I fear they may have simply vanished."

"Does George know?"

"As far as I know, George and Nick are still in hiding. There are two places where they might currently be. We decided not to be seen together in case one of us is compromised." He did not point out that the British likely cared more about George being compromised, for Eva, like many Hungarians, had an innate mistrust of foreigners, the English among them.

She watched him drain the contents of his cup. "Is there anything I can do?"

"Not anymore. Everything has become too dangerous. I will leave in the morning and then I want you to get out of Budapest."

"But the operation …"

"Everything is unclear at present and until I have definite word from the newly formed government and they have been installed, the capital will continue to be too dangerous to accomplish anything. The Germans and Russians are already engaged in street to street fighting in some places. It is simply too dangerous. We will not be able to use you anymore so you must get out."

"Do you think you have been sold out to the Germans?"

He thought back to his meeting with the leader of another group, who said they would be ready with as many machine guns as they needed when the time came. It was not possible that the man had gone against them. He had been recommended by a friend. "I am not sure what to think but my contacts are all good ones."

For the next few hours, they talked about plans for the future and how things would be when the Nazis had been defeated. Then the sounds of shots being fired far away made them both cringe. Every few minutes the shots were heard and they knew exactly what it meant. The Germans, aware of the advancing Russians, were shooting their prisoners.

Sam stood up. He would go to his American contact, the man from the OSS whose apartment was near Andrassy Street. Ironically, that was also the street where the Arrow Cross had their headquarters and he had no guarantees that they were still not hiding out there as the Russians advanced. *He he did not care about the risks as time was no longer on their side.* "I have to go to someone, to find out what is happening. Come with me and he will see to it that you get out safely."

"And how do you know he is to be trusted?"

"He's with American intelligence – and that's our last hope."

Eva reluctantly stood up. "I will need time to pack …"

"There is no time for such niceties. My contact will be able to ensure that you are safely escorted from this place. It is evident that the Russians are advancing, and the Germans panicking. You will no longer be safe – one of your neighbors might easily report you to the Nazis if they so much as suspect you have been in touch with the underground. The Germans and Arrow Cross will be setting examples, killing those who they fear will speak against them …"

A loud explosion suddenly shook the room and blew out the window. Sam yanked Eva behind him, near the door, to shield her from the flying glass and debris. "The bridges," he muttered. "They are blowing them up already."

When he made his way toward the open space where the window pane had been, he could see half of a bridge on the Buda side, but on the Pest side of the Danube it was completely gone. There was a plume of dust and debris rising over the city. He was about to back away when he looked down and perceived the two men in suits running toward the apartment. "Is there a courtyard exit?" he said suddenly, grabbing Eva by the hand. "They're coming up the front right now! They must have traced me here as well! They must be Gestapo …"

"We can get out at the courtyard, where part of the wall is broken. We can climb over it."

Together they ran down the stairs at the back of the lowrise, then out to the courtyard. They stepped over flower boxes and the low, crumbling section of the wall that had been partly destroyed by a bomb two nights earlier. Sam's hold on Eva's hand tightened as they raced through the chaotic dawn. People had ventured out onto the streets, in a surrealistic daze, as though they could not comprehend what was happening. The dark cloud overhead was so thick, it looked as though it would prevent the sun from rising over the city.

They ran through narrow lanes and back alleys until they had reached the top part of a familiar main street and turned a corner. Sam looked up and squinted, recalling the address he had memorized for such an occasion. He saw the neo-Renaissance building, with its elegant little balconies, and was relieved that it had not been destroyed. The apartment he had to reach was on the main floor. Just a few more steps …

Some shouting behind them made him reach for the gun in his pocket. Shots were fired. Eva screamed. Sam turned around to face his assailants but it was too late. A stinging pain seared through his shoulder and then everything went black.

Geneva, Switzerland

Sam's head was throbbing and he had a searing pain in his shoulder, which was thickly bandaged. He was just starting to realize where he was, what had happened to him. The white walls and the fact that he was lying in a crisp bed indicated that he was in a hospital. His fiancée Suzanne was standing at his bedside, smiling sweetly. *Good. He wasn't in a prison hospital.*

"You're awake." She stroked his cheek and he noticed that she was wearing her engagement ring. Everything that had happened now felt like a blur.

"What happened?" His voice was hoarse.

"You were shot next to the American's apartment. You and Eva were running there because two men were following you." She squeezed his hand. "I am so lucky that the American came out and got you off the street."

"Eva?" He raised his dark eyes to her. "She is all right?"

"She's fine. Both of you were whisked off to Switzerland and safety."

"I'm in Switzerland?"

"Geneva, at an excellent hospital."

"That's far from Hungary."

95

"Yes, it is. Sam, the American who got you out is here, too. He wants to see you before he leaves Europe. Are you up for it?"

"Send him in. We have to talk – and the sooner the better."

She bent over to gently kiss his forehead and then stepped out, leaving behind the scent of jasmine perfume. He tried to prop himself up but it was no use. The pain was too sharp so he slid back down again.

Marty was there in an instant, having entered the room without having made a sound. He was wearing a casual shirt and pants and his face, as always, was cleanly shaven. "How are you holding up? You gave us quite a scare!"

"You saved my life and probably Eva's as well." Sam was not a man who minced words.

"Lucky for us," Marty went on, "the Germans showed up when they did and sent those two running in the opposite direction. The Germans were too busy chasing them to even notice that you'd been shot so Eva and I dragged you into my apartment. As I was scheduled to be leaving the city, you chose a good day to drop by."

"And then we were transported to Switzerland, where I had the operation."

"You got it!"

Sam frowned. Marty had made it all sound so easy the way Americans liked to do - and yet there was a certain hesitation in his voice. "What about the others in the group?"

"Your network has all sorts of people scattered …"

"I meant the main ones. Besides myself, remember, there were George, Nick, and Karoly. Maybe they're all in hiding somewhere until the Germans are defeated."

Marty cleared his throat. "The Germans will be defeated, but the street to street fighting is pretty fierce in Budapest right now. It's quite chaotic."

"It already was when I'd left. You still haven't answered my question about my friends."

"The news isn't good, Sam. They're all missing and my contacts suspect they've been arrested."

Sam's face darkened. "By the Germans?"

"No, by the Russians."

"That is not possible. We're a British led group, we're with the Allies."

"I am well aware of that fact."

Sam went on. "As you know, we take our orders from George, who is now British intelligence. He reports to Jack, an ISLD agent. We get messages from Bari, we deliver Allied POWs to them, and they get our reports at the Center. The Russians have no reason to arrest us. By the way, who was chasing me back in Budapest?"

Marty sighed. "There's no easy way to tell you this. Rumor has it the Russians have put a price on the head of an international diplomat in addition to certain resistance elements. The trail on your three friends has gone cold, Sam. They all fell into the hands of the NKVD and they are now presumed dead. If you go back to Budapest, it is believed that you too may be dealt with by the Red Army in a similar manner. I'm sorry but you cannot return to Hungary as long as it's under Russian occupation and if the rumors about Stalin's intentions are true, that could be for a very long time. You were being chased by the NKVD."

CHAPTER 11
ABWEHR

Bucharest, Romania – mid-January, 1945

Karoly and the Dutchman were in the process of being transported to the Soviet Union. For more than a month, their captors had run the same gamut of individually interrogating them and accusing them. Karoly was careful not to utter the name of anyone in the network other than George. George was the official member of British intelligence who headed the group and would therefore be easy for the Russians to make contact with via Bari – if they wished to verify the status of Karoly and the man he had promised to deliver to the I.S. Thus far, however, they did not appear to have done so.

Things were not looking very promising. They were accompanied by heavily armed Russian guards and it was cold. *There was still hope – in the form of a chance meeting which Karoly discovered along the way.*

A group of Americans had emergency landed and a Canadian major who was in charge of a partisan airfield was with them. They watched as the two men were marched to the military plane. For a moment, the two prisoners were stood side by side. Karoly glanced at the Dutchman. The Dutchmen returned his gaze and nodded. Karoly then pretended to ask the guards where they were taking them, in very loud Hungarian and then in German. They had no interpreter present and told him in Russian to be quiet. Karoly knew that he was risking his life but it was well worth the risk, if only to give the Dutchman a few seconds so that he could establish some sort of contact with the men.

He must have managed to gesture, for the Canadian major soon approached them.

The Russian guards waved him away and shoved the two shackled prisoners forward, at which time the Dutchman whispered "I mouthed my name to him as well as my nationality." He then pretended to cough.

Karoly did the same.

Once they were on the plane, instead of accompanying them, the guards walked back outside. It gave Karoly and the Dutchman a chance to continue their conversation.

The Dutchman leaned forward. "What are they doing now?"

Karoly shrugged his shoulders and wished he could look out the window. "Perhaps they are changing the guards."

Then orders were heard barked, as though they had new prisoners. Prisoners who were considered to be high priority – prisoners that made them nervous.

There were three of them and they looked calm and defiant, their eyes cold and hard. Karoly knew immediately that they were not regular officers. They must have been from some sort of intelligence or espionage unit. The guards motioned for them to sit down in the plane and then walked toward the cockpit. They looked distracted and Karoly thought that could work in his favor. He decided to strike up a conversation with the new arrivals. He said something in Hungarian and they looked at him blankly. However, when he switched to German, their expressions indicated that they understood what was being said to them. After a few sentences were exchanged, they stated they were Abwehr, the military intelligence of the Germans. Their faces held no remorse and Karoly was not surprised. They were murderous experts in espionage, counter-espionage, and sabotage, among other things. Apparently, their captors had not tortured them to extract information – at least not yet. They refused to divulge how long they had been in the hands of the Russians.

The oldest one, a man of approximately fifty years, stared down both Karoly and the Dutchman and accused them of being plants. It was not an uncommon tactic to mix prisoners with intelligence agents masquerading as fellow prisoners.

The Dutchman shook his weary head as the plane began to move. "We were arrested by mistake."

One of the guards came back as soon as the plane was

airborn. The prisoners pretended to be asleep. He returned to the cockpit.

The oldest Abwehr snickered. "Were you working with the British?"

"British intelligence," Karoly replied.

"Why are you here?"

"It was an error, we are certain," the Dutchman stated.

"An error?" The Abwehr raised an eyebrow.

Karoly frowned. "We had orders to report to the Russians and they mistakenly arrested us."

The three Abwehrs began to laugh, as though they shared a private joke. The older one explained. "The same thing happened one week ago. They arrested him as well."

"It did not happen one week ago but that was when they took him to Moscow," one of the younger men corrected him. "It was one week ago that he was moved but he had already been arrested."

"If you can call being detained an arrest."

Karoly's interest was piqued as the plane engines continued to roar. "To whom are you referring?"

The older Abwehr laughed again. "A Serbian lieutenant."

Karoly was unable to conceal his surprise. "They took him to Moscow by armed guard too?"

"It is the same as what is now being done to you. He was arrested. He had a small group of partisans helping the Allies in the Iron Gate area of the Danube. He was instructed to report to the Russians, who were to forward him to Tito. When he did, instead of sending him to Tito, the Russians jailed him in Bucharest in the same jail that we were in. He was then sent to Moscow, under arrest, just like you."

Karoly's head was spinning. "Who told him to report to the Russians?"

"The British major who came with his weekly supply plane."

"Do you know his name?"

"No, and he is gone now, probably smoking a cigar at some gentleman's club, boasting of his overseas exploits. They have been doing this trick with the Allied resistance – the British instruct resistance leaders to report to the Russians, who then arrest and imprison them."

"But we are Allies," the Dutchman protested.

The Abwehr laughed again and Karoly wondered if they were simply playing mind games. Thus, for the remainder of the bumpy flight, he chose not to speak with them. Shortly before landing, the heavily armed guards returned and this time separated them. It was unclear whether they had overheard them conversing or it was due to protocol that they should be herded off the plane in the same groups in which they had boarded.

Once off the plane, they had to endure an unpleasant ride in a sinister black truck that was known as the black crow. Karoly tried not to think of the Abwehr's harsh words and taunting laughter. The Dutchman was tired and subdued.

It was dark and colder than ever when they reached their final destination – Lubyanka Prison in Moscow. They did not know that Roosevelt, Churchill, and Stalin would soon meet in Yalta to decide the fate of most of Europe, and that Hungary and the Baltics would be signed over to Stalin, thereby sealing their fates.

CHAPTER 12
LUBYANKA PRISON

Lubyanka Prison, Moscow, U.S.S.R. – mid-January, 1945

In 1944, Lubyanka Prison was the headquarters of the NKVD, the Soviet secret police which was responsible for the disappearance and deaths of countless people they had deemed "undesirable," whatever that happened to mean.

The building itself was tall, in the heart of Moscow. The dingy cellars were often used for interrogation/torture purposes and thousands perished there, among them not only war prisoners, including the anti-Nazi resistance of various countries and Allies who had "disappeared," but also local artists and doctors. Anyone considered a potential enemy of the Soviets, including innocent Soviets themselves, could end up in the much dreaded Lubyanka. It was a place of trumped-up charges, farcical trials, and death. More people entered than exited.

When victims perished in the Lubyanka, their heart was quickly cut out and sent to medical students for study. There were no marked graves, no burials, only the stench of death pervading every dilapidated inch of the cells.

Those who wound up there were forced to sign so-called admissions of guilt. To panic in Lubyanka was to sign your own death sentence. The guards were intolerant, the interrogators brutal, and if they so much as suspected there was something more to be gotten from a semi-broken spirit, the focus of their "investigation" was all but doomed. There were also executions but nobody talked about those much. Guards mentioned prisoners had sometimes "died" yet were otherwise tight-lipped. Records generally indicated that a number of prisoners died of natural causes, perhaps to prepare for future cover-ups on the international scene – or perhaps to attempt cover-ups even back then.

Playing on the fears of their prisoners, the captors found it convenient to pit friend against friend, in an attempt to gather information. Often there was no information but that did not deter this practice. Stalinism was based on a foundation of terror and the man who reported directly to Stalin himself, General Viktor Abakumov - the Minister of Security, and chief of SMERSH - was so very good at it. Abakumov was said to have tortured men in that place with his bare hands. *It was nothing less than a house of terror.*

Still inside the black crow, Karoly and the Dutchman heard a big iron door open and then some shouting. The gates closed with a bang. The truck door opened. Karoly knew very well where they were for he had perceived the closed gates. It was the Lubyanka, the seat of the Ministry of the Interior and of the NKVD, with an attached prison.

"Get out," he was ordered.

The officer led him inside and another guard, without a machine gun, followed. The Dutchman would be processed after him. They led Karoly through the "reception area," to a small room that was about four feet by four feet. It was painted white, though the door, which occupied one side, and the low bench were green.

He sat down and lowered his head. The light was not turned off so after a few minutes, he raised his eyes again, wondering what would come next. He thought back to his friends and family. Did they even know he was here?

There was a small round hole covered with glass and from time to time, somebody opened the lid on the outside and an eye appeared. He could hear the footsteps of the sergeant making his rounds as he went to look at the next cell. After an hour or two, he became very tired and fell asleep, leaning against the wall. He was not sure how much time had passed when a sergeant, accompanied by an interpreter, finally opened the door and demanded his name.

"Your name?"

"Karoly William Schandl."

The sergeant looked down at the piece of paper he was carrying. "Remove your clothes."

He did as instructed.

Another guard, standing behind the sergeant, examined the clothing.

"Bend forward."

He complied.

"Now you must cough three times."

He did and they looked for anything that he might have hidden in an unlikely place.

"You can stand up."

They took his belt as though they feared he might use it to attack them, escape, or hang himself. "Sign for the belongings we took from you."

He signed grudgingly.

"Get dressed."

His pants felt unpleasantly loose without the belt. They then led him to a small room which was sparsely furnished with a table, two wooden chairs behind it and another one in front. Two young officers were sitting in the chairs behind the table. Off to the side was the military interpreter.

"Sit down," one of the officers ordered.

Karoly sat down.

The officer shoved a paper before him. "This is your arrest order. The reason for its issuance was your suspected connections with anti-Soviet organizations, for the purpose of spying."

Karoly blinked and was not certain whether his light-headedness was the result of not having eaten or drunk enough, or if it were simply because what the officer had just said was so ludicrous.

"Read this and sign it."

Karoly could not believe his ears and eyes. "You must mistake me for someone else. It's an error."

"You are a British spy. Just sign it."

"Albert was ..."

"Sign it now!"

He did as they had instructed and signed it, to avoid being shot. *This was a complete farce.* He was then taken to another small room to be processed. His name, place and date of birth, citizenship, marital status, and address were meticulously recorded. They asked about his father, who had been well known before the war, and he was not sure whether that would be held against him in the long run.

Finally, he had to put his fingertips in a dark gluey ink and press them on a hard paper so that they would have his fingerprints on file. When it was done, they led him back to the little closet of a room.

Later, he again woke up to some noise at his door. Was he dreaming? He blinked.

Somebody called a name. He then realized it was at the door of the cell next to his. About half an hour later, they were at his door.

"Let's go."

He followed them, curious about what would happen next.

"Put your hands back," warned the guard who stayed behind him. They proceeded with caution, the sergeant in front appearing to be wary about meeting other prisoners or officers.

They went up in an elevator for what felt like two floors. He wondered if they were leading him somewhere to be executed.

The elevator stopped. After getting out, they ordered him into another small cubicle, where he was ordered to once more undress. He got one sixteenth of a square bar of soap and was marched to the shower room. He washed himself in the hot shower for ten minutes, grateful for the hot water, as he had been without it for so long. He then had to return to the cubicle where he had undressed, not knowing what lay in store.

A sergeant handed him a small towel, a white cotton pillow cover, and two bedsheets. He was also given a light mattress with a gray blanket and a cloth coat. On every item was the large black stamp of Lubyanka Prison. It was quite a load to carry. When his clothes were given back to him, they were hot. Evidently they had been heated in a special oven, to kill any lice and fleas. He got dressed and was led back to the elevator. He then noticed that the sergeant pressed the button for the sixth floor.

Lubyanka felt like a nightmarish maze that never ended.

They led him from the elevator to an iron door which had been painted bright white. The sergeant ahead of him knocked and someone looked through a small spy hole.

The door was opened. Karoly perceived a desk which was occupied by a lieutenant. The sergeant stopped to tell him something in Russian, then looked at Karoly, and led him to a large, well lit hall. It was surrounded by doors on three sides, with an interior staircase. They went up the stairs, to the second level of the hall and he had to enter cell number 47.

The painted brown floor in the room was cement, and the walls were white. There were two iron beds on each side. There was no window, but a lightbulb over the door, hidden by grates.

Karoly placed his musty mattress on the bed and sat down on it. There were no chairs, but there was a small wooden table. He then noticed the big tin vessel with two handles, in the corner. It served as a toilet. Apparently they would not even be opening the door for him to use the washroom.

An officer opened the door, accompanied by an interpreter. The order, like the others, was concise.

"Make your bed." He then closed the door again.

Shortly afterwards, the doctor came, with the officer, interpreter, and sergeant accompanying her. "Get your clothes off."

The doctor, a tall middle-aged woman, looked at him, from the front and the back, knocked on his chest, and listened to his heartbeat.

"Do you have any sickness?"

"No."

She looked at his eyes, pulled down his eyelids, and looked in his mouth. "He is healthy." The doctor, with her escort, then left, likely to go to the next unwilling patient.

After a while, Karoly once again heard the sounds of opening and closing doors. He could smell food. He was given only a small kettle with some hot water in it, a tin spoon, and a metal cup. That was all they expected him to subsist on?

He asked the officer who handed him the utensils whether he would be able to have something to eat.

The interpreter translated.

"Tomorrow," was the stern reply.

With nothing else to do, Karoly listened to the noises outside. He heard the doors opening and people passing. Finally it was his turn – to take the awful vessel in his room to the washroom. The washroom was filled with pungent humid air. It was about twelve by twenty feet large. Along one of the long walls was an elevation which was ten to twelve inches high. In the concrete floor of the elevation there were four funnel like holes, with room for the feet on both sides. They looked suitable for mules perhaps, but not human beings.

On the other side was a long sink with four cold water taps. There was enough room to empty the vessel and wash. He later learned that the occupants of every cell were able to visit it twice a day, in a sequence that was changed daily. The last visitors had the unfortunate duty of having to clean up the area. That day Karoly was the last visitor. He wondered if it was because he was the newest arrival. The smell didn't bother him after a while. He was so exhausted, he felt numb.

Once he was sent back to his cell, a guard opened the door. "When the light flickers, you can go to bed. When it flickers in the morning, you have to get up. You can sit on the bed but you are not allowed to lie down."

Despite the continuous light and the fact that every now and then an eye appeared at the small hole, Karoly fell asleep. He had not been asleep very long when a sergeant entered the room, with another guard at the door.

"Get up. Fast."

He complied.

"Hands back."

They led him through another maze of corridors to a simply furnished room. This time there was an older officer and a younger one, both of whom were seated at a table. The older one had a great deal of gold on his uniform. Both men had cadaverous looking faces and Karoly assumed that was why they had been selected – for their ability to instill fear with a mere glance. Yet what did the terror squad hope to gain from him?

"Sit down." The military interpreter was seated in the

corner.

Karoly sat down in the wooden chair across the table from the officers. The younger officer asked him details such as his name, family, education, and work. He made a lot of notes on cheap looking paper and never once met his eyes.

The older officer soon took over. "You are a British spy."

"No, I am not."

"Yes, you are."

"I assure you, I am not."

"Prove that you are not a spy."

"How?"

"Tell us everything."

"As you wish. I have nothing to hide."

Karoly told them about taking his orders from George so that he could get the Dutchman safely away from the Nazis. He reiterated that George was known as Albert and that he was with British intelligence helping the Allies, but that he was not an enemy spy.

"Lies."

Karoly shook his head. He wondered if they were even listening as they seemed to have their own agenda and it involved keeping him locked up. First they had accused them of being German spies, now they were British spies, even though the British and the Russians were Allies – at least they had been. It was unlikely that the Dutchman was faring any better.

The older officer repeated himself. "You are a spy."

Karoly could not conceal his irritation. "You are mistaken."

The older officer then angrily shouted that if he did not cooperate, he would be shot. He paused and added "If you cooperate, you may get away with a lighter sentence. It is up to you to decide."

There was a long silence.

"You will not cooperate?"

"If I do not know anything, how can I cooperate?"

"Tell us information."

"What kind of information?"

"About the organization The others."

Karoly pretended he had no idea what he was referring to. He had absolutely no intention of giving the names of any more individuals in the group or their network, nor did he intend to disclose anything about their resistance activities. Thus far, the Soviets had proven only one thing to him – that they could not be trusted. If they could, they would have at least attempted to verify that he had been Albert's messenger and would not keep conveniently ignoring it.

"I don't know anyone from the group. I just helped Albert," he lied. They would not extract any more information from him than that. "You can verify with the Allies …"

"Don't lie to us!"

Karoly was relieved when the two sergeants arrived and he was permitted to leave.

"*Ruky nazad*. Hands back and hurry up."

They led him back to his cell. In the morning, someone shouted at him to get up again.

He did.

The traffic with the odorous vessels started, to and from the washroom. There was a slow, steady stream of people moving up and down in the hall. Afterwards, the place became quiet again.

Karoly was shortly back in his miserable cell. The doors opened and then closed. It was time for food. A young officer accompanied the sergeant who brought in some porridge. It consisted of oats. There was also bread and some boiled water with sugar. Karoly had not eaten for what must have been a good thirty six hours so he devoured everything.

At least they appeared to be trying to keep him alive.

The investigating officers the previous night had made him tired with their questions. He was therefore sleepy and, after making his bed, stretched out on it.

When the sergeant who regularly looked through the hole saw that he was lying down, he banged on the door. Moments later, the supervising officer appeared.

He was matter-of-fact about the rules. Karoly was presently not permitted to sleep. It must have been a tactic – to break down prisoners with sleep deprivation.

The doctor also showed up and looked in. She then moved on. A sergeant came to the door and yelled in that it was time to go for a walk.

They took Karoly to the elevator and pushed the top button. On the top floor, they led him along a corridor, to what appeared to be a wooden enclosure. It was approximately twenty feet long and twenty feet wide, in the shape of a square, and was surrounded by very tall planks so that even if the tallest of men stood on the shoulders of another man, he would not succeed in reaching the top. At the very top was a barbed wire mesh. On one side of the enclosure, in an elevated small booth, was a soldier with a submachine gun. He was able to see the heads and shoulders of the prisoners making their way in the enclosure. They moved steadily like mice in a cage. *He did not think it was a place where prisoners were executed so at least there was still hope.*

Outside, you could hear a continuous whirring sound, like thousands of frogs, yet there were no frogs. Karoly's ears started to ring. When he was led back to his cell, there was someone already there – the Dutchman. His was pale, with large circles under his eyes, and he was sitting on the bed across from Karoly's. He had the expression of someone who had been tortured, yet still he held his head with pride. Karoly was relieved that the interrogators had not broken him. The Dutchman had been his responsibility – he was supposed to get him away from danger.

They talked about what the interrogators had asked them, the accusations, the conditions of the prison. Karoly then told the Dutchman about the ringing in his ears.

The Dutchman nodded. "I feel it, too. Now I know it isn't my imagination." He then fell silent.

Karoly leaned back against the wall as the light flickered again. "Once they know we are here, they will help us," he said decidedly.

The Dutchman did not reply.

"Churchill will get us out," Karoly promised.

All of a sudden a loudspeaker that sounded as if it were coming from outside the prison came on. A voice proceeded to repeat the same sentence for over an hour, but as neither Karoly nor the Dutchman understood Russian, they had no idea what it meant.

In later years, he would know what those words were. "Death to spies - Death to the English spies."

Karoly's mind wandered to his parents as he drifted in and and out of sleep. He hoped they were safe and that the refugees in the family villa would not be discovered by the Nazis.

CHAPTER 13
DECEPTION

Canada – January 16, 2005

The mysterious Riley had vanished and, for that matter, so had Lambert the historian. Of course, Kati reminded herself, Lambert was likely waiting to hear from her if she had discovered anything significant. In that respect, the ball was in her court. As far as Riley was concerned – it was not likely they would ever really know who he was or what his angle had been.

Chris was proving to be a pleasant guest at the house. Every evening, after dinner, they sat at the fireplace discussing the details at what he was now calling an unsolved case. It was something they shared, for she had allowed him to read her father's memoirs – and he had.

"He was very good at being clandestine." Chris drained the remaining drops of cognac from his glass and shook his head when she offered to pour him some more. "I'm trying to concentrate."

Kati smiled. "You haven't changed a bit. Still not letting anything overtake that great logic of yours."

"Well now, I'm flattered. I had no idea you admired my logic. I thought my level-headedness was what drove that wedge between us."

"That was only part of it. It was also the long hours."

"I should never have agreed to be a consultant on the Stedman case. That, and the teaching hours were just too much of a strain for our relationship to bear."

Kati did not disagree. She stood up and carried both of their empty glasses into the kitchen. When she had come back out, Chris was standing in front of the fireplace, leafing through a hard cover book.

"More legal research?"

"What did you say?" He looked up and then shut the book.

"Are you already doing research for your next important case?"

"Actually, this is something for you. I was going to wait until morning to give it to you as I knew you would spend the whole night going through every single word of it."

"Not another poet's memoirs," she laughed. "You really are trying to get my mind off things."

"Nothing could be further from the truth." He took a few steps forward and handed her the book. "It's the memoirs of Dan, the British agent who was hiding in Karoly's upstairs apartment at the Schandl villa on Gellert Hill, Budapest."

She accepted the book and was unable to conceal her shock. "How did you find it? I tried but was repeatedly told it was out of print."

"One of the librarians at the law library has a friend with an out-of-print books collection. He's willing to buy – and sell – if the price is right. If Dan were alive, he'd be reaping the rewards of what I paid for that book of his."

She blinked. "He's not alive?"

"No, he died a couple of years after writing that book, having had numerous problems in his life. He might have been unstable. At least that was what I heard."

Kati shook her head in disbelief. "That's odd. The way my father wrote about him and my grandmother, too…"

"Your grandmother?" he said incredulously. "You have her memoirs as well?"

"They're in Hungarian," she explained, "and much shorter than Dad's but they corroborate a lot of what he says." She opened the book and sighed. "She thought Dan was kind of quiet but liked to help around the house when he could, and liked to be involved in things sometimes, though not always. He sounds like he was maybe not all that noticeable, particularly since it was a chaotic time and neither Karoly nor Terezia had much time to pay attention to anyone really. They were too busy trying to save people and change things. Still, there was no indication that he was unstable."

"Trust me, he sounds like he was, once he returned."

"I wonder why," she mused. "I wonder if it was simply post-traumatic stress disorder, caused by the horrors of war."

"Could be."

"Or maybe he had something to hide."

"You are becoming quite the sleuth, I see."

Kati said nothing, having already opened the book to the table of contents.

Chris shook his head and began to walk upstairs. "I apologize for ruining your night with that thing. Let me know if it turns out to contain anything earth-shattering. Meantime, I'm off to take a shower and get some shut eye. I've got an early morning meeting with the chairman of the department."

Kati barely noticed that he had left. *The past had come alive again and the story would in one way or another continue.*

Dan had been present at the villa, hiding there for months. He had arrived in autumn of 1944 and had safely remained there until the end of the war, long after Karoly and the Dutchman had "gone missing" to those around them. Perhaps his book held a clue. It felt like she had just received a missing piece of a puzzle. She looked up to thank Chris profusely but he was gone and she then heard the sound of running water.

Glancing at the clock on the white mantelpiece, she realized it was almost midnight. She then sat down on the sofa and skimmed the table of contents of the book. It was organized in chronological order, starting with the training Dan had received. There would be plenty of time to pour over every word later. At present, she was more interested in learning about his reminiscences in Hungary, after Karoly's group had sprung him from the prison.

Soon she found the first discrepancy. Dan claimed in his "memoirs" that he had boldly escaped from the prison and made no mention of meeting anyone in the Hungarian resistance. Kati was stunned but then reminded herself that he was a secret agent and perhaps wanted to embellish his record so as to appear a hero. It would not be the first instance in history that a man would have exaggerated his accomplishments and certainly not the last – and Chris had brought up how the war had changed him. Perhaps he had simply wanted to re-invent himself into a great war hero, nothing more.

The following pages, however, revealed something far more sinister. It was a chapter in which he expressed his dislike of the Diplomat who had been involved in the underground movement. Dan also mentioned when he himself had first ventured to the Schandl villa and met the Schandls – after December 8, 1944. Kati read the entire chapter, shut the book, and stood up. *This was simply too much.*

She climbed the stairs and knocked on the guest room door. Chris opened it with a half smile, clad in the boxer shorts he always slept in. "Don't tell me, you miss me?" He then perceived the expression on her face and his tone became serious. "You look as though you've seen a ghost. Dan's book?"

She nodded. "Dan claimed to have only gone to the Schandl villa and met my father after December 8, 1944."

"And that's a problem?"

"According to both my father and grandmother's memoirs, Dan was already there in the autumn of 1944, months before December 8."

"It might have been a misprint."

"It is repeated too many times to be a misprint. Karoly and the Dutchman were arrested by the Soviets in Hungary on December 4, 1944 but that's not the only discrepancy with dates. He pretends Karoly was still at the house in Budapest on January 18, 1945 and makes no mention of his arrest. Plus, he does not mention ever meeting anyone in the Hungarian anti-Nazi resistance."

A frown creased Chris' brow and he looked at the pages in question as she showed them to him.

"Why would Dan want to mislead the public about that?" she said incredulously.

"It wasn't just the public," was the serious reply. "That book of so-called memoirs was actually based on his official reports – the ones he filed with his British superiors when he got back from Hungary in 1945. It says as much right there at the very front ..."

London, England - January 17, 2005

It was 6 a.m. and Marcel Lambert's mobile phone was ringing. Assuming it was his impatient superior again, he considered turning it off. He had been warned about the organization, how once you were in, you risked being hounded at all hours from any given corner of the globe.

To add insult to injury, his bed was less than comfortable. They hadn't been willing to pay for an upscale hotel – said it would have made him draw too much attention to himself and jeopardize the investigation. He could not disagree with that, particularly since an unknown entity posing as "John Riley" had already tried to contact their main source.

He reached across the night table for the phone and pressed the answer button.

"Marcel Lambert. Good morning."

Had Kati been less preoccupied with what she had just learned, she might have thought it unusual that a Swiss historian would have answered his personal phone in English, instead of French or Swiss German. "It's Kati Schandl. I'm calling from Canada."

"Ms. Schandl, how good to hear from you."

"I hope I haven't awoken you."

"Not at all. I've always been something of an early riser." He turned on the desk lamp and sat up in bed. "I trust all is well with you."

"Not exactly."

"I am sorry to hear that. Has something happened?"

"Yes, but it happened a long time ago. First, I apologize again about the early hour, but I have made a strange discovery I thought you ought to know about." She went on to tell him about the falsehoods Dan had written in his book.

Lambert listened intently. "This is very interesting information. Very interesting." He promised to contact her as soon as he had further looked into Dan and his activities, muttered a few niceties, and hung up.

Gaining access to the now questionable Dan's files, unfortunately, was not something he was able to accomplish. The organization had warned him not to, under any circumstances, disclose that he was operating for them, due to the sensitive nature of the investigation. Thus, he had to play the part of the disappointed historian when the clerk at the National Archives later that day informed him that the records he had requested were not available.

"I see. Would that mean they are not available because they cannot be found, or because there are not here, or because they are classified?"

The clerk glanced down at the completed request form. "I believe they are not here, sir. Those are military records, of personnel. Agents' records are not released to us here."

"I had assumed that as they were historical in nature, given that the war ended some sixty years ago, that they would be here."

She failed to detect the sarcasm in his voice and tried to be helpful. "From what I gather, a number of those records have been lost yet you may put your request in writing and send it off by post to …"

"No matter." He forced a slight smile, thanked her for her assistance, and walked out into the cold drizzle, deciding that his contact in London had not heard the last of him. He needed his expertise on this matter.

He arranged a meeting.

The street was quiet just before lunch time and his old acquaintance was waiting for him at the front door, an umbrella in hand despite the fact that the drizzle had stopped. With his dark trench coat and light gray mustache, he was the epitome of an English gentleman.

Lambert rushed up. "I greatly appreciate your agreeing to meet with me again. Your opinion is worth much."

"Let us go for a walk to Sloane Square."

"It's not too cold?"

"My dear fellow, I have been in London for so long, the cold and the rain are a second nature to me now. Besides, there has been a lull in the rain and my long umbrella may serve to replace my cane. It will make me feel young again – not to have a cane."

They began to walk together and Lambert explained what he had discovered, then complaining about his inability to procure the necessary records. Eventually they reached the paved tidy square, with its presently empty flower stall and fountain.

His companion stopped, motioning toward a bench facing the fountain of Venus. "Let us sit here for a while. My legs would benefit from rest."

Lambert complied and together they sat down on the damp bench.

"You are allowing your emotions to get the better of you, old chap. It is a continental phenomenon, yet one which will prove detrimental in your research should you allow it to continue."

Lambert did not deny it. "One cannot help but feel exasperation, shock, and rage, knowing that a terrible injustice has been covered up all these years."

A few piegons gathered before them, pecking at the dirt, searching for crumbs. "You are still more historian than anything else."

"Of course. That was why they approached me – for my knowledge and understanding of the past."

His contact produced from his pocket a piece of bread and tossed it to the piegons. "One must distance onself from one's subjects of study and contacts. A good double agent would have known this."

"Do you think that's what Dan was – a double agent?"

"In my opinion, it does seem possible, based on what you have told me. It would not have been the first time British intelligence was compromised during the Cold War."

"Though this was in World War II – earlier than those other, well publicized incidents."

"Yes, it was, and it also involves the disappearance of many men, including the Diplomat. Does Ms. Schandl suspect that your real motive is to find out what really happened to him?"

"Not yet. I will fill her in when the timing is right."

"I also expect the organization has ordered you to keep quiet about it."

Lambert watched him toss more bread to the congregating

pigeons. "They have, and I think I know why."

"They would not wish to admit that they had all but abandoned the case before you insisted it be revived. Was that why you agreed to join the organization last year, Marcel?"

"As the English say, if the end justifies the means..."

"Well, in any case, I recommend you step back from the whole matter for a short period of time and go over the facts."

"But Dan's official reports ...," he insisted.

"They will not contain much that leads anywhere," the retired Englishman interrupted. "These double agent types are far too clever for that. You will find the same date discrepancies but little else. What might be of use is if the Soviets ever had any files on him, yet those might be entirely inaccessible, if not destroyed or forged with more cover-ups. You must use what you already have."

"You are right," he sighed. "Thus far I know that the Dutchman was working for the Diplomat ..."

"Which you feel may have been the reason for the arrest of Karoly Schandl's entire group, I take it. Once the Diplomat came into contact with an effective, albeit somewhat untrained, unorthodox British led resistance group, that merger made both the Diplomat and the group far too powerful – a potenional major threat to the Soviets, whose sole intention was to conquer the Balkans. There was no room for individuals affiliated with western intelligence."

"I see you have done your research."

"There is still something missing. The next step would be to carefully examine any person – or persons – this Dan may have come into contact with all those years ago on Gellert Hill, Budapest – or perhaps even before he got there."

"Family? Friends?"

"You must go deeper than that, Marcel."

The Swiss historian slowly shook his head. "Witnesses? I cannot imagine it would be possible to find any after 60 years."

"My question is – were there any other such British agents who claimed to have seen him while he was in the Budapest vicinity? I refer to outsiders, you see – people who were dropped into the country like he was. Had he any official

119

associates in that land at the same time that he was there – and how do their stories hold up under scrutiny?" He then stood up, announced that it felt like it would rain, and opened his black umbrella, which shielded them both. No sooner had he done so than raindrops proceeded to shoot down from the gray skies in a cold, angry downpour.

Lambert was grateful for the umbrella and realized that the sly old fox was still a step ahead of them all, in any situation. They began to walk back together toward his flat.

"It's quite a pity that the records on that resistance group are also unavailable," the historian mused.

His companion nodded knowingly. "I expect they are long destroyed, my friend, if they were ever filed."

"But why?"

"In my opinion, no one in charge would have wanted to admit to what had happened to them, for to do so would have created quite a scandal. According to them, even the British intelligence agent dubbed Albert likely did not exist, nor did any of his associates. It was just the way things were sometimes done back then."

"A possible cover-up," the historian concluded. "One of international proportions."

CHAPTER 14
AFTER THE SIEGE

Budapest, Hungary - February 15, 1945

Hitler had ordered the Nazis to fight tooth and nail to remain the sole occupiers of Budapest. The fighting between the Russians and the Germans had been literally street to street, house to house. The inhabitants of the city had been careful not to venture out unless there was a lull. Then they would scurry about, like hungry rabbits searching for any food or scraps of wood they could burn in order to keep warm. No one was safe.

One unfortunate old woman went upstairs from her bunker too early one day and was killed by German and Russian bullets. Both German and Russian soldiers had fired upon her when hearing the movement in her second floor apartment. She left behind an already orphaned grand-daughter who was later taken in by the Red Cross.

People said it had been raining bombs on Gellert Hill. Budapest was in shambles and there were many bodies to bury. Still, everyone knew that the end was near, and most were relieved that the Nazis and their reign of terror would soon end. They could not have imagined the terror that would replace it.

Stalin had given the Soviet soldiers free reign once the city was taken. Women and young girls were brutally raped by the drunken Russian soldiers, sometimes murdered, and looting was rampant. What had begun as a liberation had become an ugly and brutal occupation.

At Terezia's insistence, all females in her household had powdered their hair white, smeared soot on their faces, and dressed in baggy clothes – to escape such a fate. They were all spared.

Terezia later ventured down to the Cave Church. She had come to see that the fathers and brothers were all well, and to talk about her son and whether anyone had heard any news of him.

Father Horvath was tired and drawn as they sat in the church together. They spoke of all the casualties.

Terezia sighed and made the sign of the cross as she recalled the Jewish family who had been murdered by the Arrow Cross at the Finnish Embassy. "I hear that the Nazis are still being engaged in battle in other parts of Hungary."

"Karoly might have been captured by the Germans," Father Horvath pointed out. "If so, he will be eventually set free, when the war is over.They will need to trade to get back their own captured men."

"I hope and pray every night for him. You yourself have heard no concrete news of my son?"

"I am sorry, no."

"He was to deliver someone to the Russians, after crossing the front lines."

Father Horvath paused.

This did not go unnoticed by Terezia. "You have heard something from his resistance group by chance?"

"I wish I had – such fine young men, but I do not know where any of them are at present. The lines of communication are not good."

"There is such chaos," she agreed, then adding. "Father, I could not help but notice that you looked troubled when I mentioned that Karoly had gone to the Russians."

"I realize that he must have been following his orders, yet there are stories – not good ones – coming out of Poland about the Soviets, their practices, and intentions," he said slowly, and then went on to explain. "The Nazis despised the well educated, and men of God, as do the Soviets. It is said that they will try and finish what the Nazis started. They intend to wipe out the educated, the powerful, the wealthy, the middle class – and the clergy. We may all find ourselves in grave danger."

"Perhaps all is not lost. The Smallholders party is expected to win the election," Terezia said. "My husband Karoly believes this as well."

"If ever those elections take place – or if the results will be honored. Tell me, how is Karoly Senior?"

"As well as can be expected. He is tired and the war has taken a toll on him."

"Does he know that your son is missing?"

"Yes, but I refuse to believe that he will never return. I feel my son is alive." She went on to tell Father Horvath how the statue of the Virgin Mary holding the baby Jesus had been the only remaining item in his bombed apartment, and the priest nodded sagely.

"Miracles do happen."

"Yes, they do, Father, and together, we will all weather whatever storm comes our way." She stood up. "I am pleased to hear that none of the brothers or fathers were harmed in the extreme bombing."

"We were fortunate, unlike poor Mrs. Kovacs."

"It was so unusual for her not to have come to our bunker that night," Terezia said sadly. "And poor Sister Sara and the boy Joseph at the Bokreta Retirement Home. I pray for them every night."

Later that afternoon, Terezia returned to the villa, where Dan and Tommy were clearing shattered glass from the floor. They had donned their street clothes, as there were no more Nazis to hide from. Tommy had no more reason to be fearful and he swept the shattered glass aside. His eyelids seemed heavy. Terezia chided him for working so hard and insisted he retire to one of the bedrooms on the main floor for some much needed sleep. He smiled sheepishly, left the broom against the wall, and said he would continue to help later. Dan picked up the broom and walked off, to put it in the back closet.

Karoly Senior looked out the front window. "He is here."

Before Terezia could ask to whom he was referring, a fast series of knocks was heard at the front door. Terezia opened the door, her husband standing by her side.

It was the Swedish Diplomat.

Terezia assumed that, like so many others, he had gone underground and remained in hiding until the worst of the fighting had ended. Now, however, the siege of Budapest was over. "Please, come in."

"Thank you." He stepped inside and looked around. "There has been a great deal of damage done to your home," he said sympathetically.

"Yes," Terezia agreed. "But, thankfully, our lives were spared. We were not expecting you. Please forgive the mess the bombing has left us in."

"It is a rather impromptu visit, I realize." His eyes flickered for a moment and Terezia sensed a certain urgency in his demeanor.

"May I speak with Karoly?"

She sadly shook her head. "He is not here."

"Do you know where I might find him?"

"He is gone. He had to take the Dutchman to the Russians and we have not heard from him since."

"When did they leave?"

"Over two months ago."

The Diplomat looked alarmed.

"The British agent is still here," Karoly Senior said. "He has not left."

The Diplomat appeared relieved. "May I have a word with him?"

"Of course." Terezia walked out behind the villa, where Dan was standing, looking at some bushes in the back garden. She was too fatigued to wonder why. "The Diplomat is here. He would like to speak with you."

Dan's face became stony. He nodded and, without a word, went into the villa. A few moments later, Karoly Senior joined his wife in the back garden.

"It is cold," he stated simply.

Terezia took him by the arm, smiled, and together they walked back inside. In the kitchen, she sat him down and cut him some bread. There was no butter, yet he ate it heartily. She was relieved to see that her husband's appetite was good and set about re-arranging the few plates the Russian soldiers had not broken –

124

as though the simplicity of the task would lessen the complexity of what might lay ahead.

Eventually, they returned to the living room, discovering that it was empty.

Both Dan and the Diplomat were gone.

*Terezia would later tell her son Karoly about the Swedish Diplomat's visit. However, as no one else had been present at their private meeting, no one can say what Dan, the British agent, and the Diplomat actually discussed on February 15, 1945, at 16-18 Kelenhegyi Street, across from the Swedish Embassy ... ***

* In the 1990s, a man who had been working for the Swedish Diplomat also reported having seen him around the same time (mid-February 1945), outside, near the Embassy on Minerva Street. According to Mr. Tomas Kaufmann, the Diplomat was surrounded by Russian officers, who drove away with him shortly afterwards. *

A few weeks later, the mother of William Kis, who had asked Terezia to hide their suitcase of documents, showed up on the front doorstep. No longer the pleasant neighbor she had once been, she was clearly not pleased to be there, for she had heard that the Schandls were certainly not in favor with the new regime.

Already there was talk of how it was looked unfavorably upon that they were so close to the Church. In addition, Karoly Schandl Senior had been the president of Hungary's National Credit Cooperative and before that had been a member of Count Bethlen's Cabinet.

The Communists generally sought to wipe out such families and Mrs. Kis could not have been happy about having to venture to the villa. Never mind that they had hidden her suitcase of important family documents as per her son's request, and had asked nothing in return. One had to be careful about where one was seen, particularly if one wished to win favor with those who were already installing themselves at the forefront of the new Hungary.

Terezia offered her some tea.

Mrs. Kis shook her head in agitation. "I am pressed for time. Where is it?"

Terezia nodded. "You are here for your suitcase?"

Tommy, who was now like family, had overheard and offered to help.

Mrs Kis looked even more impatient. "Where is it?"

"Follow me." Terezia walked downstairs to the basement with the pair at her heels. When they reached the bottom, Tommy took a shovel and started to dig in the coal.

"I saw one of the priests from your home speaking with some Russian soldiers," Mrs. Kis said suddenly.

Terezia was surprised. "Are you certain?"

Mrs. Kis went on to describe Dan.

Terezia shook her head. "You must have been mistaken." She did not add that Dan was in reality a British agent who had been disguised as a father while in hiding from the Nazis.

"How is your son, William?"

"Busy."

Mrs. Kis was about to inquire about her husband but then

stopped. She reminded herself that Karoly Schandl Senior had been a wealthy and powerful man before the war – and such men had fallen out of favor with the new occupiers. Thus, she said not a word.

When the suitcase was finally found, Terezia marveled that it had not a scratch upon it.

Tommy grinned. "The Russians never even suspected it was there."

Mrs. Kis still said nothing but, with great difficulty and irritation, dragged the suitcase up the stairs. Tommy said he could carry it out for her but she shook her head and left them without so much as a word of thanks, dragging the large, heavy suitcase behind her along the crumbling road.

It was a sign of things to come. Only Esther the sweet hairdresser would be among the very few who thanked Terezia Schandl for having helped them during the war.

CHAPTER 15
THE SWEDISH DIPLOMAT

Canada – Spring 2005

The living room was no longer full of boxes and papers. They had all been re-organized, with some of the important ones stored in a single box which was returned to the attic, along with the other boxes. Kati would refer to them in the near future, after the next phase of her plan had been completed.

The spacious living room was tidy, the only thing out of place being the suitcase in the front hall. When Chris knocked at the door and Kati opened it, he walked in, saw the suitcase, and whistled.

"Going somewhere?"

"Budapest, Hungary. My plane leaves in …" She glanced down at her watch. "Five hours. I'm catching the red eye."

"I assume it's not a leisure trip."

"You guessed right."

"I knew that would be your next move – to go to Budapest when the time permitted. You will be looking for documents, no doubt."

"And answers. Something tells me I wouldn't be able to find all the answers here, though there was an interesting bit of information I learned today."

"And there I was thinking that these past couple of months, you'd abandoned the project."

"You know me better than that."

He removed his jacket and sat down in an armchair across from the sofa. Kati sat on the sofa and gracefully crossed her legs.

"I received an email from my mother."

"She's still on the scientific cruise?"

"Yes, but as of this week, they can send email."

"And?"

"I asked her about Dan and she remembered hearing about him."

"What exactly did she say?"

"Not only did he get out of Hungary without a hitch in 1945 after disappearing from the Schandl villa, but he actually refused to meet my father in later years when Dad was released from the Soviet prison."

"You can't be serious. So, the guy stays at his apartment hiding from the Nazis all that time and then refuses to meet with him again, only to write a book once Karoly is dead – a book which contains bogus dates and other inaccuracies, presumably based on his reports?"

She nodded. "Dad was used to people being afraid, though, and that's why he didn't think much of his refusal to see him. After he was released from the Soviet prison, even some people in Hungary who had been his friends asked him to stay away from them."

"I understand. The stigma of having been affiliated with British intelligence while living in a Communist country. I am surprised he was able to track down Dan once he escaped to the free world. I would have thought Dan was using an alias the whole time, being a British agent."

"He was." She half smiled. "That would not have stopped him from learning it, however. His group was pretty capable as far as intelligence went."

Chris suddenly looked concerned. "How do I know you'll be safe in Budapest? If you waited a few months, I could go with you and …"

"That's nice, but there's no reason to worry."

"I do, which is why I am still staying here a few days every week."

"That's nice too, but no one is after me."

"They could be. There was the mysterious Riley who called from nearby, and also the threatening message."

"Nothing has happened since then, though."

"It still could," he warned.

"An indication that the sooner I get the proof I need, the

better."

"Now you're talking like a lawyer. Let's backtrack for a minute. What proof exactly are we talking about? Translation – what documents?"

"I'll be procuring documents to prove that Dad was arrested in early December, 1944 and also a record of Dan's whereabouts before that time. The first one I will find in government archives which I, as his daughter, will be granted access to, and the second will be found in another place. Of that I am certain."

"That sounds cryptic. I am starting to see you take after Karoly more than I'd realized."

"I'll let you know if it worked as soon as I'm back."

"And you'll email me?"

"Every day."

"All right," he sighed. "Now, how long are we talking about?"

"Just a week. Everything I need will be in Budapest so I shouldn't require more time than that."

She glanced out the bay window and noticed that it had started to rain, enough to cause a twenty minute delay in traffic. "There is so much more to this investigation than meets the eye."

Have there been any other developments you'd like to fill me in on?"

Her gaze met his. "I think Lambert omitted to tell me his real reason for pursuing this."

"He did check out okay, even though you haven't heard from him for a while."

She stood up, walked toward the fireplace, and turned off the gas, in case she might forget before leaving. "I have been doing some thinking and I am sure that his angle is the Diplomat."

"The Dutchman who was arrested with your father?"

"No, I mean the Diplomat. According to my father, the Dutchman was working for the Diplomat." She paused and then stated the Diplomat's name.

Chris nodded. "It's no wonder people have been contacting you. The entire world was trying to find him. I heard he went missing in January 1945 ..."

"It was February 15, 1945."

"I read all about it and ..."

"I heard that it was February 15, 1945."

"Where did you come up with that date?"

"My father, Karoly, told me. There were some things he didn't write down, even in his memoirs, but when he was older, he talked about them. The Diplomat was on the news some years ago as people were trying to solve the mystery of his disappearance. That's when Karoly told me that the Dutchman had been working for the Diplomat. He was helping people escape the Nazis with false papers. Dad said he had never met the Diplomat, as he'd already been in prison in the Soviet Union at the time he came looking for him at the house on Gellert Hill. His mother, Terezia, told him about it and she also remembered the exact date, being a religious Catholic. It was the day after Ash Wednesday. She said it was February 15, 1945. That was when he met with Dan – and shortly after that meeting, they were both gone. I hadn't realized until recently that he was the diplomat his friend Sam had mentioned in his letter. I had been thinking he was a Hungarian, but I was mistaken. It was a reference to the Diplomat who was in Budapest at the time."

He nodded. "The Swedish diplomat."

"Yes. The Swedish Embassy was just behind the Schandl villa."

"I read he was arrested by the Soviets."

"He was, and he died in one of their prisons not long afterwards. That was what my father told me back in the 1980s once, when I brought the topic up."

Chris slowly shook his head in awe. "This is simply amazing information, Kati, but why would everyone think his arrest happened in January if it was really February?"

"I'm not sure, but if the Soviets admitted to arresting him after the siege of Budapest was over, then that would have been when the war was over. That means it would have been a completely illegal abduction. Well, it was anyway, but the fact that it was not a wartime mistake would make them look that much worse. Perhaps they either forged documents or put fake dates on them to cover it up. Either way, according to my grandmother's recollection to my father, it was February 15, 1945. She told my father but no one else, as they had both been involved in the underground.They talked privately about these things."

"I am the first one to admit, I am way out of my league here in piecing the puzzles together. Did the Soviets actually do that? Did they abduct non-Soviet bloc citizens in other countries?"

"They did with an American sergeant called Bob. He was kidnapped in Vienna, Austria and ended up in prison in the Soviet Union. Of course, I bet the Soviets denied it, just like they originally denied having taken the Dutchman and the Diplomat way back then."

"Dates aside, it was a terrible thing that they arrested that great man and imprisoned him."

"I agree," Kati said solemnly. "And how tragic that he was likely murdered like so many others they felt might pose a problem for them in the future."

"How can you be sure he died in the prison?"

"That's what Dad told me a long time ago. The Diplomat died in Lubyanka. At least that was what the guard said after the tapping stopped …"

"Tapping?"

"Morse code. It's how the prisoners used to communicate between the cells in Lubyanka Prison."

CHAPTER 16
SOVIET PRISONS

Lubyanka Prison, Moscow – mid-1940s

The Dutch government had asked the Soviets about the Dutchman – of that Karoly was certain. It had become evident when they had last interrogated him. They had been extremely agitated about it and must have been irked that somehow the Dutchman and Karoly had managed to get a message out before being whisked off to Lubyanka. The American pilots and/or the Canadian major must have reported that the two prisoners were transported, along with the Abwehr, from Bucharest to Moscow. That was a good sign. Karoly would not learn until years later that the Soviets had lied and denied even so much as seeing them, despite what the Americans and/or the Canadian major had reported to their superiors. However, in the 1940s in a wretched little cell in the Lubyanka, that was not known, and so the realization that the sighting had been reported gave him a faint flicker of hope.

The Dutchman was still absent from their cell, having been dragged off for yet another interrogation. Karoly shut his eyes and tried to count how many days and nights they had been imprisoned there.

That was when he first heard it.

It was the distinct sound of tapping, coming from somewhere along the wall. The walls of the prison did not prevent sounds from traveling. Often you could hear the sounds of men having a stroke when it seemed to get very hot inside, after which the guards and doctors would run by, carrying ice. It was all quite loud and awful, but this was different – close and yet distant, and ever so meticulous, as though a man's graceful fingers were intentionally tapping for communication purposes.

He recognized it immediately as Morse code.

He walked to the wall and, without hesitation, tapped that he was present, adding his name. There was a pause.

He did it again and waited.

The tapper hastily spelled out his name.

It was the Diplomat.

A few messages followed. He did not know why he had been arrested, like both Karoly and the Dutchman. He did not know what would happen next.

Then, as quickly as it had started, the tapping ceased.

When the Dutchman eventually returned to the cell, Karoly's expression was one of both hope and animation. He waited until the guard had left them alone and then whispered "The Diplomat is in this prison as well." He was careful to keep his voice as inaudible as possible to the microphones he knew were hidden in the cell.

The next day, they waited for the tapping to resume but it did not. A few days later, Karoly, who had been picking up some Russian phrases from the guards, boldly inquired what had happened to the prisoner in the next cell.

The guard shrugged his shoulders. "He died."

That was the last he ever heard about the Diplomat.

The rhythm of life in Lubyanka was terrible, even in the regular section of the prison, where they were being held in those early days. Every morning the cell felt unusually warm, followed by an inexplicable cold period. Afterwards, there was the inarticulate shouting of some of the prisoners in nearby cells and one wondered if they had been able to survive whatever it was the Soviets were doing to them in that forsaken place. Both Karoly and the Dutchmen would become drowsy after the cold period, with a certain heaviness in their muscles. One could do very little to stay awake.

The hot periods in the morning seemed to give one a

feeling of high blood pressure, with dry eyes and nostrils. Then the cold period came and their noses became unusually runny. That was when they had excessive amounts of fluid in their bodies, including saliva, urination, and fluid from the bowels. By afternoon, when the guards brought "lunch" around, it felt hot again, yet immediately after lunch, there was another bizarre cold spell.

Fortunately, after a little while, they were permitted to lie in their beds, unlike some other prisoners, whom they later understood to be entirely sleep deprived. Was this because their captors felt there was no further information to extract from them in their repetitive, futile interrogations? If so, then why did they not let them go?

At night it often felt icy in the cell. Karoly soon discovered that the best thing to do was actually sleep during the day and lie awake at night. That way, the physical symptoms were not quite as severe.

Somehow it felt as though those hot and cold periods were linked to the sounds they had heard since arriving in the prison. There had been German and Russian voices for the first few days. They had discussed it at the time and concluded that the voices must have belonged to prisoners and/or guards who were in close proximity. It would later become evident that the voices had been meant to confuse and intimidate them. Karoly would later realize that the voices had been fed into their cell, perhaps to place psychological pressure on them. The languages, however, were not the mother tongue of either man at the time, so they knew they were not imagining those voices. In addition, they heard the same voices at the same time.

Soon something was to occur that would make them realize just how dire their situation really was. They were moved from Lubyanka to Lefortovo Prison, to cell number 111. The conditions were worse than in Lubyanka, though the wretched rhythm of life, with the hot and cold periods, remained the same.

Lefortovo, located in Moscow, was near what must have been some sort of motor repair or assembly plant, with a continuous whirring sound. The conditions in the prison were worse than those of Lubyanka. What was even more dismal was the fact that Lubyanka was where prisoners were generally kept while "under investigation." Thus, the transfer to Lefortovo was an indication that the Soviets had no intention of freeing either Karoly or the Dutchman.

There was something tragically final about being in Lefortovo, yet Karoly reasoned that once the war was over, they would have to release them. By then, the mistake would have been discovered and the British would have somehow learned where they were. He continued to reassure the Dutchman that Churchill would get them out, still having no idea of what was going on in the outside world.

One day, a woman's voice was heard in the cell. She was speaking German.

"Good morning, Second Lieutenant," she repeated several times. "You are a nice man."

"Good morning, Second Lieutenant. You are a nice man."

"Good morning, Second Lieutenant. You are a nice man."

It seemed to be a mind game they were trying to play. Karoly had a plan. He waited for her to repeat the phrases at least a hundred times, then walked toward the part of the cell he had heard the voice from, and replied, also in German, "You are a nice woman. You are a nice woman."

There was silence and then he heard the sounds of people laughing, coming from somewhere around the heater. A few minutes later, the repetitive recording continued.

Laughter. There were voices on the other side – and those voices were in real time, belonging to real people.

He would remind himself of this in later years, as the voices went on and on, and sometimes even seemed to enter his thoughts, having been placed at a very high pitch so as to trick prisoners. He had been fortunate that at first, the voices had been played in Russian – a language he could not at the time understand. Only shortly after their imprisonment had they switched to mostly German, still peppered with Russian texts, likely depending on who was in charge of the recording.

There were also staged conversations. Sometimes the guards stood at their door and repeated the same sentence in Russian, which Karoly later understood to be that "The diplomats did not allow the persecution of the English spies."

The Soviets seemed to despise the English.

There were other things to contend with in their day to day existence, however. One day, he and the Dutchman began to discuss the continuous ringing in their ears which had never stopped. They attributed it to the whirring from the plant surrounding the prison. It was just another thing to make one's existence that much more difficult. After a while, however, it became evident that it was a permanent condition. They were unsure as to what exactly had caused it.

Time passed slowly in the "special" section of Lefortovo prison. Very slowly. Then something happened over which Karoly had no control, something that would haunt him for the rest of his life. On January 15, 1946, one year to the day that they had arrived in the Soviet Union, the guards came and removed the Dutchman from the cell. He was taken away with his bed, leaving Karoly alone to wonder what the NKVD would do to the young man he had been ordered to deliver to safety over thirteen months before.

He felt terrible. George, as British intelligence officer "Albert" had received the order to have the Dutchman escorted to the Russians back in 1944 and had instructed him to take on the task. George too had been following orders with the best intentions.

Karoly was of the opinion that no one could have foreseen that the NKVD and SMERSH would have arrested them and carted them off to the Soviet prison, accusing them of being German and then British spies. Still, he was the messenger and therefore felt responsible for the Dutchman, whom he had often attempted to console while in their cell.

"Churchill will get us out," he had told him several times. "Churchill will save us."

It never materialized.

Once he was out from behind the Iron Curtain. Karoly would say that they had tortured the Dutchman in the prisons, though he would not elaborate.

While still in Lefortovo, he would hear that the Dutchman had committed suicide by hanging himself in the cell he had been placed in shortly afterwards. Years later, the Soviets would finally admit to having arrested and imprisoned the Dutchman, but they would never admit that he had killed himself in Lefortovo. They would claim he had "died" in the prison hospital. Perhaps it was not wise for any of the guards or sergeants to admit that there had been a suicide in Lefortovo. Even the guards and secret police were not above being executed.

After he was freed, Karoly would tell certain international government officials that the Dutchman ought to have been honored, for having provided false documents for so many in World War II Hungary. He said the Dutchman was a hero.

There is presently a memorial to the Dutchman in Moscow. Every year the Dutch place tulips upon it. A hero forever.

After the Dutchman had been taken away, the strange sounds in the prison continued and Karoly was bombarded with them. It was as though there were bands of texts or sounds being played at different frequencies at different times of the day. During the cold periods, only a few voices were heard, whilst during the hot periods, there were many louder voices.

One time, he heard a German voice announce "Churchill will save you." Had they listened to his conversations with the Dutchman and were they trying to torment him by playing them back, hoping to thus break him? It was true, he had not given them the names of any others in the network. Was that what they were really after or was he perhaps losing his mind and was that the reason for the increase in the voices he heard? If he were imagining the voices, it would have been due to something they were giving him.

Karoly began to wonder if they were tampering with his food and decided to make an experiment. If he did not eat for a few days, he reasoned, and the voices went away, then he would know for certain that they were administering drugs in his food and that was why his words seemed to be played back to him.

The first day of his experiment, he took the food they gave him, but later disposed of it, unseen by the guards. He consumed only the hot water and small portions of bread that accompanied it. Nothing changed, so he decided not to eat his bread. Still nothing changed so he stopped drinking the hot water. He went without water for days. Soon dehydration set in and he became very ill.

At night, it felt as though the entire brick building was rocking back and forth. He heard not only the usual texts they played to him, but other voices as well and those voices were in Hungarian – his first language, a language he had not yet heard spoken in the Soviet prisons. He became sick to his stomach and so weak that he could not stand up. Hallucinations followed, and his hearing felt as though it were slipping away. He should not have let his nerves dry out in such a manner and resolved to get better by drinking all the water they gave him, in addition to eating the food he now believed was not poisoned. The lack of water especially had made him unwell. It would take a long time for him to recover.

What did his Soviet captors have in mind – did they believe the British would trade him for someone? Or did they think that his father would come through with international connections interested in proposing a trade? After all, Karoly Schandl Senior had not been without contacts. Perhaps the Soviets did not realize they had all been solely in Hungary.

The fact that they were not poisoning him made him realize that the earlier voices had been recordings played into the cell, and not his hallucinations.

Karoly drank as much water as possible after the incident, though his ears were still not "clear." During that period of his recovery, they changed his food. They gave him a meager portion compared to the regular ration. Eventually, when his ears started to improve, he could remember the few Russian words he had learned and overheard a sergeant explain the reason for his portion to a new guard.

"He has to get it to heal his ears …"

He later learned how ironic a place Lefortovo Prison was when the unthinkable occurred. They placed two older Nazi Germans in his cell – a General and a Sonderfuhrer, each of whom must have been responsible for the murders of countless innocent Jewish men, women, and children during the war. Karoly was disgusted. He had been a member of the anti-Nazi resistance and had worked hard to ensure such people would not prevail. He despised what they represented.

Unfortunately, he understood German perfectly and therefore understood every hideous word which they uttered. They persecuted him continually. After a while, he could tolerate it no more and set out to have his voice heard by the Commissar of the prison – but how?

He would simply go on a hunger strike.

He drank water and ate small amounts of bread, but overtly refused his food. Soon he had the desired results.

On the third day, the guards removed him from the cell and took him to see the Commissar.

He was a young captain. "Why do you not eat?"

Karoly told him how he loathed the Nazis and could not tolerate being in a cell with them. He then did the unthinkable – he asked to be transferred to another cell.

The Commissar was surprisingly pleasant. Aware that Karoly had been trying to understand more and more Russian words, he promised him a dictionary, adding that he expected him to be released by Christmas. "If you are not home by Christmas, I will come to your cell and break the window myself."

Karoly was taken aback.

The Commissar added that the next time the Germans proceeded to throw their hate filled ideas his way, he should simply tell them to "Kiss my ass."

He said the sentence in German.

Karoly was led back to the cell. Shortly afterwards, he heard the same vulgar sentence played in the cell at a high pitch, only this time it was in Hungarian.

They were apparently becoming quite sophisticated with their mind games. The problem of the Nazis in his cell, however, did not go away.

Karoly learned something quite interesting the next few times he refused to take his meal. They now tried to punish him in the prison for trying to go on a hunger strike. The text recordings were stopped and were replaced by a high pitched pounding sound which caused coldness in the head and body, followed by nausea and swollen feet. At least those were the symptoms a younger man experienced. The older Nazi officers in his cell took it far worse. When their persecution of him started again, he decided to take action. He refused his next meal.

The punishment was swift. The cell became cold and the intensity of the sounds played into it was increased. Karoly felt unwell but the Sonderfuhrer especially took it hard. He became violently ill and collapsed, losing consciousness for a while. The Sonderfuhrer did not recover for weeks but stayed in the cell with his fellow Nazi prisoner - the murderous General - and the young Hungarian lawyer who continued to lament that he was cooped up with those evil ones whom had worked so hard to defeat a few years earlier, in the Second World War.

The days dragged into months and the months dragged into years.

Budapest, Hungary – 1947

The man at the door was wearing an expensive suit. Terezia Schandl recognized him immediately as having been Karoly's law partner. She would have been hopeful but there was no sign of good news etched upon his somber face.

"I simply had to come."

She led him into the living room. "I will get Karoly Senior. We can have tea together."

A few minutes later, they all sat in the living room, drinking tea.

Karoly Senior began to reminisce about the old days at the OKH, the National Credit Cooperative, of which he had been president prior to the war. It seemed to be the only thing that gave him joy anymore – to reminisce.

Karoly Junior's law partner had also been a lawyer at the OKH. They had shared a private practice together as well. Clients were still asking about his whereabouts, as was the law society, which, unbeknownst to all present, would soon be dissolved by the Soviets.

"Has there been any word?" he said suddenly. "Anything new?"

Terezia sadly shook her head. "We tried but no one knows anything – that is what they are saying. We went to the police headquarters and they told us they did not know where he was, just that they thought he was on his way home."

"But he has not arrived," Karoly Senior pointed out. "He has not arrived."

"The Russians said he was on his way," Terezia sighed. "They said they have not seen him but that he was on his way."

"Two years ago," Karoly Senior lamented. "He was on his way back two years ago. That is what they claim."

"And we do not believe them," Terezia said suddenly. "They have already arrested many of our friends and sent them to Soviet prisons."

The lawyer nodded pensively. If only he could give them good news, yet it was not forthcoming. For all practical purposes, Karoly Schandl Junior had simply vanished. Thousands had met with a similar fate during the war, though there seemed something more complex at work here, with the deception. It was almost as if there were some sort of cover-up.

His father then brought up his son's involvement in the anti-Nazi resistance and how he had delivered the Dutchman to the Russians. It did not look optimistic. They had vanished after the pre-arranged meeting with the Russians.

The truth of the matter was that his father believed him to be dead, his mother continued to pray, yet no one could imagine that the Russians had lied and arrested him with the young Dutchman and locked them in Lubyanka and Lefortovo prison.

All involved in the British led anti-Nazi resistance in Hungary were being systematically "liquidated" by the Soviets.

The Diplomat too had vanished without a trace, though no one was sure when exactly it had happened.

Different sources gave different times and sightings.

CHAPTER 17
THE SACRED

Budapest, Hungary – Autumn 1950

The Soviet occupation of Hungary was a fait accompli. Following the war, there had been elections which the Smallholders party had easily won. The Communist party at that time had been granted the power to run the secret police, though not the country. That was what the elections indicated, though it was doubtful that they had even legally obtained the mandate to run the secret police. The orders which came from Moscow, nevertheless, required that things be done a certain way, likely in order to lessen international fallout.

In 1948, non-Communist parties and their supporters were "liquidated."

Any kind of democracy, unfortunately, was not in the works for Hungary, and the Soviets, along with their secret police, set about fabricating charges against those they felt would stand in their way. They were followed by arrests, mock trials, imprisonment in either Hungary or the Soviet Union, and/or execution. In the Kremlin's mind, anyone who had been involved in any sort of resistance activities – including the anti-Nazi resistance – was a potential threat to their longterm intentions, as were the wealthy, the middle class, the non-Communist political, the clergy, and anyone in close contact with any such persons, not to mention anyone thought to have been sympathetic toward them. In short, it was a time of lies, trumped-up charges, and criminal acts.

The AVO - *Államvédelmi Osztály* - was a very dirty player in the game. They were the much dreaded Communist secret police, which had been set up in Hungary by the Red Army. They were run by the Soviet secret police which would in later years be known as the KGB. Ironically, their headquarters were in the very same building that the Arrow Cross had used in Budapest. Some said it was a sign of the times – different regime, but driven by an evil which equaled that of the hate mongering Arrow Cross and Nazis. Even more shocking was the fact that the AVO had gone so far as to recruit some former Nazis to join their ranks.

They often operated as follows. An arrest warrant was issued, the victim having been accused of being suspected of anti-Soviet activities. Generally there were none. In blatant violation of international human rights, the victim was then collected by the arresting AVO officers and transported to the AVH/AVO Headquarters, whose basement housed dungeons and extra thick walls to drown out any screams. The intimidation tactics consisted of starvation, sleep deprivation, and physical torture which ranged from beatings to pulling out nails – or far worse. Once broken down, the unfortunate focus of the endless interrogation was then forced to sign a confession of trumped-up charges. If not, the unlucky person was either executed or handed over to the Soviets. If he signed, he might still be executed or handed over to the Soviets.

More than once, the victim was led to believe that he was being released, only to take a few steps and find himself then arrested by the Soviet secret police, who whisked him off to the Soviet Union, where hundreds of thousands were reported to have vanished in gulags.

There were also the sudden night-time abductions of men and boys, who were sent to the Soviet Union "to work" and never returned. Lives were lost and families were destroyed. One wife of an unfortunate young man who had been taken away was so hopeful that she went to the train station in her town every day of her life to see if her husband would return on the next train coming in from the east. He never did and she died of old age decades later, never having seen him again.

The clergy, as later became well known, was a major target of the Communists. In 1948, Cardinal Mindszenty was arrested, tortured, and forced to sign a confession of false charges. After his mock trial, he was imprisoned.

Time was running out for a number of people, and more

and more were attempting to flee the country. It was a risky undertaking, for the AVO often cleverly entrapped them, after which they would be imprisoned for trying to flee the country - something that had been declared illegal by the Communists, likely because they did not want the rest of the world to hear first hand accounts of the brutality and oppression of their regime.

During their imprisonments, the potential escapees, many of whom were wealthy or considered "undesirable elements" by the Soviets, would have their homes and properties confiscated. Private or family run businesses were "nationalized."

It was all very well orchestrated, so as to minimize international pressure and give a sense of legality to the crimes upon which the new order of the Kremlin's newly acquired land was to be built. Sometimes friends informed on friends, perhaps due to being threatened by the secret police or perhaps because they were no more than opportunists willing to partake in anything for profit or favors. Either way, the outcome would be the same. The "friend" would be arrested, imprisoned, and possibly executed. Such were the times. It made one extremely cautious about whom to trust, especially by 1950.

The fathers of the Paulist Order remained in close contact with Terezia Schandl. Karoly Schandl Senior and his wife Terezia had a number of junior priests staying in their retirement villa in Felcsut. It had not been entirely completed and the amenities were minimal, but it was located away from the capital and the prying eyes of the secret police and the less than trustworthy authorities. It was a time when it was dangerous to be a priest, for the Communists were self-proclaimed atheists and were determined to exterminate the clergy.

Father Horvath of the Paulist Order was still a good friend. Sometimes he visited the Schandl villa, while other times Terezia ventured to the Cave Church to attend his services and seek an audience with him.

He was the only one who assured her that she could very well be right in her heart and that her son Karoly Junior could still be alive. She had not lost hope and prayed every day to the Virgin Mary to spare her son and let him one day return to her.

One afternoon, she and Father Horvath took tea together

and discussed what was taking place in their homeland.

"Is there any possibility that they will free the Cardinal?" she inquired.

Father Horvath shook his head. "I do not believe it will happen in the near future. One must pray."

"But he has done nothing wrong and he is a man of God."

"Those who illegally arrested him are Godless."

Terezia put down her half-empty teacup and then toyed with the ring on her finger, the way she did when she was nervous. "Then it is only a matter of time. Father, I fear for the priests as I fear for my missing son and my tired husband. What is to become of us?"

Father Horvath wished he could provide an answer. Unfortunately, he could not.

"They must already be watching us very closely. Why do they simply not let us all leave the country?"

"Stalin's Godless Communists do not work that way. They will stop at nothing to accomplish their goals. That goal is to rid themselves of the clergy, anyone connected with them, the intelligentsia, and all whom they consider to be the 'undesirable class' in a manner that would do the least damage to their international reputation. I have even heard rumors that they took Count Bethlen to the Soviet Union some years ago and imprisoned him, after which he died."

"I pray for him. My husband so admired Count Bethlen. I wonder if the Communists are aware that he was a member of Bethlen's Cabinet when the Count was Prime Minister ..." Her voice trailed off.

Father Horvath told her not to despair.

Terezia sadly shook her head. "I have been giving this a great deal of thought. We must leave before they come and arrest us."

Father Horvath lowered his voice. "Though it could be a very dangerous undertaking."

"It must be done."

"You are certain of this, knowing that there are immense risks?"

She nodded. After realizing that there lay only dark times

ahead, she had resolved to flee Hungary with her husband. Father Horvath too was concerned – about the safety of some of the fathers in the monastery.

Terezia was determined to come up with a plan. In the following hour, it was decided that three Paulist priests would join the Schandls in their escape. In the days that followed, Terezia considered her options. It would be too risky to take matters into one's own hands. She would have to pay someone to help them cross the border, as others had. That was the only way – yet who could she trust? Some did manage to go west to freedom, but there were more who did not succeed and wound up imprisoned – or far worse.

She had to make it as safe a plan as possible. She had already paid a visit to the passport office and asked about applying for a visiting passport. They had said they would get back to her.

In the meantime, she met Mrs. Bellak.

Mrs. Bellak was the wife of an academic, a friend to many, and everyone appreciated her sympathetic ear. One day, when Terezia was at a social gathering of one of her relatives, expressing her concerns over the future, Mrs. Bellak, who was also present, seemed very interested in what Terezia Schandl had to say.

"Have you had any word of your son?"

"I pray for my son every day," Terezia replied. "There is still no news, at least not yet."

"I admire your strong faith," Mrs. Bellak replied. "But are you not worried about the future?"

"Everyone is," Terezia pointed out. "The key is to find a way to change it."

Mrs. Bellak's eyes widened with interest. "You sound as though you are going to leave Hungary, like so many others. Do you have a plan?"

"Not yet."

"One must be cautious, Terezia, about whom to trust. Would Karoly Senior also accompany you?"

"I would never go anywhere without my husband. The journey would not be easy for him, but I would be there to help him."

"You must tell me all about it," Mrs. Bellak whispered. She took Terezia aside so their conversation would not be overheard.

"My plan is simply to somehow flee the country. I know we will not be safe here much longer. We will go west, perhaps to Austria."

Mrs. Bellak smiled. "Nothing is easier than that."

Terezia was not certain what she meant. "We have been to the passport office but have not had any success ..."

"I can help you do it," she suddenly stated. "I can arrange for you to meet with some Russian officers in Dunantul – the area west of the Danube – at a chateau – and they will drive you to the Russian occupied zone of Vienna." Mrs. Bellak then mentioned the name of a man whom she would recommend as their guide. "It will cost you 1000 forint," she added.

Terezia thanked her and said she would give it some consideration, yet she was not comfortable with the idea of entrusting their safety to Russian soldiers. For this reason, she contacted one of the former directors of the OKH, who had been a good friend of her husband's. His warning was dire.

"Under no circumstances should you trust the man you were considering as a guide. I have heard of him and he has a reputation as a liar."

When Mrs. Bellak showed up on Terezia's doorstep a few days later, Terezia informed her of what she had learned of the man.

Mrs. Bellak had a quick response. "There is also someone from Sopron. His friend has a daughter who is studying in Vienna and he is able to visit her often, with a temporary permit. He can obtain for you such a permit in Sopron, if you like. It would be easy, for Sopron is close to the Austrian/Hungarian border."

Terezia paused and promised to give it some thought.
Mrs Bellak left.

When the head of the passport office showed up shortly afterwards, asking for 20,000 forint to prepare their passports, Terezia was taken aback, but agreed. It still did seem the safest to go through official channels, even though it might involve paying a bribe. While they were waiting for the passports, however, the passport office was investigated and the man who had promised them their passports for 20,000 forint was subsequently arrested. Terezia read about it in the newspaper.

By then, Mrs. Bellak was showing up at the villa almost every day, always warning Terezia that time was running out.

Terezia finally asked her about her friend in Sopron, the man who would be able to supply their permits.

"His name is Sandor Rose and he has helped others like you and Karoly Senior go west. He could easily help you." She smiled. "Shall I introduce you?"

Terezia was hesitant. "How can you be sure that he is trustworthy?"

Mrs. Bellak nodded. "I understand your hesitation. I have known Sandor for a long time and have also met his wife and daughter. He is very discreet and he knows exactly how to outsmart the authorities. Shall I introduce him to you?"

"Yes, that would be greatly appreciated," Terezia agreed.

"Tomorrow morning?"

"Tomorrow, then."

The following day, Mrs. Bellak made good on her promise and brought the man she had mentioned to the Schandl villa.

After the introductions had been made, Sandor Rose respectfully kissed Terezia Schandl's hand and apologized for being a few minutes late.

Terezia suggested they adjourn to the living room. Mrs. Bellak said she was glad the drapes on the windows were still drawn, as one could no longer be sure of whom to trust.

"The dog is outside," Terezia pointed out. "When outside, he barks at any movement. We will hear him if anyone approaches the house."

Mrs. Bellak sat in a velvet covered chair. "One cannot be too careful."

"Such a friendly little black dog," Sandor Rose said

cheerfully. "Er … your husband is not joining us?"

Terezia shook her head.

Sandor Rose waited for the lady of the house to take a seat and then followed. He was a very accommodating, well dressed gentleman. He cleared his throat and then proceeded to explain how he would be able to help the Schandls escape.

"I understand you will be traveling with your husband and two other relatives. In two separate groups, we can go to the train station here in Budapest. There we will catch a train to Sopron and once in Sopron, I will take you to the passport office to pick up your special temporary permits that will enable you all to go on to Vienna."

Terezia was dubious. "There is really such a thing as a temporary permit?"

"Oh yes," Sandor Rose insisted. "I know because a friend of mine has a daughter who is studying in Austria. With my assistance, he was able to get a temporary permit which enables him to visit her every month. It will cost one thousand forint for me to obtain them for you. I have contacts at the Sopron passport office who can be bribed."

"May I pay Mrs. Bellak?"

"Yes, of course, though I ask that you not tell anyone about your plans." He cleared his throat and went on. "As there are to be two small groups which will not be traveling together, there will be little suspicion on the part of any of the authorities. I have done this many times before. It is a foolproof plan. On arriving in Vienna, you will be able to join the other group. But one group will depart two days before the other group."

Mrs. Bellak expressed her assurances that Sandor Rose was very good at what he did. "And," she added, "he does have references if you need them."

Terezia did not hesitate to respond. "In that case, can you take me to one of your references?" *She had to be certain.*

Sandor Rose was obliging. "A lawyer in Pest. We can go to his office together, if you like, but it will have to be now."

They all stood up. Mrs. Bellak pointed out that she should not be seen going with them to the lawyer's office. "It might arouse suspicions if the three of us walk in together."

"Yes," Sandor Rose agreed. "The smaller the number of people seen together these days, the better."

A short time later, Terezia found herself accompanying him to a law office which was located in a building in downtown Pest, at Apponyi Square. They hadn't needed to make an appointment – it seemed Mr. Rose was on very good terms with the lawyer.

The lawyer confirmed what Sandor Rose had claimed. He insisted that such a temporary permit to Austria did exist and that Sandor Rose had helped him apply for his so that he could visit his daughter every month. Terezia was still not convinced. Before she departed, she informed Sandor Rose that there was still one more person she needed to confer with.

Father Horvath was at the Cave Church. Terezia told him about Sandor Rose and how Mrs. Bellak and the lawyer had recommended him, but she still had doubts.

Father Horvath offered to meet him.

Terezia was relieved. The following day, Sandor Rose was introduced to Father Horvath of the Paulist Order. He was pleasant and answered all of Father Horvath's questions with ease.

Father Horvath, like Terezia, was under the impression that the man was telling the truth. Sandor Rose had gained the priest's trust. It was then confirmed that three Paulist priests would be accompanying the Schandls. The plan was set in motion.

Terezia paid Mrs. Bellak the one thousand forint she had requested.

Prior to leaving, Terezia visited her cousin to bid her farewell, Her cousin was beside herself with worry. "Don't go," she implored, "for I am certain that it is a set-up. They will arrest all of you."

Terezia assured her it was safe. After all, Sandor Rose would even be bringing his wife and daughter along for the journey.

On September 1, 1950, Terezia and her husband Karoly Senior were accompanied by two Paulist priests as they went to one of the train stations in Budapest. The third priest had left a couple of days earlier with two of Terezia's relatives.

Karoly Schandl Senior had aged a great deal since the war, and now walked at a slower pace. Terezia lovingly helped him along, carrying her suitcase. Karoly Senior was carrying his small black briefcase, in which they had placed her jewelry and their important papers. Soon, she told herself, they would be in Vienna, where the Soviets and Communists would no longer threaten their safety. When her son returned, as she believed he would, he too could join them.

It was a windy autumn day.

The train station, as always, was a hub of activity. They would not be noticed among the crowds. Sandor Rose had been so accommodating – earlier on in the day, he had brought his wife and daughter to help Terezia and her husband pack.

As Terezia sat on the train, she noticed two men who appeared to be saying goodbye to Sandor Rose. She thought one of them looked familiar, but was not sure where she had seen him previously.

Had he been at the passport office or the police station?

The train finally pulled out and they were soon passing the countryside which they had often traveled. A sense of ease set in with the familiar landscape.

Once at Gyor, they would transfer to the train which would take them to Sopron. After their visit to the passport office, to pick up their temporary permits, they would be abe to travel to Vienna, Austria – and freedom.

She was looking forward to seeing her nephew who had escaped the AVO two years earlier when they had come looking for him. They had planned to arrest him only because he was managing his family's mill and they wanted the mill to be "nationalized." He had been forewarned by a friend that he had been on the AVO list of those who would be arrested in the near future – so he had fled the country and had succeeded in reaching Vienna. He would be there for them and had even promised to help Terezia find a job, if they would need one to survive in Austria.

They arrived, without incident, in Sopron. Terezia looked around the small station, with her husband at her side, intending to say goodbye to Sandor Rose's wife and daughter and to thank them for their assistance. They were nowhere to be seen, but Sandor Rose was at their side in an instant.

"Are you tired?"

"Not at all."

He was walking very fast – she could hardly keep up with him. Terezia wondered why he was in such a hurry. She could no longer see the two priests and wondered where they had gone.

Sandor Rose took the small black briefcase from Karoly Senior's hand. "I will help you carry it," he said suddenly.

Karoly Senior frowned.

"It is all right," Terezia told Sandor, coming up to his side. "My husband …" She stopped when she realized that their guide was even more hurried than before.

The Schandls quickened their pace.

Sandor Rose's pace became faster.

Terezia followed him in haste. After several minutes, she realized he was actually trying to get away from them.

"Why are you running?" she asked loudly.

In an instant they were surrounded by several men from the AVO, their Russian machine guns drawn.

They were now prisoners. It had been a trap, slyly set by Sandor Rose, who had since disappeared, along with the black briefcase. Terezia wondered if that was even his real name and whether the "lawyer" he had introduced her to had been real. Her heart immediately sank.

She and her husband were taken to the AVO headquarters for questioning.

Terezia calmly informed them that they had simply ventured to Sopron to obtain a permit in order to travel to Vienna. The AVO men didn't care. They were then lined up, facing the wall, with their hands over their heads. The men took all of their possessions, leaving only her wedding band.

Shortly afterwards, Terezia and her husband found themselves on a truck and taken to Csorna. There they were unloaded, taken to a barn, and told to sit on the floor, again facing the wall. They were not permitted to stand up or lie down. It was disgraceful treatment of an aging man who had done so much for his country. Terezia Schandl was not guilty of any wrongdoing either – unless one considered charity work a crime.

They were interrogated again.

After three days in the barn, they were put on another truck and transported to Gyor Prison. The Schandls were then separated and imprisoned for two years.

Terezia soon found herself in a cell with other women and was shocked to discover that the presumably helpful Mrs. Bellak must have herself been an AVO agent, for in the Gyor Prison were seven other people whom she had offered to help in a similar manner. The pattern was always the same – she would introduce them to a guide and they would be arrested by the AVO during their attempted escape. All were considered to belong to the "undesirable class" by the Communists, as they were either wealthy, highly educated, or nobility. Each had paid Mrs. Bellak a thousand forint. There was also a nun among them.

Not long after her imprisonment, Terezia would learn that the Schandl villa on Gellert Hill, Budapest had been confiscated by the Communists, along with the rest of their property and assets. The Gellert Hill villa was converted into Communist government offices. As the owners were in jail for having attempted to flee the country, there was no one to oppose the seizure, no one the international media could communicate with. It had all been very well orchestrated. It would never be reversed. *"They wanted our house!" she would write in her memoirs.*

The Communists' treatment of the Paulist Order was to be even more severe. In 1951, on Easter Sunday, during mass, the AVO burst into the Cave Church, arresting all of the priests and smashing the church's altar and statues.

The entire Paulist Order was shut down, their property confiscated, including the vineyards in Soltvadkert. Father Horvath and several other priests were taken away, condemned to languish in Communist run prisons, where some ecclesiastics would perish.

Father Vezer, the Head of the Cave Church, was sentenced to death.

He would be hung in 1952.

The Cave Church on Gellert Hill was closed off and would remain in such a state for the next forty years, sealed with cement that was over two meters thick ...

CHAPTER 18
CONDEMNED

Lubyanka Prison, Moscow, U.S.S.R. – 1950

After spending the last five years in Lefortovo Prison, Karoly Schandl had been moved back to Lubyanka Prison for his "hearing," if one could call it that. It was absurd that they were now "officially" accusing him of being a British spy. He had been "officially" arrested in January 1950 despite having been imprisoned since December 1944. His new, official arrest had been ordered by Abakumov, who reported directly to Stalin himself. It did not look promising.

Of course, he reasoned, a new, official arrest was the only way they could somehow justify prolonging his captivity – yet what did they hope to gain by it? He had hoped they would realize that, as the war was now over, they had even less justification to keep him imprisoned.

He had spent years surrounded by the stench of death, the sounds of horror. The Dutchman was lost and Karoly doubted the young man's family even knew what had become of him. There were so many others who had been lost, like the sick old man whom one of the guards had laughed about. Karoly would later tell how he overheard a guard laughing that the man had fallen into the hideous pit where human excrement was thrown every day. He had been too feeble to get out and he had later died.

Karoly said very little during those years. He simply observed what went on around him, and tried to listen to as many conversations of the guards as possible. They were not supposed to speak in front of the prisoners, yet if one was quiet, they almost became unaware of one's presence – at least from time to time.

He had become quite accustomed to the voices they played in his cell and had learned how to ignore them, even when they were played at such a high pitch, it felt as though they might be his own thoughts, and made him feel cold and then hot all over. A number of incidents had occurred in the past which had proven to him that they were certainly not his thoughts. Once in a while, a recording was played in the wrong language. In addition, sentences were repeated to him that he had said to others, including that Churchill would get them out.

It was that sentence he presently heard in his tiny cell in Lubyanka, as he paced back and forth. "Churchill will save you. Churchill will save you."

He shook his head and wondered how stupid they must think him. He had long since given up on the notion that Churchill or the British would get him out. In truth, he had believed it for only a short time, at the very beginning, and had said it repeatedly back then in order to reassure the Dutchman. The fact that they were playing it also proved that there were microphones hidden in the cells.

As suddenly as the recording had begun, it stopped.

He sat down in his tiny windowless cell and wondered if they would even have a trial. Perhaps they were attempting to extract more information from him and he would then be shot. He shut his eyes and thought of his parents back in Hungary, wishing he had said goodbye properly in December 1944, when he'd had the chance.

That was when he heard it.

"Nick."

He opened his eyes. There was no one present. The voice said Nick's first name and then his full name several times. It went on for hours and continued throughout the night. By morning, he was starting to think that "Nick" may have actually been one of his own thoughts, though he could not explain why his name would occur to him while he had been remembering his parents.

The following night , he was taken to another room for his hearing. He had been waiting for 48 hours. The interpreter was Lieutenant Siminov, and he was working with a major whose name sounded like either Sidorov or Shidorov - Karoly was not sure which.

After the formalities of stating his name, etc., Karoly waited.

Lt. Siminov handed him a photograph and instructed him to look at it. "A Hungarian First Lieutenant," he explained. "Under the regulations, I am supposed to give you two photographs, but presently have only one. Pretend you have two and the other one is of someone you do not know."

Karoly looked at the photograph. It was hazy, yet somewhat familiar. A man's face. He shook his head.

"Turn the photograph over and read the name that is on the back," Siminov ordered.

He did and was careful to conceal the surprise on his face. It was Nick. The photo had been idealized and showed him without his glasses. Karoly looked at the picture again. Yes, the name matched the face. Nick was in the same prison!

"You do not recognize the person?"

He shook his head and handed Siminov back the photograph. "No, I do not."

His head began to spin with ideas on what it all meant. They had arrested Nick as well, all those years ago, and he was still imprisoned. It could not have been a coincidence that he and Nick were both in Lubyanka prison, likely both awaiting their "hearings." The Soviets must have known about their group – but just how much were they aware of? Or was it a suspicion they had, based on something an informer had told them – and was that why they had attempted to trick him by repeating Nick's name in his cell throughout the night? Furthermore, why did they wish to keep the British led anti-Nazi Hungarian resistance locked away? He vowed to continue with his silence as far as the group was concerned. He would never admit to knowing Nick or Sam or any others in the network. Nothing, it seemed, had changed.

The hearing did not last long. The outcome was one which gave Karoly little reason to hope. The Soviets had decided to convict him of "being in contact with an anti-Soviet organization during the war – the British Intelligence Service." He was sentenced to 25 years in prison.

His stay at Lubyanka was over, as was his stay at

Lefortovo. He was to be transferred to Vladimir Prison, where the high profile, most important prisoners were kept. He did not consider himself to have been such an important person. In truth, he had been a messenger of the resistance group. Even if they were aware of more of his resistance activities, he doubted that was the reason they considered him as important as the generals they kept locked in Vladimir. Was it because his father had been well connected and they believed they might be able to trade him at some point – or had Karoly been in contact with someone in Hungary? Just what had Abakumov and Joseph Stalin so worried that they would send him to Vladimir, where he was to be secretly imprisoned? Had they been attempting to cover up the arrest and death of the Dutchman – or was there more to it?

Transfer to Vladimir

It was a cold day he would not soon forget. Karoly would not miss the misery he had experienced in the tiny cell that had been his home for so long – Cell 111. He was instructed to carry his mattress, his linen, and his pillow.

Once in the reception cell, he thought back to what it had been like when he and the Dutchman had first been brought here. *He had been so young.* This time the reception cell was to be his departure cell and he was without the Dutchman.

There were the usual questions about his name, place and date of birth. The young officer, who was accompanied by a sergeant, looked about the same age the Dutchman had been. When the question period was over, he was unceremoniously pushed into the black crow, where he waited. There were the sounds of many men talking and he realized they must be the guards who would be accompanying him on this journey. Perhaps he ought to have been relieved to leave the hellish stench and death of Lefortovo for Vladimir. However, he had been unjustly condemned to another 25 years in prison. It now seemed likely that he would die in the Soviet prison, for how could one survive another 25 years? And what would come after that – another conviction? The Red Cross had been kind to supply him with the occasional blanket, though that was the only contact he'd had with the outside world in years. *Did anyone even know he still existed?*

The black truck that was used to transport prisoners began to move and they drove just outside a railway staton. When the truck had come to a stop, the door was opened and he was ordered to get out.

He was immediately surrounded by six guards – each of whom carried submachine guns – and two snarling German shepherds. Apparently they would be taking no chances. Fortunately the dogs were on tight leashes.

He was led to the train station by two guards walking in front of him and two on either side. His hands were tied behind his back. When the train began to approach, he considered breaking free from them and jumping in front of it but then forced the idea from his head. He had come this far – it would be foolish to kill himself now. Besides, he would prove more useful if he lived – he would be able to tell the world what they had done to the Dutchman and others.

They walked him to an isolated coach and pushed him in. It was the prison coach. Before he got in, he heard some children shouting at the guards from a distance. "Bloodsuckers!" they yelled and then they ran away. The guards did not pursue them. *He wondered what it felt like to be despised by your own people.*

The prison coach was full of guards. There was no way to escape, as the compartments were separated by iron boards. They were closed but the noise from the outside could still be heard. Karoly had not heard the sounds from the outside for a very long time. He could hear the sound of a train as it began to pull away.

They sat him on the lower berth and handed him a blanket. After what felt like an eternity, a steam locomotive attached their coach to a train. They started to move.

He heard the voice of an older American man in the next compartment as he asked the guards to help him climb onto the higher berth so that he could sleep. "Help an old American major," he said. "I was once a soldier like you."

Karoly was surprised. He did not realize there were also Americans in the hands of the Soviets. Was there anyone they did not arrest?

After a slow stop, the train sped up. Eventually it slowed down again and then came to a complete stop. The sergeant told him to get up. He heard the other prisoners being moved out of the train. Soon it was his turn and they took him down to a platform. It was dark outside.

This time they assigned three guards and one angry dog per prisoner. He saw four or five other prisoners. The guards led him to the truck and then shoved him inside. The prison must have been close, for after they ascended a hill, a gate was opened. The truck made several turns and then stopped.

They had arrived at a large building. There was a small, paved yard which was enclosed by more buildings, all of which were tall. There were also the tall walls, to prevent any escapes.

They hurried him through an iron door and he soon found himself in a small reception cell. Next, they demanded his name, etc., and took his clothes, to place them in the disinfecting oven. He was handed linen, a long shirt and long underwear, a couple of sheets and blankets, a mattress, and striped pijamas.

The underwear and linen had on them the mark of MVD, the Ministry of the Interior. Under that, also written in black, was Vladimirskoje Tourma No. 2. It would be his new address.

Vladimir Prison was a great deal cleaner than Lefortovo Prison. It reminded him a little of Lubyanka Prison. The inside of the building was not open, like in Lefortovo, where the sergeant sat in the center of a big star-like structure from where he could see all the corridors and doors. The building in Vladimir was separated into distinct floors, and each floor was subdivided into two major halls.

He was taken to the second floor and Cell No. 44.

In Lefortovo there had been a toilet and tap. Here there were neither. Instead, each cell had a tin "parasha" and at the beginning and the end of each day, the prisoners were marched to the washroom, in a different order.

Karoly's cell was a private one, unlike the larger, general cells which were full of international "guests." Cell 44. They had placed him in the special section of the prison, away from the others, and he was now in solitary confinement. He wondered if

Nick had met with a smiliar fate.

If so, at least they were both still alive.

Prison Life in Vladimir

Karoly was not certain how long he would be locked in solitary confinement, so he decided to re-live as many days of his life as he could remember in order to keep his sanity. In fact, he thought of one day of his life every day and attempted to relive that day in his mind. He was thus able to avoid the insanity which plagued many who ended up in solitary confinement. He ate, slept, tried to move around as much as possible to allow his blood to circulate – and thought. It was something his captors were unable to control.

Unfortunately, the voice recordings continued to be played in this prison, still at a pitch so high, he felt it affecting his nervous system. The hot and cold periods one experienced in the other prisons were present in Vladimir as well. During the hot period, one could hear the other prisoners and they sounded agitated. That was the time one heard a lot of texts. The cold period always created a sense of urgency, during which time the nose, eyes, and bowels excreted fluid. During the cold period, there were fewer texts – and they felt distant. Nothing had changed – only the location of the prison. He was convinced that the hot and cold periods and the strange sounds were somehow connected. One day, he vowed, he would find out how.

He knew that there were still living people on the other side of the sound system, and was therefore careful not to speak out loud. There were hidden microphones in the cell to enable them to listen to anything he would say – whether while sleeping or awake.

It seemed they also wished to control his dreams. He had heard German spoken in Lefortovo Prison for so many years that he occasionally dreamt in German. One night he woke up, after mumbling a few German words in his sleep. When he sat up, he could hear some Hungarian words, which he had not heard often in Lefortovo. He then heard someone curse in Hungarian and the recording stopped. It was replaced by a German text. In the future, they would use both languages in their transmissions to him, though it never would work. *He could not be brainwashed, nor would he been driven insane, like some of the less fortunate prisoners he later spoke of.*

Time passed slowly in the special section of Vladimir Prison. Karoly noticed that during the time that the guards were changed and the recordings momentarily stopped, he could hear parts of conversations and other sounds coming from the room where the recordings were being transmitted from. He heard news broadcasts and even American music.

One time he heard voices which repeated various obscenities concerning priests and nuns. Then it stopped and a voice sternly said "It is strictly forbidden." Evidently, a supervisor had entered the transmission room and put an end to any talk of the Church, whom the Communists abhorred.

There was a great deal of commotion heard at the time Stalin had ordered the arrest of a number of Jewish doctors. From his cell, Karoly could hear one of them protesting that he was a well known doctor who had attended international conferences and they had no right to imprison him. The doctor must have been placed in the cell opposite his, Karoly reasoned, though he did not hear him for a little while after that.

One afternoon, however, the guard operating the recordings was not careful and Karoly could hear the broadcast of the opera "Rigoletto" in his cell. The doctor then proceeded to sing, making it apparent that they were on some of the same "sounds." Karoly closed his eyes and drank in the music as the doctor sang the entire opera, in his "solitary exuberance." It was the most beautiful afternoon he had experienced in years.

He hummed along as the doctor sang the 'Donna e mobile' aria.

He never knew what became of that doctor.

Karoly was sure that the switches of sound were not permitted, for one of the radio broadcasts was later interrupted by a nervous voice saying "He's coming" in Russian. After that, they must have been more careful, for there were few, if any broadcasts.

The rhythm of life in Vladimir continued, as did the frequent ringing in his ears. He wondered if the high pitch noises created the same effect on the prisoners in the general section or if they were unique to the special sections of the prison.

He would later discover, in his research, that the Soviets had been bombarding him with ultrasonic sounds.

In 1953, Joseph Stalin died.

In 1954, Abakumov was executed by a firing squad.

On April 5, 1954, Karoly Schandl was moved from the special section to the general section of Vladimir Prison. By that time, he had spent 9 years in Soviet prisons, with a total of 4 years and 3 months in solitary confinement.

It was somehow strange and surrealistic to be among a group of people again, all of whom were international prisoners. As before, opposite sides had been placed together.

One of the first things Karoly did was to check the large holding area for hidden microphones. He found none but was still convinced they had placed them near the walls, as he warned everyone. The other prisoners seemed to think he was paranoid; they had not been exposed to the special section and were therefore not as aware of the Soviets' tricks.

It was not easy to be among people again, particularly because they were in desperate circumstances. Some prisoners informed on the others in order to receive favors. Those who were permitted to help in the kitchen were especially believed to be in such a category.

Each person had his own story, his own experience to tell. He soon met Mark, a Polish officer who had been working in the Eastern Department of the Polish War Office. He had been imprisoned since 1939.

Karoly was genuinely surprised. "They brought you from the War Office to here?"

The officer explained, his voice low. "The Russians took me to the camp in Katyn but transported me to Moscow for imprisonment in 1939."

Karoly nodded. "And you thereby escaped being shot in the back of the head, which is what the Soviets administered to the rest of the Polish officers when the Germans were nearing in 1941. Thousands were executed."

"Yes, that is true. I heard of it from others in here."

"I wonder if the world will ever learn of these atrocities."

Mark was silent for a moment. "Now you must tell me your story."

Karoly was grateful to have found someone to speak to in earnest, someone he could trust and exchange experiences and information with. He told the Polish officer, who had been languishing in Soviet prisons for the last 15 years, about how his friend "Albert," the British agent had told him to report to the Soviets with the Dutchman, and what the Abwehr in Bucharest had claimed while en route to Moscow. He also told him how Albert had received orders from Bari, the Allied Headquarters when Europe was still embroiled in the Second World War.

"The Dutchman was here also?"

Karoly shook his head. "No. He died in Lefortovo Prison seven years ago."

"And Albert?"

"I am not sure where he is."

Mark thought for a moment and then said "I have a theory. You may not wish to hear it, however."

Karoly assured him that he did.

"I am of the opinion that all groups in the resistance against the Nazis which contained potentially anti-Soviet elements were delivered to the Soviets by the British, for liquidation."

Karoly was shocked. It had not occurred to him that somewhere in the ranks of the British there could have been a leak – or more than one.

"Albert, your friend, who was British intelligence, likely

166

received his order from Bari," the officer went on.

"It could have been intercepted," Karoly pointed out.

"There are many different scenarios," Mark agreed. "Nevertheless, I still believe I am right – that the British delivered the resistance from the Balkans to the Soviets for liquidation."

Karoly said nothing, for he was not so sure he agreed with that theory.

"Do you know if they arrested any others in your group?"

Karoly paused and considered telling him about Nick being in the same prison but then decided against it. At least for the time being. "No."

A prisoner who was known to have been a former member of the Gestapo appeared to be listening to their quiet conversation, so Karoly changed the subject. Such was life in Vladimir Prison. One found oneself surrounded by former friends and foes, under the most dire circumstances. It was a rarity to have a decent conversation, much less one that was not later reported by the prisoners who were permitted to be kitchen helpers. They were believed to be informers, desperate to pass on information in exchange for food.

The outside world could not have imagined how many "missing" people were trying to stay alive behind the tall walls of the Soviet prisons.

In Vladmir Prison, the Soviets were also holding an American, "Sergeant Bob," whom they'd abducted years earlier in Vienna. There was also a Japanese general, who insisted he was innocent of all charges brought against him and offered to teach Karoly the Japanese alphabet.

Karoly was relieved to discover that the "sound treatment" was less intensive in the general section, yet there were still spies among the prisoners, and hidden microphones which must have been recording the more audible conversations. One had to be careful, for here, on a different scale, the Soviets were still playing their usual games of mind control, intimidation, and manipulation.

In 1955, two guards abruptly came in and took Karoly

Schandl to a small office, where two officers were sitting. He wondered if they had come to the conclusion that as he was not someone who could be traded, he was no more than a liability and needed to be exterminated. Would he now be executed? He waited.

They ordered him to sit down.

He did.

One of the officers then read aloud the decree which he was holding in his hand. "Karoly William Schandl, effective immediately, you are to be released into the custody of the Hungarian People's Republic, where you will be rehabilitated."

He asked where exactly they were sending him.

"To Hungary."

He was still not convinced that it wasn't a trick.

In November 1955, after a few months in a Soviet work camp, he was transported to Jaszberény Prison. In May 1956, he was "officially" released into the custody of Hungarian Communist authorities, who would keep him imprisoned for another four months ...

Budapest, Hungary – 1955

Every Christmas Eve, Terezia Schandl had set a place for her missing son Karoly at the dining table. Times had been hard, the Russians had years ago claimed he had been on his way home, and her husband was now in his seventies. The future did not look bright.

After enduring two years in prison, they had been released, only to find that all traces of their former life had been removed, including property, homes, savings, and numerous items of a personal nature. The National Credit Cooperative had been dissolved.

Escape presently seemed impossible and it was certainly not likely that they would ever be permitted to leave the country. Still, they had each other, some relations, and a small apartment to dwell in. Many former friends and acquaintances had vanished, some having been carted off by the Soviets for no reason, others having become too worried about associating with a man who was once the State Secretary of Agriculture and the President of the National Credit Cooperative, neither of which seemed to fit in with the agenda of their Soviet occupiers.

One had to be careful about whom to trust, and the belief that the AVO might still wish to bring up nonexistent charges against them had not left Terezia Schandl. Thus, it was with great hesitation one evening that she answered the door when someone knocked loudly. Hungarians often dropped in on neighbors, yet there had been a certain urgency to this knocking.

She cautiously opened the door ...

"I have come to tell you something important." It was an old friend of her son's from the law society.

Terezia hastily led him in. "You have news?"

He nodded and respectfully removed his hat.

"It is about Karoly, your son."

Terezia was beside herself. "He is not ...?"

"He is alive!" was the excited reply. "I know for certain for I myself have seen Karoly! He was in a work camp."

Terezia made the sign of the cross. "When was this?"

"I was released a week ago. I would have come sooner but it took me some time to find your new address. Your husband is ...?"

"Taking a rest before dinner. Please tell me everything!" she exlaimed. They both sat down at the table and he told her how at the work camp he had seen Karoly Junior and that he knew it must be him, although his hair was thinner and he had a gray beard.

"Was he in good health?"

"I saw him only from a distance but he looked fine."

For eleven years she had not given up hope. Terezia went in the other room, to her sleeping husband. When he had woken up and heard the news, a single tear trickled down his cheek.

"You see, apuka," she whispered, "I was right. I always knew he was still alive."

CHAPTER 19
PASSAGE TO BUDAPEST

Geneva, Switzerland – Spring 2005

Marcel Lambert had just received an unexpected email from Kati Schandl and he read and re-read it several times. She was on her way to Budapest, she explained, to find some documents that would show how someone on the ground close to Karoly and his resistance group had lied about the time he was in contact with them. Naturally, the historian was intrigued. Was she referring to Dan? Kati, like her father, seemed to be rather secretive.

He had assumed she wanted no more contact with him, as he had not heard from her for a couple of months, and was therefore surprised to learn that she had not abandoned the "investigation." She also sent him a scanned copy of one of the pages of her father's memoirs, with revealing details about how his resistance group had been formed. Perhaps she had sent him the scanned page as a gesture, to show that she had not lost interest in cooperating with him.

Lambert was not disappointed that the attachment took long to open. He was looking forward to reading the words of Karoly Schandl, a man whom he had never met. The attachment finally opened.

"In the 1930s, I was a Boy Scout, and my group of Boy Scouts (the Piarist Catholic Boy Scouts) made some friends in Poland, where we attended a Jamboree. One of our Polish friends, 'Jack,' later fled to Hungary in October 1939. We helped him, sheltered him. He was naturally in contact with the Polish Legation in Hungary, as long as it existed, and remained there as an agent after the Legation left Budapest.

One by one, all unmarried members of our Boy Scout group got involved in the 'illegal activities' of the resistance. We had vowed to help not only our friend Jack and the Poles, but also our Jewish friends and whoever we were able to help.

It was the Boy Scout spirit that survived, even after the dissolution of the Boy Scout organizations. One of my friends in the group, a young Hungarian lawyer of Jewish origin, George (name changed), visited Alexandria (Egypt) through the Tito partisans and was dropped in Hungary later from Bari, as an official agent of the British to organize and lead our group. He was then known as 'Albert.'"*

A few sentences later, there was something very new and revealing to Lambert on the page. "Jack," the Polish friend in charge to whom Karoly had referred, was an agent with the Inter-Service Liaison Department - ISLD, an organization which was later better known as MI6. George, or rather "Albert," had reported to him. Karoly and the others took their orders directly from George. Hence the significance of their group. There was now an ISLD/MI6 connection.

Lambert wondered what had happened to the records of that group. He also wondered how exactly the Soviets had managed to learn of their existence.

Canada – Spring 2005

Chris had insisted on having a glass of wine with Kati before her flight, to wish her a bon voyage.

They toasted their glasses and he nodded. "To a safe and productive trip. You will keep in touch, won't you?"

"Of course." She sipped the white wine. By now Lambert would have received her email. She hoped he would not try to contact her before she departed. She needed to keep a clear head and focus on her destination.

"Where will you be staying?"

"Somewhere very interesting."

* *"The Yagoda Siren," Dr. Karoly William Schandl, 1961 (memoirs).*

171

"On Gellert Hill?"

She smiled. "What do you think?"

"I am starting to think you might be as elusive as your father was. There is still one thing I do not understand. Whatever happened to the family villa on Gellert Hill, Budapest, the villa in Felcsut with 100 acres of fertile farmland, and whatever else your grandparents might have owned?"

"There was also a house in Veszprém," she added. "That was where my grandfather was from."

"You never talked much about your grandfather. I'd love to hear about him, Kati."

She nodded. "I think I last saw him when I was about ten years old. It must have been shortly before he passed away. He had white hair and he looked distinguished but very unhappy. I knew he had been someone important halfway across the world but from my child's viewpoint, he always looked as if he would rather have been somewhere else."

"Like Hungary."

"Yes. He was very patriotic. He is still in the Hungarian Almanac from the 1920s and also the 1930s and it can now be found on the Internet. His picture is in the Almanac, too."

"To get back to Hungary … What happened to all that family real estate and land that had been seized, after – when the Soviets pulled out fifteen years ago and there was no more Communism? Was it returned?"

"Not to us, no. The Gellert Hill villa on Kelenhegyi Street alone – without the large lot that had belonged to it – was valued around a million U.S. dollars at the time, and the descendants were collectively presented with less than 1 percent of the value, with absolutely no chance of getting it back. I am almost relieved Dad didn't live to see that," she added soberly. "His parents had planned to leave him the villa when they retired in Felcsut. That's what my grandmother Terezia always said."

"What happened to the large lot which belonged to the Gellert Hill villa?"

"The Communists sold it to the Finnish Embassy."

Chris paused. "I bet the value of the villa and all the other properties has greatly increased since then."

"Yes."

"That's a real shame. Your grandfather helped build the country, then his son got unjustly arrested by the Soviets, imprisoned for over eleven years and then had to flee Hungary to save his life, only to have his descendants awarded less than 1 percent of the family assets when freedom supposedly hits." Pause. "Somebody must have kept it all."

She put down her wine glass and sighed. "Are you trying to get me depressed before my flight leaves?"

He put down his now empty wine glass and stood up. "It was only half a glass so I can still drive you to the airport. Let me do at least that much."

Kati stood up as well, and casually slipped a blue notepad in her handbag, next to her tickets and passport. "I accept."

As they drove in the fast lane toward the airport, she stared out the window, wondering whether the sky in Hungary was different from the sky in Canada. She had never been to Hungary before. When she was thirteen years old, there had been a family trip through Europe, yet Hungary had been conspicuously absent from their itinerary. While she and her siblings slept in their room in a Swiss inn, their parents had spoken in hushed tones in Hungarian. Karoly wanted to return but knew they would be looking for him again, despite the so-called "reforms" which had supposedly taken place after the 1956 revolution. *As long as there was a Communist regime, he knew he could not return. It was as simple as that.*

Her thoughts were soon interrupted by Chris. "What will be your first stop once you arrive? Based on what I've read of your dad's memoirs, I'd guess it would be the Cave Church."

"You're right about that, but it's not just because of his memoirs." Pause. "It's because of what I know happened there."

"You mean you have a hunch?"

She smiled as he turned into the terminal. "There are records which put Dan the British agent at the Cave Church with the Hungarian resistance in November 1944. Those, in addition to other documents, will prove that he lied in his reports about the dates, and will prove that he was already hiding at the Schandl villa when my father was arrested. It is documented that he attended meetings of my father's resistance group, which has also been referred to as a British led cell."

"Because it was overseen by Jack, the ISLD agent who recruited them."

"Exactly."

He stopped the car and turned to face her. "How can you be so sure there will be such specific records?"

"I already know there are. I've been doing some research."

"On the Internet? I have noticed you spending more time online lately."

"It is amazing what one can find if one looks in the right places. The Paulist Order was not only revived after the fall of Communism, with the Cave Church re-opened, but they now have a website in Hungarian. I recently discovered it - and on that website there is a summary of the church's history. It reports that in November of 1944, British Agent Dan met with the Hungarian resistance in the Cave Church. It also mentions how my grandparents and some Paulist fathers were arrested by the AVO in 1950. Priests are great record keepers." She smiled. "And they kept their records well hidden for all those years."

Chris shook his head in disbelief. "November 1944. He pretended he wasn't there yet."

"There are other things which implicate Dan – and they too are in that book he wrote. The church records, in addition to other documents, will make everything clear."

She kissed him on the cheek and got out of the car. He got out as well and handed her the suitcase.

"It was nice of you to drive me."

He made her promise to let him know when she arrived safely.

She agreed.

He still couldn't shake his worry. Sixty odd years after the deception, Karoly Schandl's eldest daughter was about to expose the lies of a British agent who sounded like he'd had a great deal to hide. He may have been dead, yet what if he'd had accomplices who were younger back then and were still alive?

After returning to the house, where he intended to stay

during Kati's absence, Chris decided to have a look at Dan's so-called memoirs. She had mentioned that there were other things he wrote which implicated him, but had not elaborated.

The book had been left on the coffee table in the living room. He opened it, sat down, and read the first chapter in which, much to his astonishment, Dan, the once British agent, admitted that he had been a lifelong and very active member of the Communist party ...

CHAPTER 20
GELLERT HILL

Budapest, Hungary – Spring 2005

It was evident on the taxi ride from Ferihegy Airport into the city that Budapest had seen better days. Kati looked out the window as they sped past what appeared to be semi-abandoned, dilapidated warehouses or barracks as they headed closer and closer toward Pest.

Budapest was divided into two parts by the fast flowing Danube River – Buda and Pest. On the Buda side, one found the medieval Castle district, the upscale residential area of Rose Hill, and, of course, Gellert Hill, which had been named after Saint Gellert. Pest was considered downtown, with shopping districts, cathedrals, synagogues, museums, squares with statues, a number of very old apartment buildings – and some seedy districts which a tourist would have been well advised to avoid.

One of the most famous landmarks of Budapest was the massive Parliament building which had been built during the Austro-Hungarian Empire. *Karoly Schandl Senior had given several speeches in the Parliament, calling for land reforms.*

It was Sunday, so there were few pedestrians on the streets. The sidewalks were wide and there were charming cobblestone lanes scattered here and there. The nostalgic architecture was an interesting mix of East and West, though most buildings were crumbling at the façade, in dire need of repairs. The whole city looked like a crumbling fairytale that refused to die.

Many of the buildings still had bullet holes left over from the Second World War, when the Germans and Russians had fought to the bitter end for the land which in principle belonged to neither.

Kati had asked the driver to take her to Gellert Hill, where she had rented a room for the week. She felt as though she were returning home for the first time in her life.

When they pulled into central Pest, she noticed both Gothic and baroque architecture. The city was rich with its historic past. Centuries earlier, the occupying Turks had also had left behind their architectural influence and a number of baths for which the city was now famous. Budapest had more than one hundred hot springs. It was vastly different from the landscape of a North American city.

Within minutes they were crossing the 200 meter long Independence Bridge and approaching the foot of Kelenhegyi Street.

She had crossed the ocean to venture here.

Kati stared in wonder at the massive rock cliff ahead, with the tall white cross on top. "*Sziklatemplom.* The Cave Church."

"I see you have done your homework," the taxi driver responded pleasantly, then adding, "It was closed until a few years ago."

She said nothing, partly because this moment was beyond words, but also because Chris had warned her to be on her guard. He had not been comfortable about her venturing to Budapest in search of answers.

The car pulled up past some trees and stopped in front of a villa nearby. When Kati got out of the taxi, she immediately noticed that Gellert Hill smelled different than anything she had ever experienced. The air was sweet, with the aroma of flowers, which thrived in the temperate climate. There was a balmy breeze. Small turtle doves were cooing in the background, hidden somewhere in the lush trees which lined the street. She paid the driver, who insisted on carrying her suitcase through the tall iron gate, up the steep stairs to the front entrance.

Later, she found herself walking up Kelenhegyi Street, wearing jeans and comfortable walking shoes. There were birds chirping, and trees, with their lush leaves, flanked almost every house on the narrow, winding street. *No wonder her grandmother Terezia had loved it here.* At the top of one hill was a sturdy gate with a sign that looked too official to have been residential. Even further up, next to it, was a sprawling villa which was not in as good condition as it had been all those years ago. It was painted yellow and practically covered by trees.

The Schandl villa. Her grandparents' home and her father's home.

Kati looked up at the second floor where her father's apartment had been and longed to reach out and touch a part of it, or at least to walk closer. *Karoly had occupied the entire second floor.* She was unable to get anywhere near the villa, however, for it was surrounded by a wrought iron gate, with an alarm to keep out intruders. She shook her head, looking in from the outside. The lot, the large garden, the tennis court were long gone, as were any traces of the Schandls ever having been there.

A few steps down was the more official looking gate which led to the Finnish Embassy "Reserved for the Finnish Embassy," the sign warned, so as to discourage anyone wanting to park or stop in the area.

Kati continued walking up the affluent street her father Karoly had walked on so many times. Behind Kelenhegyi Street, she soon found herself on Minerva Street, just across the Schandl villa. The Swedish Embassy had been on Minerva Street back then, in an imposing edifice. On it was a plaque remembering the Diplomat and the wonderful work he had done in 1944.

Kati paused to take a photograph. She then turned back to Kelenhegyi Street and proceeded to take more photographs, mostly of the villa where much had transpired, and also the embassy gate next door.

The street was empty except for one other person - a dark haired man standing in front of a parked white van. He was staring at her. Kati stopped taking pictures and made her way back down the street.

Reaching Kemenes Street, she walked down twenty-two stone steps and kept walking, turning past the Gellert Hotel, where a homeless man selling freshly cut flowers was begging passersby for a few forint as a yellow tram noisily rode past.

She stopped, took out her wallet, and silently gave him two thousand forint. He thanked her and handed her the flowers.

They had more in common than he realized, for despite her family legacy in this land, she too was homeless in Budapest.

After passing the hotel, she crossed the street and walked up the winding path toward the entrance of the Cave Church. It was closed during services, yet presently there was no service so the entrance was open. In the outer hall was a display which described the church's history in Hungarian, German, and English.

The cave was originally formed years earlier as the sedimentary rock slowly rose from the sea and the hot springs made the layers which became spaces in the cave. In the 1920s, some pilgrims to Lourdes asked that the cave be transformed to a grotto which would be a replica of the Lourdes shrine of miracles. The cave was enlarged, with additional rooms added. Then, in the 1930s, the monastery was attached to the rock. Its turrets could be seen outside, beside the church.

In 1934, the Paulist order returned to Hungary, after 150 years of Austrian suppression, and took up residence in the Cave Church's monastery. In 1951, it was stormed by the Communist secret police as Father Vezer was saying midnight Easter mass. He was arrested and executed and several of the fathers and brothers were unjustly imprisoned.

On the left wall was a relief of Cardinal Mindszenty, who had presided over many services in the church prior to his arrest by the Communists.

One of his quotes was inscribed at the bottom:
(translated from Hungarian)

"If one million Hungarians pray, then I will not be afraid."

The dimly lit church was a maze of silent, limestone passageways in the cave, filled with various altars and chairs for the faithful. *It would have been the ideal place for clandestine meetings.* There were numerous rooms, all connected, and in the main passageway, an old woman was sitting next to a table which was covered with white candles and souvenirs.

Kati had already sent the Paulist fathers of Hungary a copy of Karoly Schandl's memoirs, which meant that they now knew as much as she did - in addition to what existed in their own records.

When she later emerged from the church grotto, she strode back onto Kelenhegyi Street, mindful that she still had an errand to run. Kati then turned onto Bartok Bela Street and walked toward the nearest bank.

After she had changed sufficient dollars into forint at the small bank, she walked down one block to Budafoki Road, which ran parallel to Bartok Bela Street. Passing by Krusper Street and Bertalan Lajos Street, she soon reached a side street where there was a small, family-run restaurant. Unfortunately, it was closed. She turned back onto Bartok Bela Street and walked a block to Orlay Street, then turning back up to Kelenhegyi Street and the Schandl villa.

It had been a mere 20 minute walk from the bank back to Kelenhegyi Street. She took a few more photographs and then decided to return to the nearby villa where she was staying, to pay the owner in cash, as promised, and also to email Chris. *It surprised her that everything was so close around Gellert Hill, that everything was within walking distance.*

She would let Chris know that she had arrived safely and that all was proceeding according to plan ...

Budapest, Hungary – September 27, 1956

Karoly Schandl smiled as he posed for a photograph at the Danube River. Freshly shaven, he was wearing a brown suit – his first in almost twelve years. Anna took his picture and then suggested they go for a walk before returning to the apartment. He agreed.

Aware that he would never truly be free of the Red Army, whom he suspected would come looking for him at any given time, he had arranged to stay at the apartment of an acquaintance. Anna had lost her husband during the war and was pleased to help one of his old friends.

Karoly had been free for just two days – and he still had more questions than answers. His mother, Terezia, had been overcome with joy when he had shown up on her doorstep two days earlier, announcing it was the happiest day of her life. His father had been too emotional to find any words.

Their joy had soon turned to disappointment when he had taken his leave, after explaining he was certain the Russians would wish to find him again sooner or later, and he was taking no chances this time. Now he was more than familiar with the Soviets' tactics, and he had no intention of experiencing another "stay" in the Lubyanka, Lefortovo, or Vladimir prisons. He had kissed his parents and promised to come back at least once a day to see them – whenever possible.

As they walked along the banks of the fast flowing Danube, Anna whispered of all the changes that had taken place since he had been taken away. She told him of the much dreaded AVO, the endless arrests, and the fear that had paralyzed the country since the Russian occupation had started in 1945.

Karoly listened. He eventually stopped and pointed across the river, to Buda, where the cliff with the Cave Church still stood, though it was sealed and the cross had been removed.

"They cannot kill God," he said matter-of-factly.

Anna quietly asked him not to point toward the church again. "They might be watching us."

"They cannot be watching us for they do not even know I am staying with you. The day before yesterday I gave one of them the slip and jumped on a passing tram before he could catch up and see where I was going."

"They have informers everywhere." Anna rubbed her hands, as it was becoming cool, and then suggested they return home for dinner.

"You go ahead," Karoly said. "I have to visit someone."

She knew that it would have been futile to ask him whom he planned to visit, for he would not have answered her. She suspected, however, that it had to do with his past resistance activities. "Please be careful." Then she quickened her pace and was gone.

Karoly put his hands in his jacket pockets and took in his surroundings, grateful that he was able to walk through the city instead of pacing in a miserable prison cell. The only problem was that the land he had returned to was under oppression. He still needed answers, though, and that was what prompted him to walk to the front entrance of a stately home which had been divided into flats. He rang the doorbell and waited.

The man who came to the door eyed him for a moment and then took a step back in disbelief. "It cannot be!" He had heard of his release, yet had not expected him to wind up on his doorstep.

Karoly nodded. "It is me, Schandl Karoly Vilmos, in the flesh. I just got out two days ago, after 11 years 10 months as a guest of the Soviets." He grinned and added "It was a good way to diet, at least. How are you, Ferenc?"

His old friend ushered him inside and then locked the door, nervously rubbing the back of his neck with a hand. "I heard you were alive but am surprised you found me."

"I did my research and learned they let you stay in your house, even if you can only occupy one of the flats."

Ferenc nodded but did not offer him tea, nor did he ask him to sit down anywhere.

Karoly was perplexed by his behavior. "You are in good health?"

"Yes, quite."

"I need to know about George. What happened to him? I know that Nick was in the prison at the same time I was and is now likely somewhere in Hungary, and Sam escaped, though my parents have had no news of George."

Ferenc nervously lit a cigarette and inhaled deeply. "You should not have come here, Karoly. It will bring no good to either of us. The KGB killed George years ago, from what I have heard. It was back at the end of the war, when they were called something different – SMERSH, I think. If you are not careful, I do not doubt that the KGB will come looking for you again, too."

Karoly banged his fist against the wall, sickened with grief. All that time George had been dead? He had been murdered by the Russians, as had the Dutchman and the Diplomat? It did not make sense.

Some of the ash fell from Ferenc's cigarette to the floor. He did not seem to notice. "Things are different now, my old friend. The Soviets consider the West, including the British, the enemy. You would be well advised to avoid this topic of conversation again. The AVO is teeming with informers and if word gets out that you are talking about the resistance, they will have your head on a platter."

"I think my release was a mistake," Karoly said suddenly. "A clerical error. It seemed they thought I was someone else and I did not contradict them. It was a new clerk and he was confused by the bureaucracy."

Ferenc extinguished his cigarette in a dirty ashtray on a ledge. "Still sly as ever, I see."

Karoly sighed and nodded at his old friend. "I am going to a meeting one of my old contacts is holding. There will be meetings, to discuss the future of Hungary. Things simply cannot go on like this." His head was still spinning from the tragic news of what had befallen George. *He had not survived his treatment at the hands of the NKVD, the SMERSH. He had not lived to see his thirtieth birthday.*

Ferenc raised a shaky hand to prevent him from continuing. "They kill people for so much as speaking of these things."

"What exactly are you saying?"

"I do not wish to endanger myself."

"You will not come?"

Ferenc shook his head and motioned to the door. "It is too dangerous an undertaking. Frankly, it is equally dangerous to be seen meeting with you. Therefore, I must unhappily ask that you never venture here again."

"What are you talking about?"

"I cannot risk being seen with you, Karoly. Everyone knows that you are a marked man by the Soviets and there is speculation that they released you so that you could unknowingly lead them to any 'collaborators.' Please never contact me again."

Moments later, Karoly found himself darting between street alleys, to ensure he was not being followed to his next destination. Ferenc had been so nervous, who was to say he would not contact the authorities or one of their informers, to "report" Karoly and thus distance himself from their conversation?

He soon found himself standing in front of a dreary little café. Catching his breath, he slowly opened the door and entered, passing an old man who was smoking and reading the newspaper at a wooden table.

His contact, Peter, was seated in the corner, pretending to be reading the newspaper. On the table was a white porcelain cup, half filled with espresso. Peter raised his brown eyes and nodded.

Karoly nodded, pulled out a chair, and sat down.

They spoke in low voices.

"You were not followed?"

Karoly shook his head.

Peter folded the paper and placed it on the table. "What do you think of the new state of things?"

Karoly frowned. "It was a good thing to get out of the jail, but a shock to return to an oppressed society." He made no mention of how he had just learned the tragic fate of the young idealistic lawyer who had led his anti-Nazi resistance group some 12 years earlier. *He made no mention of it but it never left his thoughts.*

"There are others who think the same way, Karoly, and that is why I wanted to meet with you – to tell you that there are those of us who want things to change." Peter paused to drain the remaining black coffee from his cup, then placing it back down in its saucer. "Mark my words, things will change – and sooner than anyone thinks."

"Do you have guarantees from the outside?"

"We have contacts who …"

"Guarantees," he repeated. "I know only too well what contacts may or may not do. I once had many such contacts and wound up imprisoned by the Soviets for almost 12 years. My friend was murdered by the NKVD, the SMERSH. What did the contacts help us back then? You need more than outside contacts. You need guarantees from them as well."

Peter peered at Karoly for a moment, thinking that perhaps he was too caught up in the past to feel the present. "About the changes I mentioned, the ones that will occur..."

"Count me in." Karoly nodded decisively before standing up. "I too will do whatever it takes to rid Hungary of the Red Army's occupation."

Peter was visibly pleased. "And I can reach you at Anna's apartment, if need be?"

"Yes." He glanced outside and was relieved to see that it had started to rain and there was no black AVO car in sight. "We can meet here again next week, if you like."

"I'd like that very much, Karoly. Your opinion means a great deal to me - and a great deal to the cause."

CHAPTER 21
HUNGARIAN REVOLUTION

Budapest, Hungary – Spring 2005

Andrassy Street was not as wide as it appeared to be in pictures when one compared it to a North American avenue. Perhaps that was because, as elsewhere in Budapest, the sidewalks were wide enough for pedestrians to actually feel they were part of the street. It was lined with trees and the architecture was understated elegance – tall, grayish old buildings and what had once been stately homes which had been converted into apartment buildings. The famous State Opera House was near the bottom of the street, next to a small luxury hotel.

Kati quickened her pace and turned onto a side street, where the coffeehouse her contact had mentioned was located. He had kept their telephone conversation that morning brief, stating where and when they should meet. One could not help but be intrigued. Had he been successful in finding what she had requested?

That morning, there had been a brief, typically Budapest downpour so the streets and sidewalks were still wet. At the time, Kati had been strolling down the well known Vaci Street – a shopping street where cars were not permitted. At the first sign of drizzle, elegant waiters in white shirts and black pants had rushed outside, to hastily pull back the café tables and chairs from the street, placing them under the canopy. Moments later, the skies had darkened and a ten minute ensuing downpour had descended upon Budapest, drenching all in its path. When it was finally over, the blue skies had returned and the waiters had put the tables and chairs back out on Vaci Street. *Such was Budapest – a place where darkness never lasted.*

A low series of rings indicated that her cell phone was ringing. Kati stopped in front of the coffeehouse and pressed the answer button.

"Hello?"

"Sorry, I have been delayed." It was her contact, Miklos. He sounded serious. "You are all right?"

"I'm fine." She wondered why he thought she might not be all right.

"I will be able to meet you in an hour. Is it okay?"

"That would be great." She assumed he had gotten bogged down with one of the many projects he was working on. The university had recommended him as an excellent researcher - he must have therefore been in demand.

"Very good. It would be better to meet at the Centrál Kavéház." He gave her the address.

Kati agreed and Miklos quickly hung up. As he had told her at their first meeting, he did not like to give away too much on the telephone, just in case …

Walking back to Andrassy Street, she decided to venture to the building at number 60.

60 Andrassy Street. Once the headquarters of the Arrow Cross, then the headquarters of the Communist secret police known as the AVO, it presently housed a museum which served as a reminder of both terror regimes. It was called the "House of Terror." An hour would pass quickly here, though she was not quite sure what to expect.

The ticket she was handed was a black and red booklet. When she entered the building, she felt a chill and remembered the fate of someone she had never known.

Sam had been one of Karoly's friends in the group. Sam's only brother, like the members of the group, had also been involved in anti-Nazi resistance activities. He had not managed to escape Hungary. After the war, the AVO had arrested him and dragged him to this building, where he had been held and tortured, because he had been involved in an anti-Nazi Hungarian resistance group during the war. After a few weeks, the AVO had abruptly released him late one night, telling him he was free to go. He had taken a few steps, only to walk into the clutches of the Soviet secret police and Red Army guards awaiting him. The Hungarian AVO had washed their hands of him by handing him over to the Soviets, who in turn arrested him and transported him to a gulag. Like thousands of others who had met with such a fate, he soon went "missing" in the Soviet gulags, never to be seen or heard from again. And of course the AVO likely had no record of him, as they had probably given those over to the Soviets as well.

Sam had made it to the United States. His brother had not. His death sentence had been handed down at 60 Andrassy Street.

"Pardon me, you are English?"

She blinked and realized she had been standing in front of a dark elevator, with a few people waiting inside. One of the casually dressed men continued to address her.

"They said we are supposed to take the elevator up to the second floor and begin the tour from there." He spoke near perfect English with a slight German accent.

Kati thanked him and stepped in the elevator. The heavy doors slowly closed and they were soon transported up into what appeared, through the glass windows, to be some sort of dark labyrinth with endless floors and corridors. No one spoke.

The doors opened and they followed the dim hall. The House of Terror certainly lived up to its name, though not in the exaggerated, freakish way a North American might have expected. Here, housed on three levels, were many of the past horrors that had been committed by two evil regimes. Apparently the Communists had gone to great lengths to cover up all traces of the crimes against humanity which had been committed at 60 Andrassy Street, but to no avail. Records and footage had been found, victims had begun to speak, and even the execution area and cells in the basement had been recreated, some containing the actual hoses which had been used to wash away the blood of those they had tortured.

The unguided tour began with exhibits of the atrocities the Nazis and Arrow Cross had inflicted back in the 1940s. One glass case held the faded uniforms of Arrow Cross soldiers. Kati stared at them and wondered how many innocent men, women, and children the Arrow Cross men wearing those uniforms had slaughtered. Sister Sara and Joseph had been among them.

Had any of those uniforms belonged to the Arrow Cross men who had been observing the Schandls back then?

On small screens nearby, one could see footage of naked bodies being bulldozed into a hill of corpses. Kati could not bear to watch it so she moved on, past the German tourist, who was now openly weeping.

After the horrors of the Holocaust came the displays of the 45 years of terror the Soviet Union had inflicted upon Hungary.

World War II had left the nation in ruins. Forty percent of the national wealth was gone, and a million people were estimated to have been killed during the bombing. Those who remained and were considered the "undesirable class" by the Communists had been all but annihilated.

On the wall were written the words of the Deputy of Dzerzhinsky, the founder of Cheka, the Soviet secret police which had been the predecessor to SMERSH, the NKVD, and the KGB. It clarified a great deal *(translated from Hungarian)*:

"We are not searching for evidence or witnesses
and we don't want to expose anti-Soviet acts
or propaganda. The first and foremost question
we are interested in is: what class do you belong to,
what class were you born into, and what kind of
upbringing did you have? Answers to these questions
will decide the destiny of the accused.
This is the essence of red terror."

Kati continued with her tour of the essence of red terror. Moments later, she found herself standing on the wooden floor of the former office of the man who had been in charge of the AVO in the 1940s and 1950s. It must have been from this room that the arrest of her grandparents had been ordered. She stood in the middle of the room and stared at the large desk in the corner. Mrs. Bellak and the man who had called himself Sandor Rose must have been specifically chosen so as to set up Karoly Schandl Senior and his wife Terezia. The man in this office had decided that they were a liability to the criminal plans of the

Communist party and should therefore be tricked, arrested on false charges, and subsequently imprisoned. It had all started here.

Kati stood there for a very long time before moving on to the next rooms, the next displays. She quietly took them all in, and stopped for a few minutes to watch the televised mock trial of a former Prime Minister who had campaigned for democracy. The witnesses and other accused men appeared to be cringing, as though they had been tortured. The AVO judge smirked just before handing down the death sentence to the accused, Imre Nagy, who was not given a chance to speak. He was cut off when he declared the trial a sham. *The AVO had paid their judges a hefty salary for presiding over the most murderous kangaroo courts.*

Kati continued past some old Communist propaganda posters until she came to a room which, at first glance, appeared to be empty. When she entered, her ears were filled with the ethereal sound of monks chanting. The centerpiece was a massive white cross in the middle of the floor, surrounded by jagged cuts in the wood around it. The cross reminded her of the white cross on the Cave Church.

In 1949, seventy percent of Hungarians had been Roman Catholic.

She slowly walked toward the robe of Cardinal Mindszenty, which was displayed in a glass case at the end of the room. The Communists had arrested the Cardinal, tortured him, and imprisoned him until the 1956 revolution, when protesters had set him free.

Father Vezer, the head of the Cave Church, had been less fortunate. He had been hung in 1952.

Kati saw a guard watching her as she walked through the room, feeling as though she were in a trance. Everything she had read about her father's resistance activities, the involvement of the Cave Church, had become a reality. She wondered if her face showed that she knew a great deal about these times – a great deal more than anyone might have suspected.

Time had passed in Hungary, with a new generation of the oppressed. In one of the last exhibits, one encountered people singing Hungarian songs. Kati entered the Hall of the 1956 Revolution. Projected on the walls all around her was endless footage of young men and women, arms locked, happily marching, singing. It was the start of the student uprising. Every way she turned, she could see their faces, their autumn coats, their carefree strides as they marched in solidarity. One felt as though one were marching with them, except they were not really there anymore – and all Kati saw of herself in the bright footage was a lone shadow on the wall of the former AVO building on Andrassy Street.

The 1956 uprising had been crushed by Soviet tanks.

Kati sighed and moved past to the last exhibit – a wall of photographs and names. A somber guard was standing next to it so she assumed it was not open to the public and walked out of the museum at 60 Andrassy Street.

Budapest, Hungary – October 1956

Years of living in fear had taken a toll on the people and the young, in particular, hoped for a better future. Thus, when thousands of idealistic university students showed up for a peaceful demonstration on October 23, 1956 at the statue of General Bem, preparing to walk together to the statue of beloved Hungarian poet Sandor Petőfi, they believed that it was going to be a beautiful day – a day of change.

Petőfi had recited his poem "National Song" on March 15, 1848, signaling the beginning of the peaceful demonstration the youth had started – to free Hungary from its Austrian chains of oppression.

> *"On your feet, Hungarians, your country is calling*
> *The time is here, it's now or never ..."*

One of the student leaders stood and read aloud their demands for change. There were sixteen points. Every time he paused, the crowd cheered. Passersby could scarcely believe their eyes. To have such a gathering was against the law, forbidden by the Soviet occupiers and their AVO thugs. The students did not care. They were fueled on by the fresh autumn air, the sight of each other's hopeful faces, and the knowledge that there was strength in numbers. They would not be ignored, they would no longer live in fear. The students would later be joined by workers.

It was the day the Hungarians rose up together against Soviet rule.

The demands of the people were not unreasonable. They wanted the Soviet troops to withdraw from Hungary. They wanted Imre Nagy to be reinstated as Prime Minister. They wanted free elections and freedom of the press. They wanted the chance to own a little land. They wanted freedom of speech and thought. In short, they wanted their independence.

Not surprisingly, the radio, still run by the Communists, began to broadcast lies about the peaceful rally, which was growing in numbers by each minute. The radio broadcast falsely claimed it was not true that the people wanted to end ties with their Soviet occupiers.

Word spread quickly and the sea of people marched to the radio station, which was heavily guarded by AVO men with Russian machine guns. The people would not be deterred, they would not be terrorized any longer. Some tried to enter the building, hoping to have the chance to read their own statement on the air. They were turned away. They tried to enter the building again. The AVO men fired into the crowd. Dozens of innocent, unarmed demonstrators were killed in the hail of bullets.

Peter and Karoly were meeting at a café halfway across the city. They heard the news of the demonstration and radio station incident from one of Peter's contacts – a man from Csepel, a working class district. When Karoly heard that the

AVO were still guarding the radio station and the crowds were confident they would prevail despite the shooting, he appeared grim.

"They will try and smuggle bullets and weapons into the radio station, right under the noses of the people standing outside," he warned. "Every vehicle must be checked. I can come and …"

"You are the son of a former politician and also a former political prisoner of the Soviets," the man began. "We are asking that the sons of politicians and former prisoners not join us – at least not visibly."

"He is right," Peter agreed. "The Soviets would claim the old regime was simply trying to overthrow the new one and would use it as an excuse to discredit the demonstrators and claim they were pawns."

Karoly was unable to conceal his displeasure. "For now I will honor your request, but you simply must warn the people at the radio station that the weapons and ammunition will be sent soon. If they do not intercept it, there will be a bloodbath with hundreds, if not thousands of deaths.."

The man nodded and then hurried away.

Karoly stood up. Peter did the same. Patrons who had just heard of what was happening rushed from the café, to go and see for themselves.

Karoly thought of Anna and began to worry. She would have been on her way home from the school where she was a teacher. What if she had taken a detour to buy bread?

"I must go back to the apartment."

"I will come by and give you an update on the situation at the radio station when I know more." Peter then put on a workman's cap and disappeared into the excited crowd.

When Karoly arrived at the apartment, he found Anna asleep on the sofa. Not all of Budapest, it appeared, knew what was taking place. She opened her eyes and sat up. "You look serious. What is it?"

He told her about the demonstrations and what was happening at the radio station.

Unbeknownst to him, at the same time, an ambulance was

making its way through the crowd which had surrounded the radio station. The driver claimed to be on his way to pick up some of the wounded inside the building. At first, the crowd let the ambulance through. Then some decided to look inside, to verify the driver's claim. Inside the ambulance were bullets, grenades, and weapons that would be used against the people by the AVO men still inside the building. The driver was an AVO man. The crowd dragged him out of the car and executed him.

Fighting soon broke out between the demonstrators and the secret police, in different parts of the city. Some streets were quiet, whilst others had heavy fighting. News spread quickly. Armed peasants later marched into Budapest, to help their fellow countrymen.

Russian tanks were ordered onto the streets of Budapest. Instead of being frightened, both young and old became angered. Boys and young men took on the tanks despite their lack of weapons. Boys played a game of cat and mouse with the Russian tanks, sometimes baiting them by throwing stones at them and then running into alleys, where the tanks were ambushed with molotov cocktails. Other boys bravely neared tanks and tossed their molotov cocktails inside, then running away as the tanks were incinerated.

Karoly, having insisted that Anna remain inside and keep the door and windows locked, donned a workman's cap and made his way toward a main street which had been visible from the window. He had spotted a few Russian tanks far off in the distance and knew they would be approaching in a matter of minutes. He was not the only one who had spied them. In a side street was a man handing men and boys molotov cocktails. Karoly said nothing, but took a cocktail, and waited for the tanks with the rest of them.

Budapest was not going to give in to the Soviets without a fight.

It was a long, noisy day, and when he returned to the apartment, his face and hands full of dirt and scratches, Karoly was smiling. For the first time in 12 years, he had a reason to hope. Anna was beside herself with worry. He assured her that he hadn't been recognized by anyone with that workman's cap on.

"Besides," he added, a twinkle in his eye, "what does it matter? I for sure was already a marked man by the Soviets."

He then told her of the tanks they had destroyed nearby that day, and she shuddered.

"They would hang you if they knew."

"Who?" he laughed. "The AVO? They are being hunted down by some of their former victims as we speak. Furthermore, Stalin is gone – at least from Hungary."

Anna observed him as one would look at someone who had lost his mind. "What do you mean?"

"His statue from the City Park – the demonstrators toppled it today. They dragged Stalin's head through the streets and the people spat on it. Things are changing fast – and for the better."

"I do not know what to do about food, Karoly. Is it safe to venture out?"

"It will be soon, I am sure. In the meantime, we can make do with what we have." He grinned and placed a kiss upon her cheek. "Today was a great day, Anna. The first time I have had a good day in over 12 years!"

The following day, Imre Nagy was declared Prime Minister of Hungary. He agreed to put an end to the Soviet occupation. The battle against the occupiers raged on. More and more citizens poured into the capital. Even children were involved in the fighting. Working men from Csepel arrived with weapons. More gunfire erupted. The freedom fighters continued to battle with Soviet troops and tanks. The tanks were taking heavy losses but so were the Hungarians. On October 25, in Parliament Square, hundreds of unarmed marchers were gunned down by AVO and Soviet troops.

That same day, however, also marked something quite remarkable. The Hungarian army changed sides and joined their countrymen in the fight against the Russians. The commander of the Killian barracks joined the revolutionaries, as did a Hungarian general. The fighting raged on.

On October 28, Prime Minister Nagy stated that the Russians would withdraw from Hungary. There was to be a ceasefire. The AVO, the much dreaded security police that had inflicted terror upon thousands, was dissolved. Still, sporadic fighting continued.

Karoly was disappearing more and more and spoke little of where he had gone, what he had done, but, as from the start, he always wore that workman's cap. After a few days, Anna decided that it sounded peaceful enough to venture to a breadline. It was a gross miscalculation on her part.

By the time she arrived at where the breadline would have been, the hungry masses had been reduced to bloody corpses by Russian troops that had been waiting around the corner with machine guns.

Anna returned to the apartment in tears, where she found Karoly nursing a gash on his arm.

"They were massacred," she sobbed. "What kind of animals would massacre women waiting for bread?"

Karoly finished wrapping a torn cloth around his arm. "You mustn't cry, Anna. They died heroes, like so many others who have fallen." Despite his words, he had a terrible sadness in his soul which could not be expressed in words. So many innocent casualties – so many brave men, women, and young people sacrificing themselves for the hopes of the future.

By October 30, however, the revolutionaries seemed to have won. The Kremlin appeared to be at a loss and the Soviets pulled out of Hungary. Cardinal Mindszenty and other prisoners were freed.

Then came 5 days of hope – hope that the future would be as free as it seemed. Newspapers reappeared. Western movies which had not been permitted were shown at the cinema, including "The Count of Monte Cristo."

The cells in Gyor Prison, which had once housed Terezia Schandl and her husband, had been emptied, as had the other prisons. Prime Minister Nagy had appealed to the United Nations and also to the West for help. There were rumors of imminent outside help – rumors of promises. People on the streets believed the Soviets would not return – that the Western troops would beat them into Budapest. They genuinely believed that they had seen the last of the Soviets. On those glorious mornings, the people finally awoke without having to be afraid.

Word spread quickly throughout the country and the evil Red Star was removed from buildings.

Karoly's contact Peter came to visit him at Anna's apartment once during those happy times, and brought a bottle of red wine to celebrate.

They made a toast to the future and Anna told Peter how Karoly had kept leaving during the fighting with that workman's cap on.

"I knew it wouldn't be possible to keep you away," Peter chuckled. "I tried to tell the others that you would never simply stand by!"

"What happened to your contact from Csepel?" Karoly shook his head when Peter tried to refill his glass. "Have you heard from him?"

"He is somewhere, I am sure, but I have not heard from him. By the way, I checked up on your parents before coming here. Your mother was relieved to hear you are well and said you were wise not to return home." He paused. "The Russians did come looking for you there."

Karoly was not surprised and said as much.

"It is a good thing we have ousted them for good." Peter poured himself more wine.

Anna's eyes widened. "How do we know the Russians will not return?"

"The United Nations will be on our side," Peter stated simply. "Hungary is now a democratic country run by Hungarians. It would be a criminal act for the Soviets to touch us and this time they could not use the excuse of needing to liberate us - as they did after the Second World War was already over and the Nazis had been defeated."

"They 'liberated' many people of their lives," Karoly said, a sense of irony in his voice.

He thought back to George and remembered his young, smiling face as he'd announced he had joined British intelligence so that he could continue doing the work he had started during the war – important work for the good of the free world. Even George's own family had been unable to tell Karoly the precise date he had been captured by the Soviets and taken away. Karoly wished he had been able to learn more. Their time had also been one of hope and belief in the future. Sam had been ready to run for a seat in the Smallholders Party, Nick was an enthusiastic engineer, and he would likely have continued his law practice. Now, however, George was dead, Sam was long gone, his practice was gone, and God only knew where Nick was now - or if he was even safe.

Twelve years. By now Karoly would have had a family. Instead, he had dark memories of dark, deathly places, no home to speak of, and more questions than answers.

It was difficult to keep up with the present, particularly since he still hadn't put together the pieces of the past.

"The council is having a meeting this evening so I really oughtn't stay any longer." Peter stood up, thanked Anna and Karoly for their hospitality, and left.

When he was gone, Anna cast Karoly a look of surprise. "You did not want to join the council meeting?"

Karoly shook his head. "The next few days I will spend here with you, Anna - just to make sure that you are safe." Recalling the past had made him dubious about what was going to happen. The mood was jubilant at present, though things were not always as they seemed.

The following day was October 31. It was the Vigil of All Saints. Budapest was remembering the fallen. Cardinal Mindszenty was presently in Budapest, giving the people hope. The Vatican had chosen him to head the Hungarian Catholic Church in 1945. Since that time, he had been arrested, tortured, and imprisoned by the Communists, yet he had survived.

Some believed that the Cardinal's survival had been an act of God.

As they listened to a requiem being played by Radio Budapest, Terezia Schandl said as much to her husband, Karoly Senior. "God is on our side, apuka. He has freed the Cardinal."

Karoly Senior nodded, a faraway look in his eyes. He was remembering how the Cardinal used to give sermons at the Cave

Church, how thousands of the faithful had flocked to hear him speak.

Across the city, their son Karoly was also listening to the same requiem on Radio Budapest, yet he was worried.

It did not go unnoticed by Anna. She sat across from him in the small living room and watched him toy with his now cold cup of tea. "You are troubled about something."

"Things are just not clear to me," he sighed. "I am not certain if it is because I was just recently released from almost 12 years of imprisonment and have thus lost touch with the current state of the world – or if there is more to it."

"What do you mean, Karoly?"

He shook his head, his hazel eyes laden with concern. "I learned a great deal about the Soviets when I was in Lubyanka, Lefortovo, and Vladimir prisons all those years. Do you know that my first thought when I heard about the demonstrations – my very first thought for a moment or two – was that the whole thing might have been staged by the Soviets, to flush out any potential revolutionaries. That thought was for a fleeting moment. As time passed, I realized that the demonstrations were very real. Still, this sense of doom and confusion has not left me. "

Devastation

On November 1, Prime Minister Nagy announced that Hungary would withdraw from the Warsaw pact, which had proclaimed the military alliance of Soviet bloc countries. It was also learned at that time that Soviet troops were preparing to make their way back to Hungary. The Soviets claimed they simply wished to help Soviets still in the country to evacuate. People were starting to worry. When would the West assure their protection from the Red Army?

At around 4 a.m. on November 4, 1956, the residents at the top of Rose Hill, on the Buda side of the city, were awakened to a continuous, even, rumbling sound. They did not know what it was at the time. Over 1000 Soviet tanks had amassed in Buda, to take back control of the capital. *It was the beginning of the end.*

The Soviet troops invaded. Their tanks were soon out in full force, crushing all resistance. Thousands were massacred, their bodies left on the streets. It was a blow from which the Hungarian freedom fighters would not recover, though in courage they far surpassed the enemy.

In his last radio broadcast, Imre Nagy begged the West for help. People on the street believed the West would send troops to help them. They whispered and waited.

They never came.

Imre Nagy was arrested by the Soviets.

He would be executed after a secret mock trial in 1958 – a trial which would end up being shown on a screen for all visitors to see – at the House of Terror museum at 60 Andrassy Street, decades later.

Cardinal Mindszenty took refuge in the American Embassy, *where he would stay until 1971, when he was granted amnesty and had to leave for the U.S.*

Meanwhile the Soviets set up a puppet government.

Thousands of men, women, and children were arrested and deported to the U.S.S.R. There were a number of executions.

The Russians came looking for Karoly at his parents' apartment several times. His mother begged him to leave while it was still possible to cross the often unmanned border, while he still had a chance.

On December 4, 1956, exactly 12 years to the day when he had been apprehended by SMERSH, he sadly realized that she was right.

He had to leave Hungary; the Soviets and their evil regime had finally seen to that. In 1956, over 200,000 Hungarians successfully crossed the border into Austria, then dispersing into various western nations. Karoly William Schandl was one of them.

After making it to Vienna, he walked into the British Embassy, seeking political asylum. He was now a free man but, unlike the other refugees, he still had some unfinished business – and it concerned a matter which had started in 1944 ...

CHAPTER 22
WHITEHALL

London, England – Spring 2005

Marcel Lambert was in the city for a history conference, where he'd been an invited guest speaker. Amid the lengthy papers and presentations, he had found the time to meet with an old contact whom he now considered a friend. It was a friend whose opinion he valued greatly, and Lambert wished to update him on an important case. They had agreed to meet at Sloane Square again. It was his contact's favorite part of the city, as it afforded both a pleasant environment and a certain degree of privacy. It had never been his style to have serious conversations where they might be overheard or where there was even the remotest chance of being bugged.

Lambert had a great deal to say. He felt there had been immense progress in the investigation.

His old friend listened patiently as the historian filled him in on Kati Schandl's trip to Budapest and speculated she would find concrete proof that Dan the British agent had lied in his reports about the dates. Lambert was chain smoking as he spoke and gesturing enthusiastically.

"Documentation is an excellent thing to have, to back things up," his friend agreed.

"It will prove everything!"

"Marcel, you seem to believe the end is nearing – the light at the end of the tunnel."

He sat next to his friend on the bench and crossed his foot over his knee. "I am convinced of it." He believed he finally had the lead he had been seeking for so long and it pleased him a great deal.

His old friend nodded thoughtfully. "You see the end whereas I perceive the beginning."

"The beginning only?"

"Perhaps Dan and his lies were the tip of the iceberg. More research would need to be done on that – all his contacts would have to be investigated. For example, where were they at the time, what did they claim, that sort of thing. He would certainly not have acted alone. He may have also reported to someone who was there as well."

"You did already mention that the last time we spoke," the Swiss historian pointed out. "I have not forgotten and there are those who will undoubtedly be able to follow up on it."

His friend paused and then spoke slowly, as though carefully weighing his words. "There is also another important thing to consider."

"Such as?"

"We must look at those who were affected in this case before we make any assumptions. What, thus far, do you know about Karoly Schandl's father? I assume you know more than I."

"I can tell you the following about Schandl Senior. From 1921 until 1928 he was the State Secretary of Agriculture in Hungary, and was also a lifetime member of the Upper House. He was appointed by Count Bethlen, a Transylvanian who was Prime Minister of Hungary from 1921 until 1931."

"What kind of era was it?"

"Count Bethlen was a liberal-conservative who spoke out against anti-Semitism more than once. He was not a fascist."

"Do go on."

"Evidently, Schandl Senior had been a protégé of Bethlen's, though they were never on a first name basis. Schandl himself was from a somewhat modest background and he gained an excellent reputation early on in life by working hard, starting various associations, and campaigning for farmers and small land owners. Apparently he made many important speeches in the Parliament, calling for land reforms. No one ever had an unkind word to say about him."

"And his family life at that time?"

"His wife Terezia married him when she was quite young. She, like Karoly Senior, was a devout Roman Catholic. The family had a very close relationship with the Cave Church and the Paulist Order. The church was located down the street from their Gellert Hill villa. During the war, Karoly Senior remained at home in the villa with his wife – in addition to the refugees who came and went. His wife Terezia was somehow supplying false papers for Jewish refugees whom she also hid in the five Catholic charities on whose board she served – unbeknownst to the other board members, that is."

"Was he aware of what was going on?"

"Yes, he was, though he was not as energetic as he had been in his younger days. By 1944, he already had a good sixty years and a lifetime of hard work behind him."

"And what of the Prime Minister who appointed him – this Count Bethlen. You are the historian. What more can you tell me about him?"

"The Soviets arrested Bethlen without justification in December 1944 and imprisoned him in the Soviet Union, where he presumably perished around 1946 or 1947."

Lambert's contact watched a pigeon as it proceeded to peck at a morcel of discarded bread. "I expect the Soviets went to great lengths to keep these things covered up."

"Apparently they denied knowledge of his whereabouts for quite some time."

A frown creased the elderly gentleman's brow before he continued. "Let us now discuss late 1956 and early 1957. Here we have Karoly Jr., whose parents are in danger of being imprisoned again at any given time, and he himself has just succeeded in escaping from behind the Iron Curtain. What do you think he will do next?"

Lambert allowed some ash to fall from his cigarette to the ground. "Proceed with caution."

"Only if he feels the need for it. Thus far, it appears there was a leak. Schandl was no fool."

Lambert nodded. "He would have felt it, you are right."

"I believe he would have wanted to get to the bottom of the matter and get something done. One simply cannot imagine that all those arrests and deaths he knew of would have been forgotten by him. He must have thought of them every single day he had to endure in those hellish prisons. He must have been counting the days he could get out and tell the free world about all the dirty little secrets he had learned, ranging from illegal abductions to murders."

"Yet in late 1956 and early 1957 he was a political refugee in a foreign land. How might he have done anything at that time?"

"By going to Whitehall – whom he still trusted – to tell them in person all he knew, all that had happened. After all, his anti-Nazi resistance group was led by the late George and George was British intelligence. The question, my dear fellow, is what, if anything, came of it?"

Spring 1957

Karoly Schandl was a free man working as a researcher and interpreter in England. London had been hit by a wave of Hungarian refugees following the 1956 revolution, and everyone was still impressed by the courage which had been demonstrated by the freedom fighters against their Soviet oppressors. Thus, people were very interested in hearing about the Soviets and their brutal tactics.

In February of that year, Karoly was invited to make a speech to the Newcastle Rotarians about his experiences in the Lubyanka, Lefortovo, and Vladimir prisons. He spoke of the psychological torture he'd endured and the ultrasonic sounds. He did not mention any names of fellow prisoners, but went into detail about the effects of those ultrasonic sounds. The prisoners, he explained, had been bombarded with them continuously, and suffered the physical effects as well. One simply could not escape. He told them of the feeling of heat in the morning, the nose bleeding, seasickness, which was then followed by feelings of stiffness, restlessness, and sleeplessness. The audience listened with great interest in what he had to say. Few people had survived over 11 years of captivity in Soviet prisons and lived to talk about it.

Following his speech, a number of people approached him to thank him for sharing his experiences. His talk was reported in the Evening Sentinel newspaper.

Karoly liked England and the people of Britain a great deal. He had spent a memorable year there when he'd been an economics student at Cambridge. He knew London quite well and was therefore comfortable venturing anywhere in the city.

He was welcomed in all parts of London, with the exception of Whitehall. He had tried numerous times to make an appointment, to get through to see someone about information he had – important information – but to no avail. They had turned him away.

He was going to try again.

"May I help you, sir?"

He introduced himself and then added "I need to see someone. I have important information."

The clerk did not appear interested. "I am sorry, sir, but it is not possible to …"

"I recently got out of Soviet prisons and I know there are British citizens there."

The clerk became suddenly silent.

"The Soviets are pretending they do not have these people, I am sure. There is one who was an RAF pilot and he is still there."

Silence.

He began to feel exasperated. "The RAF pilot is among them. He was helping the anti-Nazi resistance group I was in during the Second World War. He is one of yours!"

The clerk paled. Another clerk came. Karoly repeated what he had said. That clerk became nervous as well. They asked him to leave. Karoly left and wondered why they acted as though they were afraid of him.

He tried several times to get through to Whitehall, stating he knew of innocent men who were being secretly held in the Soviet prisons, but to no avail. The people out front always became nervous, and always asked him to leave. They never let him speak to anyone.

The sheer joy of being a free man among the welcoming British people was no longer enough. Whitehall did not want to listen to him about their own citizens – and others – who were languishing in Soviet prisons. Disbelief eventually turned to disgust. Every step he took now reminded him of those still imprisoned, those whom he had been unable to help. It was time to leave. Furthermore, he would have to be careful about whom he trusted in the future, for somewhere in the ranks of British intelligence back in the Second World War, there had been a leak – and it still appeared to make Whitehall extremely nervous.

CHAPTER 23
TOMMY

Budapest, Hungary – Spring 2005

The Central Coffeehouse – *Centrál Kavéház* – was located in Budapest's inner city. It had recently re-opened and was once more a popular place for writers, businessmen, and academics.

Kati Schandl entered with the Hungarian historical researcher she had arranged to meet. Miklos asked for one of the secluded tables at the far end – specifically by the window. The waitress smiled, suggested they go sit down, and then added that she would soon bring them menus. He thanked her and walked ahead, clutching his worn briefcase under his arm, as though he feared the contents would spill out at any given moment.

Kati followed him to the small table and sat in the luxurious chair opposite him.

"It is good that the table beside us is empty," he muttered. "Good to be ensured of privacy." He peered through his glasses at the waiter who approached their table and asked what they would like to drink. He ordered an espresso. Kati asked for a soda water. The waiter scrurried away.

"You are thirsty," Miklos remarked, placing the old briefcase at his feet. "Did you go shopping before we met?"

She shook her head. "I visited the House of Terror Museum. The one on Andrassy Street."

"And?"

"It was very interesting – and very sad."

"Historically accurate, much to the displeasure of some."

The waiter returned with their beverages, set them on the table, and handed them each a menu. He then rushed off. The waitress was nowhere to be seen.

Miklos poured a generous amount of cream into his

coffee. "How are you liking Budapest?"

"It is very nostalgic."

He eyed her thoughtfully. "I have obtained the record you requested – the one which proves your father, Schandl Karoly Vilmos, was arrested in Hungary by the Red Army in early December, 1944."

Kati nodded. "I knew you would."

"They interrogated him for a few days and then made the official arrest on December 8, 1944. Your father's memoirs were accurate. The British agent lied about the dates."

Kati sipped her soda water and glanced out the window. Across the street, a well dressed employee was rearranging the window display of a modern art gallery. "Thank you for your help. Will I be able to take the record with me?"

"Of course. I did everything through proper channels. I have an official copy for you in my briefcase. After lunch, as we part company, I will slip it into your pocket. The jacket you are wearing does have real side pockets, does it not?"

"Yes, the pockets are real." She looked at Miklos, who nervously lit a cigarette. "Do we really need to be this secretive? It was all long ago." She hadn't told him about the mysterious Riley, whose identity she would likely never know, or the threatening note. His apprehension was therefore something of a mystery.

"It is possible you are being followed, watched. The British agent was not only a communist in theory, he was a very willing participant in the party." He paused to exhale. "The files indicate that your father never came back to Hungary."

"There was still Communism in place, until he died. He felt it would be too risky."

"He was a very wise man. You know, Dan came back more than once."

"My father did mention that Dan showed up again in 1947 but didn't elaborate. I think it may have been because he was already in prison at the time so he didn't actually see him, he just heard about it second hand."

"I am talking about the 1970s and the 1980s as well."

The waitress appeared and asked whether they were ready

to order. Miklos dismissed her with a wave of the hand, continental style. She said that she would give them more time and then left again.

Kati was unable to conceal her surprise. "The 1980s?"

"He was one of them, that's what I've been trying to tell you. The KGB must have been quite pleased about his cooperation. In the early 1980s, he came back and did interviews for their propaganda television news here in Hungary. They showed the house at 18 Kelenhegyi Street, where he had been hiding during the war. This means that in the 1980s, the Communists remembered the Schandls, and that Dan had stayed in their villa in 1944. The NKVD arrests and killings were not, of course, reported on the Communist propaganda television broadcast. I assure you, the Communists would not have been happy to see Karoly had he returned. Even in the 1980s they remembered very well what had happened to those affiliated with the Schandl villa, but conveniently made no mention of it. I would caution you to watch your step here in Budapest."

Kati slowly closed the menu. "It is simply awful to hear that my father would still not have been able to safely return here in the 1980s. I guess his instincts were right. But why would I need to worry about it now? Communism fell fifteen years ago."

"Tell me, did you notice at the end of the House of Terror tour a wall of photographs and names?"

"Yes, but I do not know who they were."

"Those are known victimizers," Miklos explained. "The photographs and names of Nazis and AVO men and women, mixed together in the Perpetrators Gallery. The guard must stand there at all times, in case someone is sent to remove any of them. There are still some former AVO men with power in this part of the world. You see, when the Soviets pulled out, it was agreed that there would be no prosecution of former AVO who were still alive. That was one of the conditions of the withdrawal. They do not like bad publicity. Furthermore, certain elements would not want what really happened to be known, as it paints them in a very bad light. In addition, Dan may have had accomplices who now reside in foreign lands. They could have easily been aware of your travel plans."

The waitress was at their table again. Miklos looked up and ordered a light pasta. Kati said she would just have some chicken soup. She had lost her appetite.

The remainder of their time together was filled with a somber silence. At the end of the meal, Miklos paid the bill, slid the copy of Karoly's record into Kati's jacket pocket, and walked out with her, onto the street. He then muttered for her to be careful in the event she was being followed and suggested she call him if she ran into any problems.

Kati thanked him for his invaluable assistance and would have added that it was a pleasure to meet with him, but Miklos had already disappeared into the afternoon crowds.

Her stay in Budapest would soon be coming to an end, but there were still some important places she would have to visit. After a brief stroll, she found herself in Saint Stephen's square, walking up the eighteen stone steps to the grand entrance of the Basilica. She opened one of the doors and entered. After making the sign of the cross, she sat in one of the pews. On the left wall were statues of two cherubs holding a cross. On the right was a white statue of Ladislaus triumphantly holding his sword in the air.

There was no mass about to take place so the enormous Basilica was relatively empty. There was an old woman in a floral dress seated in front of her, occasionally dabbing at her eyes. A man with dark hair and dark sunglasses, wearing a dark suit, took a seat in the pew to the front left. Kati watched him dubiously, wondering why anyone would be wearing dark sunglasses in a dim church.

She decided to wait and see whether he had been following her. Miklos had seemed genuinely worried. After five minutes, the man in the dark suit stood up and took his leave. Kati was relieved, and after a few minutes also stood up. She walked toward the back and was surprised to see the man in dark sunglasses observing her. He had simply positioned himself behind her. She looked directly at him. He moved a few steps toward the candles and proceeded to light one. She did not believe for an instant that he was truly interested in lighting a candle. She did not leave but came to stand next to the candles as well. The man in the dark sunglasses must have realized he had blown his cover, for he hastily walked out the door without even looking back. *How long had he been following her?*

Kati continued walking around the Basilica and soon found herself before a statue of Saint Terezia. It gave her some comfort about the future, but certainly not the past.

She still had a voice. She still had a future. Others had been less fortunate.

Karoly had met Tommy Lazar at St. Stephen's Basilica over 60 years ago, and had then taken him home, to hide him, to save his life.

No one could have known back then that despite surviving the dangers of the Second World War, Tommy Lazar would still have his life cut short ...

Australia – 1959

Tommy Lazar was a free man living in a free land. He'd lived through the Nazis and later made it to Australia, where he now enjoyed the hot climate, frequent days trips, and the company of family and friends. Everyone who came into contact with Tommy loved him. He was just that kind of person.

Despite all that he had been through, all the hatred, he had also witnessed firsthand the goodness of mankind. In June 1944, he had come within hours of being shipped off to a concentration camp, where persecution, despair, and death awaited him. One brief moment in Saint Stephen's Basilica in Budapest had changed his fate.

Karoly Schandl had been there for him.

People often remove buttons and other such accessories from their clothing without giving it much thought, yet there had been a great deal of thought behind it when Karoly had ripped the yellow star from Tommy's jacket and thrown it to the stone floor. He had been denouncing the wicked, intolerant ideology of the Nazis, regardless of the consequences.

Together, in that upstairs apartment of Karoly's at 16-18 Kelenhegyi Street on Gellert Hill, on the Buda side of the Hungararian capital, they had both survived. The Nazis had searched their rooms, but had found nothing. The secret door to the secret closet where Tommy was hiding had never been found.

Terezia Schandl would later state that their good fortune had been not only due to their courage, but also because God had been watching over them the entire time. Tommy had prayed with Terezia often and he had attended mass with her every week in the Cave Church. Of course, the good fathers knew that he was not a junior priest as his frock indicated, for they themselves had provided said frock. They had also provided frocks for members of the Hungarian resistance.

It had been 15 years since the Nazis had wanted to ship Tommy out to the camp in Auschwitz all because he was of Jewish origin – 15 years since he had met Karoly at the Basilica.

He had survived. After rising from the ashes of Budapest like a newborn, with years of hope ahead on a faraway horizon, Tommy had chosen to celebrate life and all that it had to offer. Still in touch with Karoly by mail, his letters reflected his contentment in Australia. His parents were there as well.

Australia was a world away from any remnants of the Nazis, the Arrow Cross, and was untouched by all things Soviet. There was no evil regime or secret police. There were no reasons to be afraid. Everywhere Tommy looked, he saw beauty. There were long stretches of sandy beaches, parks full of eucalypts, stone caves, and the Sapphire coast – a region that had been settled by Europeans in the 1800s.

Tommy had made his home near Sydney. The Sydney coast, with its abundant marine life and caves, was a place he enjoyed. He also enjoyed the freedom to get into his automobile whenever he so desired. It was a long distance between cities, yet he reveled in every moment of every drive.

He was, in the truest sense of the word, alive.

Life had proven relatively serene and uneventful in Australia, and he had blocked all thoughts of the past from his mind – until recently.

During the Second World War, he had been hiding at his friend's villa and that villa just happened to be steps away from two significant embassies. They had both been frequented by the Diplomat and for years the Diplomat had been missing. Hence the interest of certain governments who looked forward to speaking with Tommy Lazar. He had been at a significant place in 1944 and 1945, quite by chance, on Gellert Hill, Budapest. People wanted to interview him.

They had approached Karoly as well. He, however, was still guarded in anything he said to outsiders, as his parents and former resistance members were still behind the Iron Curtain. In 1956, the world had not listened to the pleas of the Hungarians. Thus, by 1958, one knew that there was little hope of any global intervention at any level. The Hungarians were at the complete mercy of their occupiers and any potentially anti-Soviet elements would continue to be liquidated. On the surface, there had been reforms, yet the "undesirable class" or anyone suspected of even harboring thoughts of resistance – past or present – was in grave danger.

Tommy's situation had been different from Karoly's as he himself had not been involved in the resistance activities during the Second World War. He had almost been a casualty of the Nazis and had wound up hiding and surviving.

He believed that the most dangerous part of his life was over. He had survived the Holocaust. He had also survived the 126 hits on the Schandl villa during the siege. His discovery of a gun collection, left by retreating soldiers, had likely spared them all of being shot by the Russians. Tommy, Mr. Schandl Senior, and British Agent Dan had buried those guns in a crater.

It all seemed a world away in Australia in 1959.

It was the Christmas season so everyone and everything was quite festive. Tommy had a smile on his face as he got into his car and proceeded to drive along the long stretch of road ahead of him.

There was another car, then sudden darkness.

Tommy Lazar was dead.

"Tommy Lazar" died in a car crash in Australia in 1959.

CHAPTER 24
CONTACTS REVISITED

Budapest, Hungary – Spring 2005

It was a warm day in Budapest, but not everyone was basking in the outdoors. Miklos and Kati were back at the crowded Central Coffeehouse. She wondered why he had requested another meeting. She had assumed their business was finished. The air inside felt heavy.

This time he held in his hand a file which he did not appear to be nervous about. "More papers," he said seriously. He slid the file over to her and silently watched as she opened it, not bothering to touch his espresso. "Are you able to read in Hungarian?"

Kati stared down and first noticed the name of her father, then more dates. "Not official or legal terms but I do all right with the easier texts."

His dark eyes softened for a moment and he took back the file. "Here, let me read the important parts to you. I will translate what it says. This is a more detailed record of the exact whereabouts of your father the whole time."

She nodded earnestly. "The previous document with the dates was very helpful. It proves he was already arrested in early December 1944 and Dan lied in the reports he filed."

Miklos lowered his voice lest they be overheard by the man reading a book at the next table. "This is, as I said, more detailed and I think there is something you would wish to know, for personal reasons. After the Soviet prisons, Karoly was sent to a camp in September 1955. In November 1955, they took him by train across the Hungarian border and he was placed in the Hungarian prison of Jaszbereny." Miklos paused. "And then in May 1956, he was taken to the secret police headquarters in Budapest, where he stayed until the middle of September. That was when he was returned briefly to Jaszberény – and finally released."

"When you say the secret police headquarters in Budapest, do you mean …?"

"60 Andrassy Street." Miklos slowly shut the file and slid it across the table. "Back then it had been renamed, first Stalin Street and then, after they denounced Stalin, it suddenly became Avenue of the People's Republic, but everyone called it by the original name. It was always Andrassy Street. Here, I made this copy for you."

"So the odious tiny cells I saw in the cellar of the House of Terror …"

"He was held in one of them, from May until September of 1956."

"I see."

"You are okay?"

"I'm fine."

"Those were dangerous times. Thousands of people passed through that place."

"I know."

Kati placed the file in her bag and thanked Miklos for his help. They shook hands and then parted ways.

She had one more important meeting awaiting her before she was to leave Budapest. Instead of hailing a taxi, she decided to walk. It was a long way, but she needed time to think, to clear her head. She'd had no idea when she'd gone through the cells in the basement at 60 Andrassy Street that her father had been one of the prisoners there. So many human rights abuses, so many international war crimes had gone unnoticed by the world. *She hoped that all of the AVO's faces were plastered on the Gallery of Perpetrators. It was the very least they deserved.*

With every step she took, she retraced her earlier steps at the building at 60 Andrassy Street. It would simply be too painful to return there now, yet she went over every single detail of the place in her mind. The tiny reconstructed cells which were located in the dungeon-like basement where they had been all those years ago had reminded her of prison cells from a dark, sinister castle in the Middle Ages. The maze had extended even further. Apparently, there had been so many prisoners that several undergound blocks had been used to make more cells, and they had all been connected to 60 Andrassy Street. It was like some gigantic parasite extending its tentacles unseen in the labyrinths beneath the city.

She hoped the museum – the House of Terror – would stay there forever, as a poignant reminder to the world of how one evil regime had been replaced with another. She hoped no one would ever forget those who had suffered behind its thick walls and the Iron Curtain.

After a while, she found herself crossing the Independence Bridge, the beautiful fin-de-sièce bridge which led to Gellert Hill. On top of the bridge's pillars were mythical Magyar turul birds. The turul was a legendary hawk-like bird, a historical representation of divinity. In Hungarian mythology, it was said to carry a flaming sword. The sword of the turul was believed to have the power to defeat all evil – and it was called the Sword of God.

Kati could see Gellert Hill getting closer and closer as she crossed the bridge on foot. The massive rock cliff of the *Sziklatemplom* towered over all, its white cross bright in the sky. Higher up stood the towering "Liberation Monument," a majestic lady who looked as though she might have been the first cousin of Lady Liberty in New York – *though they had led very different lives.*

Originally designed as a tribute to a Hungarian, in 1947, the "Liberation Monument" was hastily finished, erected and suddenly proclaimed a tribute to the Soviet soldiers who had "liberated" the city and her people. There was also a statue of a Soviet soldier. In 1991, the last Russian soldier left Hungary. In 1992, the statue of the Soviet soldier was removed. The lady, however, stayed. She, like the holy grotto of the Cave Church, was now a testament to survival, for had she not been watching over the city the whole time, silently waiting for the darkness to end?

Within the hour, Kati was back in her room, seated at a dark mahogany desk which had a cardboard box on top. It was a box she had brought with her and it contained memoirs and other important items which were related to "the case." She carefully pulled an old snapshot out of the box. There were three men in the picture and one of them was holding a toddler. All were middle-aged and despite their smiles, their faces had the look of those who had seen and lived a great deal. There was a tall man in a dark suit carrying a dossier, a smiling man wearing a pair of brown knee-length shorts with a white shirt, and a thin man dressed in a white shirt and dark pants. The thin man appeared to be the eldest in the group. The tall man was grinning at the toddler, as though impressed by the fact that the child even existed. To an outsider, they would have seemed like a group of middle-aged men who had some catching up to do, yet it was far more significant.

It was the summer of 1961 in New York City, and Karoly was meeting with Sam, as well as Mark, the former prisoner from the Soviet Union who knew how the Soviets operated. *There had been important things to discuss at that meeting, important decisions to be made ...*

June 1961

The New York Yankees had just defeated the Minnesota Twins and New York City was buzzing with the news. Karoly, his young Hungarian wife, and their first-born child arrived in a city which was vibrant and full of excited people. *It was a far cry from the dark labyrinths of the Soviet prisons.*

The Statue of Liberty was like a giant jewel towering in the sky. It was a beautiful day to be in New York, a beautiful day for a family outing at the park.

Karoly's wife slowly walked their excited toddler toward a small fountain and together they watched the bubbles and spray.

Karoly glanced around, searching for a familiar face. It had been over 16 years since he'd last seen Sam and he wondered if he should have exchanged photographs with him. A lot had happened in those 16 years. He was no longer the carefree, idealistic young lawyer he had been at the onset of the war, and

Sam was likely different as well. He had lost his brother somewhere in the evil stretches of the Soviet gulags.

"It's been a while, my old friend."

Karoly turned and found himself face to face with a slightly older, more sophisticated version of Sam. His hair was still dark, though graying at the temples. The two men embraced.

Karoly introduced his wife and child. His wife smiled. The toddler was more interested in the fountain bubbles.

Sam laughed. "It's good to see you Karoly. You look no worse for wear."

"Though my head of hair has diminished more than yours," Karoly joked. He then suggested they sit on the bench nearby. Sam nodded. He was wearing a dark suit and carrying a dossier full of papers.

"Your wife is as beautiful as you said in your letter."

Karoly sat next to him on the bench as they watched her holding the child up to catch some of the splashing drops from the fountain. "Yes. We hope to have more children. As I am now a professor in Canada, the future looks brighter."

"It is indeed a long road from Lubyanka to North America."

"What happened to Nick?" Karoly said suddenly. "I found out, quite by chance, that they were holding him in Lubyanka in 1950. They showed me his photograph just before my 'hearing.' Is there anything new? I had heard he was in Hungary but cannot be sure."

Sam lit a cigarette with a lighter and inhaled deeply. He then placed the lighter back in his suit pocket and shook his head. "He was released but the trail then went cold. I too fear he is still somewhere behind the Iron Curtain."

"And thus in grave danger," Karoly added. "I worry about my parents as well."

"Karoly Senior and Terezia are still in Hungary?" His dark eyes were filled with concern. "The Communists will not let them leave?"

"No. Every three months they put in their application to leave, to join me in Canada, and every three months it is rejected by the Communist officials."

Sam watched as a boy with a New York Yankees cap sped by on his bicycle. "How many times have they applied to leave and been rejected?"

Karoly shook his head as he recalled. "Many."

Sam thought back to his brother, and remembered how helpless he had felt hearing how he had perished in a Soviet gulag. "So much loss," he said suddenly. "If only one could do more."

"Are you still in touch with Marty, the fellow from the OSS who helped you escape from Hungary?"

Sam tossed his cigarette to the ground and stood up. "Indeed, Karoly, but they are the CIA now. Would you like me to speak to him? He might be able to help your parents. I can arrange a meeting."

"That would be greatly appreciated."

"By the way, what happened to Tommy? Have you heard from him?"

Karoly told him how he had died tragically in a car crash in Sydney, Australia in 1959, and how Tommy's grief stricken parents had written him about it.

"Poor Tommy," Sam said.

"I was very sad about it for a long time. Tommy was like a younger brother to me."

"Another good one lost to the world."

Karoly stood up as his wife and child approached them. Moments later, the group found themselves walking toward a small restaurant where someone was waiting.

It was Mark.

Mark had spent over 15 years in the nightmarish prisons of the Soviet Union, yet one would never have guessed it by looking at him. A Polish Officer, he had been sent to the Soviet prison in 1939. More than 15 years lost for nothing. Instead of being bitter about the life which had been stolen from him – the youth, salary, family and opportunities which could never be recovered – he had an aura of endless good fortune and a certain wisdom about him. At least, as he always pointed out, he had not been executed at Katyn, where the Russians had shot thousands of Polish officers and intellects.

Karoly made the introductions. The men shook hands. Mark was the eldest in the group and Karoly valued his opinion tremendously. He now worked for a candy company in New York and was already planning his retirement in a quiet town in Upstate New York with his wife.

They sat down to have lunch and conversed about a number of topics, which ranged from sports to John F. Kennedy. Karoly's wife was charming, albeit preoccuped with the toddler, who took to running around the table after dessert had been finished. The men watched and laughed.

Mrs. Schandl finally caught the child and smiled. "Perhaps we should go out for a little walk and leave the three of you to catch up."

Karoly smiled and placed a kiss on her cheek.

When they had walked out the door, Mark complimented him on his family. "And," he added, "they are of course your main priority now."

Sam lit another cigarette and observed Mark with a pair of dark eyes. "You think it's not over."

The former Polish officer shrugged his shoulders. "It is never over with the Soviets. We all know that the KGB has our names and they periodically dispatch assassins to take care of any anti-Soviet elements wherever they happen to be. You are both former resistance members and I simply know too much."

Karoly finished his tea and placed the empty cup on the table. "I am still unable to piece together exactly what happened. Somewhere there was a leak, though I am not sure how, when, and where. George is dead. He will never be able to tell us from whom the order came." He then told them of his attempt to speak to someone at Whitehall – and how they had turned him away.

"They already know there was a leak," Mark deduced.

Sam's face was dark. "I had no idea George was signing his death sentence when he accepted his orders from his superiors. I wish I knew the names of the men in Bari with whom he was in radio contact."

"There would have been men on the ground as well," Mark interrupted. "Men who were there to do reconnaissance, but not in the way one usually assumes. Men who would have been watching in the wings, reporting back to the NKVD so that they would be able to pick up those they were after and then vanish without a trace."

Karoly frowned. "Who was the British chief giving those orders? First I would like to find that out and then ask …"

"People who dig deep holes often end up falling into them," Mark warned. "You have a family now. Why start asking questions? They will hear about it and decide you are still an anti-Soviet element, my friend. They are likely still watching you."

"I am always guarded in what I say …"

"It is better to be completely silent than merely guarded." Mark motioned to the waitress for a refill on his black coffee. Once she had poured more coffee into his cup and walked away, the men resumed their discussion.

"It seems our pact must continue even on this continent," Sam said sagely. "As long as we cannot be assured of the safety of all group members, we must keep details about the group a secret and refrain from mentioning any members' names."

Karoly reluctantly agreed.

There was simply too much at stake.

"Things were so different back when it started," Sam said quietly. "Maybe one day the world will be able to learn about what really happened."

"Have you heard from Jack?" Karoly suddenly inquired.

Sam extinguished his cigarette in the ashtray and shrugged his shoulders. "I'm not sure where he is."

When Karoly's wife returned with the toddler a half hour later, the three men stood up. They all walked outside together and were about to say their goodbyes when Karoly suddenly produced a new camera. "A picture," he insisted. "A picture so that I will always remember this day – the day I met a former member of my resistance group who was able to escape the Soviets, and also an important Polish officer whose acquaintance I made in a Soviet prison. The day I met them in New York City. Three men who escaped the Soviets and met for lunch in the free world."

Sam nodded. Karoly's wife offered to take the picture. Karoly stood between the two men and the toddler tried to rush forward. Mark laughed and held onto the child. Karoly laughed too. Sam grinned. Karoly's wife took the picture.

That's what that day was like back in early June, 1961.

Budapest, Hungary – Spring 2005

Kati placed the old photograph back in the box and then, one by one, took out every document and every page of Karoly Schandl's memoirs. *She was about to help along an investigation which ought to have been started decades ago.*

Once she had finished checking that all of the mansucript was there, she paused. The picture was too personal and she had no guarantees that Mark or Sam's image would not be used somewhere. For this reason, she reconsidered and took the photograph out of the box. The historian could have the documents and memoirs, but not the 1961 photograph. Her father would probably not have wanted her to show the world the image of Mark and Sam, both of whom had since passed away.

Her thoughts were soon interrupted by the loud ringing of her cell phone and she reached for her handbag, to answer the unexpected call …

CHAPTER 25
THE EXCHANGE

Canada – Autumn 1961

Karoly's thoughts were interrupted by the loud ringing of the doorbell. *They were on time.*

He stood up and walked toward the door, which his wife had already answered. The toddler was taking a nap.

The two tall men who stood on the doorstep were cleanly shaven, with short hair, and were wearing dark suits. "Good day, ma'm." The toddler must have woken up, for there was a little noise coming from one of the bedrooms. Mrs. Schandl smiled and excused herself.

Karoly shook hands with the two men and introduced himself.

They told him their names, after producing their official IDs.

He said he was very pleased to see them and shut the door. The three walked into the living room. He asked his guests to sit down.

"Thank you." The older man sat on an armchair across from the sofa. Karoly and the younger man sat on the sofa.

"Would you like coffee or tea?" Karoly offered.

They politely declined.

"We understand you were a prisoner in the Soviet Union, sir," the older man began. The younger man took out a notepad and pencil.

Karoly leaned forward and nodded. "Eleven years, ten months as a prisoner of the Soviets. I was imprisoned first in the Soviet Union for 11 years, including 4 years in solitary confinement - and then as a 'rehabilitated' man in Hungary."

They both appeared surprised. "A lot of years," the younger man said.

The older man went on with his questions. "How did they arrest you?"

He told them of the resistance group, how he had been asked to transport the Dutchman, and how the Red Army and the NKVD had taken them both on December 4, 1944, then delivering them to SMERSH.

"And what prisons were you in, sir?"

"Lubyanka, Lefortovo, and Vladimir."

The younger man shook his head in disbelief. He had never met anyone who had survived all three prisons – three of the vilest places on earth.

The older man also appeared to be taken aback. "You must have met a lot of people there, sir."

"Yes. Citizens from many countries and some of them are still there."

"Do you remember names, by any chance?"

"I can tell you the names of the prisoners I saw there," Karoly offered.

For the following hour, the younger man wrote down everything Karoly said. When he told them about Sergeant Bob, they became especially interested.

"Do you know which part of the U.S. he was from?"

Karoly shook his head. "No, but I know that when the Russians illegally abducted him, he was in Vienna. That was where they snatched him from." He went on to describe Bob.

The older man asked some more questions and then glanced at the younger man. They both stood up.

Karoly stood up as well. "About my parents …"

The older man turned to face him. "There are going to be some exchanges in the future, sir. As soon as we have more information, we will notify you. It will be soon."

They all shook hands.

The two men in suits thanked him for his help and left.

A few months later, Karoly received a phone call from the older man.

"Once again, we appreciate all your help, sir."

"I was glad someone wanted to hear. At least some will

have a chance now."

"Your parents are still in Hungary?"

"Unfortunately, yes."

"As I said earlier, sir, there are going to be some secret trades. They will happen in the near future, so please tell your parents to put in another application immediately for permission to leave Hungary. The Communists won't refuse it this time. If they put in their application now, I guarantee it will be accepted."

Karoly thanked him.

When he hung up the telephone, he smiled at his pregnant wife. "They will be able to get out now. Our children will know their grandparents."

She gave him a hug. "Wonderful news! But how can you be sure?"

"The men who visited a few months ago arranged everything."

Karoly's next step was to write a letter to Karoly Senior and Terezia, advising them to put in another application to leave Hungary immediately. They did.

It was accepted.

They would soon be coming to Canada.

After his meeting with the two men, Karoly felt he had more he wished to share with the powers of the free world. Hence his decision to begin his memoirs, a copy of which he would send to the CIA …

Canada - 1962

Karoly never learned exactly whom that "exchange" had involved and he knew better than to ask.

What he did know was that in 1962, as the two men in suits had promised, Terezia and Karoly Senior were both finally permitted to get out from behind the Iron Curtain. They had put in their application again - after their son had advised them to- and it was suddenly approved by the Communist government. Terezia, now in her late sixties, was excited at the prospect of seeing the small grandchildren she had never met. She was grateful to leave behind the bad memories of the evil regime. She had her faith and hopes for the future.

Karoly Senior, on the other hand, was almost eighty years old. Though always happy to be in the presence of his wife, the moment he left Hungarian soil was probably one of the saddest days of his life. One can only imagine what was going through the mind of the patriotic statesman as, out of necessity, he bid farewell to his homeland. He arrived in the New World impeccably dressed, in a European suit, his head held high. His hair and mustache were snowy white, his gaze often faraway. He walked with a cane and said very little. His face did light up after meeting his grandchildren, though.

Karoly Junior was now a university professor with a toddler, a baby, and a young wife who stayed at home in their apartment. The rugged coast of eastern Canada in the early 1960s was not exactly teeming with Hungarians.

Karoly Senior was a tired outsider. He spent his time recalling the old days, silently lamenting for hours, and sleeping as the passage of time lay before him. While he was State Secretary of Agriculture, from 1921 until 1928, as many as 200,000 peasants had been granted their own land. Thus, when people saw him in his constituency, they sometimes wept and rushed forward to shake his hand. He had been beloved by his people and now they were nowhere to be seen. There was no one left to be helped.

"He is dreaming," Terezia would whisper when his eyes closed, and from her tone of voice, one had the impression that she sincerely hoped he was.

The climate of eastern Canada was not as temperate as Hungary and took some getting used to. Seasons were cooler, the air was salty, and the wind quite strong. The lighthouses and rocky beaches were charming, but it was all very unfamiliar terrain.

For the first time in her married life, Terezia Schandl did not have a household to manage. Sometimes Karoly Junior invited his father to accompany him to the university, to read in the library, though Terezia did not wish to join them. Realizing she had a great deal to say about the past, her son suggested she do as many Europeans - and write her memoirs.

And so, in 1962 in the tranquility of Nova Scotia, Terezia Schandl proceeded to write about her incredible experiences.

When finished, she gave the manuscript to her son Karoly so that he could pass it on to her grand-daughter Kati when she grew up.

CHAPTER 26
INVESTIGATIONS

Budapest, Hungary – Spring 2005

During the last week, Kati Schandl had become something of a regular at the Gellert Espresso. The grand Gellert Hotel, where it was housed, faced the Danube River and was steps away from the Independence Bridge. Kelenhegyi Street ran up one side of the hotel and on this corner the Cave Church stood, highly elevated on the rock which it had been carved into – as though reaching for the heavens.

The Espresso had tables both indoors and outdoors and it was indoors where Kati was presently seated, observing her surroundings while Marcel Lambert, in a chair seated across from her, continued to read Karoly Schandl's memoirs. It was impossible to read the historian's expressions so she focused instead on the décor and life around her.

Lambert had requested a meeting in Budapest, as he knew she was still in the city, and promptly caught a flight from London to meet her.

The chairs of the espresso were upholstered in different shades of red and neatly arranged around small tables with shiny green surfaces. It was all very art nouveau, with chandeliers hanging overhead, and a continental ambiance provided by the grand piano in the corner, where a well dressed pianist sat, playing French melodies. One could see the day's fresh pastries tidily lining the glass case next to the coffee bar.

The usual waitress who served Kati's table every afternoon was off duty and there was presently one waiter for all the tables. He appeared to be suffering from the heat as he rushed around, balancing small cups of coffee on his tray. He did it smoothly and pleasantly but beads of perspiration had begun to appear on his slightly tanned face.

Kati raised her own cup of coffee to her lips and glanced at Marcel Lambert, who was reading the last pages of Karoly Schandl's memoirs.

When he had finished, he placed the papers back in the envelope. "Enlightening," he murmured. "Most enlightening." He then opened the next envelope, which contained a copy of Karoly's prison record, in addition to the record of Dan's attendance at the Hungarian resistance meeting in the Cave Church – which had occurred in November of 1944.

"I see you have procured the official documents showing Karoly's arrest. As this military archives document indicates, he was officially arrested by the Red Army in Hungary on December 8, 1944. That, along with the record of Dan's November 1944 meeting at the Cave Church, prove that British agent Dan lied about the dates."

"Yes," Kati agreed, putting down her cup in a white saucer with gold trim. "He is now proven to have lied about arriving only in December and seeing Karoly throughout December and January."

"What I find particularly interesting is that Karoly and the Dutchman waited for the Red Army at a designated meeting place, the estate of a family friend, south of Lake Velence. That indicates that the Russians knew they would be there and they knew exactly who they were. The Russians did not simply find them – they went there with the sole purpose of capturing them."

"Yes," she said absentmindedly.

"And then there is the dramatic visit to Whitehall." The Swiss historian placed both envelopes in his briefcase. "Though why do I get the feeling that you have not told me everything about the Karoly's group?"

"Because there were more of them. George, Sam, and Nick were closest to Karoly, but there were more in that British led group. There were a handful of them, with dozens of people helping. However, I do not know all their identities. I know about George, the I.S. (British intelligence) agent who led them and was presumably murdered by the NKVD, Sam, who escaped, and Nick and my father, who did not escape and were imprisoned by SMERSH. I also know that they were all recruited by Jack, the

Polish friend who was an ISLD agent. He officially headed up that whole British 'cell.' George reported directly to him."

"And Jack was the new friend they made at that Boy Scouts Jamboree in Poland in 1932?"

"Yes. They were the Catholic Piarist Boy Scouts and all very idealistic – friends since high school. When Jack fled Poland in 1939, they helped him."

"What else can you tell me about Jack?"

"I don't know what he ended up doing after 1944, though he had a few aliases."

Lambert said nothing, but carefully closed his briefcase. "The Soviets went to great lengths to round up these young men. You still seem preoccupied. Is there anything else you have not told me?"

"There was one detail yet it seems rather minor."

"Ms. Schandl, no detail in this investigation is a minor one."

"It concerns the old lady, the nurse who was killed during the siege. My grandmother Terezia wrote in her memoirs that they took her body to Orlay Street. Orlay Street was the designated temporary burial ground at the time."

"Go on."

"Dan said something else."

Lambert raised his eyebrows. "Indeed?"

"For some reason, he claimed in his book that they buried the old lady and 'others' in the garden behind the Finnish Embassy."

"The one on Kelenhegyi Street, which had been in the villa that was destroyed?"

"Yes. But that is not where they took the old lady and that is certainly not where the neighbors were burying the dead. It was defintely in nearby Orlay Street."

Lambert took a small notebook from his trouser pocket and scribbled a few notes in it.

"I was also wondering, " she said suddenly, "did anyone happen to follow you when you came here?"

He placed the notebook back in his pocket and frowned, pausing for a moment when the waiter placed his coffee and

Gellert chocolate roll on the table. The waiter quietly returned to the coffee bar. Lambert pondered her words. "I believe I have been unnoticed. Were you followed?"

Kati continued. "One time on Kelenhegyi Street, there was a man in front of a parked van. That might have been no more than a coincidence, but the man in sunglasses at the Basilica was definitely watching me." She shrugged her shoulders. "If someone was worried about something and hired him, then they wasted their time, for I have now given all of the papers and pertinent information to your organization."

"My organization?" The surprise in his voice was evident.

"I have long suspected that your interest in my father's activities had something to do with how you came across his name – while researching the Swedish Diplomat. I am sure you have now noticed my father's reference to the Diplomat. He said that the Dutchman was working for the Diplomat. Also, based on what my grandmother Terezia told him after his release, Dan met with the Diplomat at the Schandl villa in early 1945."

Lambert drank some black coffee. "You are right. The Diplomat was the original focus of the investigation and there is indeed an organization for which I am working."

"I don't expect you will tell me the name of that organization."

He slowly shook his head. "I am afraid I cannot do that. However, I can tell you that in my opinion, Dan's documented lies are the tip of the iceberg – the thread which will head to the major web which was spun by more than one person all those years ago in Budapest."

She nodded. "And I am sure one of you will manage to solve all of it."

The Swiss historian looked down at the rich chocolate roll on his plate – a dessert for which the Gellert Hotel was renowned. "One of us?"

"Mr. Lambert, you must realize that I was not only in communication with you. While I never for a moment doubted your sincerity, I did wish to make the facts known to as many as possible. You were not the only historian I heard from."

"There were others?"

"In total, I have passed on my father's memoirs and recollections, in addition to the documents, to three international historians. I am certain one of you will solve the 60 year old mystery of who betrayed them. Everything is now in your possession." *She did not add that she had first sent a copy to the Paulist Order.* "In fact, I don't even have the originals anymore. But there are certain things I would like to clarify, things that do not appear in any memoirs. According to my father, the prisoners were interrogated regularly by their Soviet captors, though I don't expect it was all recorded. He would have wanted me to tell you that."

The pianist stood up and went on his break.

Kati stood up as well, pulling out her wallet.

"I shall take care of the bill." Marcel Lambert smiled, aware that their association had come to its natural conclusion. "Thank you for your help, Ms. Schandl. You have been a great resource in my investigation. I always knew it was not a mere coincidence that your father's home was between the Swedish and Finnish embassies and that he and the Dutchman were arrested by the Soviets around the same time the Diplomat vanished in Budapest. I also knew the Soviets were worried about something or somone he knew and thus assigned him an identification number in prison." His face became serious. "The world needs to know and to remember them all."

She nodded and said she had one more place she had to return to before departing from Budapest.

Lambert said that he understood and thanked her again for the documents, the memoirs.

She graciously shook his hand. "You are welcome. I know it's what he would have wanted. They all just wanted to help people – the world should know that, too."

There was no more to say so Kati slowly strode out through the open glass doors, across the patio. The scent of spring blossoms was in the air. There was no hint of rain in sight.

The uphill walk to the Cave Church was steep. Still, the path was well paved, and one could see exactly where one was going. Further up Kelenhegyi Street, there were overgrown winding paths and old stone steps which looked as though they could lead anywhere in the densely treed area. It would have been so easy for someone to slip in and out of Gellert Hill without being spotted, particularly if one had done enough reconnaissance to familiarize onself with the terrain – or if one had been accompanied or instructed by an individual who already knew every nook and cranny. *An infiltrator.*

Kati eventually arrived at the grotto entrance and walked inside. It was dim and cool, as the natural spring water kept the temperature inside the church at 20 degrees centigrade regardless of the season. There were rows of chairs set out for the next service, which was scheduled to begin in fifteen minutes.

She walked toward the woman at the table of candles and bought a white one. She then lit the candle and placed it at the foot of a statue of Our Lady of Hungary, in remembrance of all those who had fallen, all those who had suffered.

Her grandmother Terezia and her grandfather Karoly had come to the Cave Church often to worship. Her father Karoly's anti-Nazi resistance group had held clandestine meetings here. It was within walking distance of the family villa. She watched the bright flame cast shadows at the base of the statue, feeling as though they were all standing beside her, as though their spirits had never left.

When she later emerged from the Cave Church, she paused to take out a note she had received earlier. Kati silently opened the note and read it once more, standing in the warmth of the afternoon sun.

The Paulist fathers and brothers thank you.

CHAPTER 27
EXCERPTS FROM
KAROLY SCHANDL'S MEMOIRS

EXCERPTS FROM THE PRIVATE MEMOIRS OF KAROLY WILLIAM SCHANDL, 1961:

"During the Nazi occupation of Hungary, I - and my mother - helped the persecuted Jews and Poles, and I was active in the underground against the Germans and Nazis. I heard that more opportunistic persons considered me as a peculiar Don Quixote of the Second World War who tried to fight my own war and help others, instead of saving my own skin and making the best of situations I could not change...

In the 1930s, I was a Boy Scout, and my group of Boy Scouts (the Piarist Catholic Boy Scouts) made some friends in Poland, where we attended a Jamboree. One of our Polish friends, 'Jack,' later fled to Hungary in October 1939. We helped him, sheltered him. He was naturally in contact with the Polish Legation in Hungary, as long as it existed, and remained there as an agent after the Legation left Budapest.

One by one, all unmarried members of our Boy Scout group got involved in the 'illegal activities' of the resistance. We had vowed to help not only our friend Jack and the Poles, but also our Jewish friends and whoever we were able to help.

It was the Boy Scout spirit that survived, even after the dissolution of the Boy Scout organizations. One of my friends in the group, a young Hungarian lawyer of Jewish origin, George (name changed), *was active in supporting Allied prisoners (English, French, Dutch, etc.) who reached Hungary from German prison* camps. He visited Alexandria (Egypt) through the Tito partisans early in 1944 and was dropped in Hungary later from Bari, as an official agent of the British to organize and lead our group. He was then known as 'Albert.'

During the Nazi occupation, our group used to take escaped Allied prisoners-of-war from Hungary to the Tito partisans, with monthly reports to 'the Center.' The partisans had their weekly supply planes arriving from Alexandria or Bari, and the escaped prisoners were the load to be taken back.

On the request of 'Albert,' who was then an officer of the British Intelligence Service, I was asked to accompany a Dutch Lieutenant (Lt. V.d.W.) over the fighting lines to the Soviet troops in December 1944. The Dutchman, himself a hero in Holland for his acts of courage in World War II, was responsible for falsifying documents for hundreds of people in order that they could escape Nazi persecution. The Russians were supposed to forward the Dutch Lieutenant to the I.S. (British Intelligence Service), and myself to the allegedly formed new anti-Nazi Hungarian government ...

As of September 1944, the Russians occupied the territory between the Tito partisans and Budapest. 'Albert' was then instructed to send the messengers through the Russians, instead of Tito. After an unsuccessful attempt to cross the fighting lines by a Palestinian sergeant, as I knew the countryside and military situation very well, I accepted the task to lead the Dutch Lieutenant to the Russians. I left a partisan organizer, who was freed from prison camp by the group, and a Jewish school friend with my parents, and departed from Budapest with the Dutchman to reach the Russian troops ...

'Albert' told me that he himself would go to the Russian commander on the arrival of the Russians in Budapest, in his British uniform, to ask for transportation and food for the escapees in hiding (and so he did, but he did not survive the treatment he received by the Russian NKVD).

Crossing through Russian Lines, south of Lake Velence, The Dutch Lieutenant and I waited for the Russians at the estate of a family friend (December 4, 1944). We were 18 kilometers south of Lake Velence. We soon encountered the Russians but it was not the reception we had anticipated. After being robbed of our belongings, we ended up in the Lefortovo Prison in Moscow, with the ridiculous accusation that we were 'German spies' as a pretext.

On the way to Moscow, we came across a group of American pilots who had emergency landed over Russian occupied territory, and the commander of a 'Partisan airfield,' a Canadian major. The Canadian major reported the meeting because from the behaviour of the interrogators in Lubyanka, it became clear that the Dutch government had asked for the delivery of the Dutchman. In 1957, I learned that the Soviet officials in 1945 denied ever seeing or meeting the Dutch officer.

On the plane from Bucharest to Moscow in January 1945, I was transported, strictly guarded, with members of the Nazi 'Abwehr' organization in Romania. They told me laughingly the story of the Serbian lieutenant who had a small group of partisans in the Iron Gate area of the Danube. The British Major who used to come with the weekly supply plane, bringing ammunition, weapons, food, clothes, and fuel for the group, told the Serbian lieutenant to go to the Russians after they arrived and ask them to send him to Tito. The Russians did not send the lieutenant to Tito, but jailed him in Bucharest, together with the 'Abwehr' people. He was sent to Moscow, just as we were, under 'arrest,' with the plane leaving one week before ours.

It seems it was a similiar case – the same pattern of instructions from the British to the leaders of the resistance who had connections with them, to report to the Soviet authorities, followed by imprisonment and jail in the U.S.S.R.

I met a Polish Lieutenant in jail in 1954, who had been imprisoned since November 1939. He had been working in the

Polish War Office, in the Eastern Department, and therefore was taken from the camp in Katyn to Moscow, thereby escaping death by a shot in the back of the head, administered to the rest of the Polish officers in the camp at Katyn when the Germans were nearing in 1941. The Polish officer's opinion was that all groups in the resistance against the Nazis containing potentially anti-Soviet elements were deliberately liquidated by the British, by being delivered to the Russians for liquidation. In 1954 I did not believe it. Now, however, I believe it. Somebody on the line of communication between the big warlords and the resistance fighters on the spot gave orders 'with the best intention,' resulting in the jailing and killing of the 'faithful fools.' Who was the British Chief giving orders to their friends to go and report with the Russians, even after he had to know what will happen to them? Dutch, French, British officers, sergeants who were connected with the resistance in Eastern and Central Europe disappeared in Russian jails. Who is responsible for them?

In 1957, I spent a few months in England and left a job there as a researcher to come to Canada. The reason for this move was my anger against officials in Whitehall, who refused even to hear my story and help a member of our group,who was still in jail in Russia.
They acted as if they would be afraid of me ...

Soviet Prisons

I spent 11 years and 10 months in jail, including 4 years and 3 months in solitary confinement. The following are the effects of the 'Yagoda Siren' on a realistic and absolutely healthy person. These are just the facts, experienced during 11 years in the prison.

We noticed the first unusual biological symptoms in the prison of Lubyanka (Moscow) on the 2nd or 3rd day of our confinement in the 'regular' section of the prison (4th or 5th floor #92) in January 1945. I was together with my friend, a 2nd Lieutenant of the Royal Dutch Army. Later, especially in the

Lefortovo Prison (in Moscow), we discovered that all the inmates of the prisons were subjected to the same 'rhythm' of life.

Until my 'conviction' in August 1950, I was not under the 'general' regulations, being legally (?) a prisoner-of-war, so I could stay in bed until after 7 a.m. and could sleep in the afternoon.

In the morning, at 7 a.m., if I was still half sleeping, I had a dream that I was on a fast elevator or a pole, rising very fast, going up and up, and swinging at the highest points (dizziness). We woke up with a feeling of warmth, high blood pressure, and agitated. Several times in the 'morning period,' which lasted about 1 hour 30 minutes to 2 hours 30 minutes long, I had nose bleeds. A boil on my back could not heal for years, as it hurt every morning. Finally it healed as a 'blood wart,' slowly disappearing after I got out of jail years later.

After the breakfast was 'handed in,' a more or less sudden pressure was felt on the brain, throat, chest, the whole body. During the morning 'hot' period, everybody was walking in the cells around us. Sometimes we heard inarticulate shouting, like the sounds of a man getting a stroke, the calls of the 'sergeant' for ice, and the running of the doctor or the 'feltscher' to a cell. Sounds of disputes or fights sometimes reached our ears in the hot period.

If I was sleeping during the period of change from 'hot' (high blood pressure) to the 'cold' period, I had a dream of falling, gliding or skiing down a slope, usually in snowy or icy surroundings. Drowsiness, tiredness, a cold feeling in the brain, around the thyroid gland, and heart followed. It was impossible to remain angry or agitated in the 'cold' regime. I was half asleep or asleep during this period of the day. Once I wanted to do some physical exercise in this period, I got pain in my muscles, and I could not even lift my arm.

During the 'hot,' 'high blood pressure' period, our

239

nostrils, eyes were dry. At the first signs of the 'cold' or 'sinking' period, our eyes became wet, our noses were dripping. Excessive saliva and urinary excretion caused discomfort and unnatural amounts of urination. Fluid even came from our bowels, causing symptoms of diarrhea. The 'cold' regime lasted 'till about 11 a.m. or 11:30 a.m., and then sometimes by slower stages, sometimes faster, the 'hot' regime followed it.

Lunch was distributed between 12:30 p.m. and 2 p.m., during the 'hot' period. Before lunch, we could again hear the sounds of prisoners walking, agitated speaking, and sometimes fights in the cells. After lunch, the regime was changed again to 'cold,' with all the effects of it.

The cold 'regime' lasted about 3 hours, 3 hours 30 minutes, and then a gradual 'warming up' was felt. Dinner (?) or evening meal was given from 5 to 6 p.m. again during the 'hot' period. After dinner, the cold period was not so marked as in the morning or after lunch.

About 1.5 to 2 hours after the evening meal, more or less abruptly the 'intensity' of the 'Yagoda siren sounds' was changed. They became stronger and more violent, causing a very uncomfortable inside restlessness, sometimes coupled with sharp pains in the ears, head or abdomen (I sometimes felt very sharp pains in my bladder, followed by the excretion of pink - bloody - urine). Some people reacted to this increase in intensity with pains in the stomach, and by throwing up pieces or the whole of their 'supper.'

At 'otboj' or sleeping time, a very strong 'icy' feeling was felt. The icy feeling prevailed, causing dreams of falling in a snowy environment, etc. The 'cold' or 'down pressed' feeling was not uniform throughout the night; it changed depending on the 'filtering' effect of the 'texts' or 'words' interwoven in the uniform stream of a cool, icy band you could not escape.

Just at the 'wake up' time, the intensity of the 'sounds' or 'rays' dropped again, causing a feeling of relative ease and relief. For several weeks, when I was prevented from sleeping by the extreme intensity of the 'sounds,' I was sleeping during the day and lay awake during the night. For ordinary prisoners this was impossible, as they were not allowed to sleep during the day, not even to fall asleep sitting on their bed ...

It was interesting to notice the 'ups' and 'downs' or 'hot' and 'cold' spells in the cells of the Lubyanka and the prisons in Vladimir, where the washrooms were not 'built in' in the cells but at the end of the corridors, just before the prisoners were directed to the washrooms. The 'downs' or 'cold' always created the feeling of urgency. Excretion of fluid from the eyes, nose, mouth and other organs accompanied the need for excretion.

Very often the bowels discharged only the colourless water created by the irritated glands in the intestines. Control was extremely difficult, especially by older or weaker persons.

The Sounds

In the first month of our stay in the Lubyanka and Lefortovo prisons, Lt. V.d.W. (the Dutch Lieutenant) and I remarked that we could hear the sounds of people speaking Russian or German. We thought that some sounds were coming through from the other cells, and we did not pay too much attention. We even discussed that it was strange that sometimes they repeated the same sentences for almost an hour, and that they seemed to come even from the loudspeakers attached to poles or the walls of the prison outside our cell.

Often we heard the same Russian sentence repeated. We did not understand it, so we did not pay attention to it.
('Death to the spies - Death to the English spies.')

The Lefortovo Prison was surrounded by an airplane motor repair or assembly plant, the motors running for days, not far from the building. So when our ears started to ring permanently, we attributed the ringing to the whistle of a high-

speed electromotor. Later it was embarrassing that the whistling never ceased, and we realized that it was not an electromotor, but our ears. We attributed it to the noises of the motors of the repair plant.

Exactly one year to the date of our arrival to Moscow, Lt. V.d.W. was separated from me, his bed removed from our cell, and I was left alone.

The sounds became more audible, as the bare walls of the cell acted as the walls of a 'sound box.' From this date – January 15, 1946 – to my transfer to a bigger, 'general' cell from the special 'section' of the prisons, on April 5, 1954, I had ample opportunity to observe the pattern of the sounds, their nature, and their effect.

There appeared to be not a single sound, or single text, but a series, or a 'band' of different texts, or sounds. Most of the words, or 'texts' were felt during the 'restless' or 'hot' periods of the day. During the 'cold' periods there were fewer texts, sometimes only 2 or 3. I heard simultaneously several persons speaking during the 'hot' periods, as if I would be sitting in a crowded pub, where everybody was shouting. Where the 'intensity' of the impact was stronger, from about 6:30, 7 p.m. 'till next morning, the hearing of sounds, together with the itchy feeling over the body, inside and outside, was especially unbearable.

I knew that the sounds were the product of an outside source, and not creations of my own, because I heard them initially in Russian, a language I did not understand or speak at the time.

Later I made some tests. I had to listen for hours one morning to the voices of some women in German (which I spoke). 'Good morning, Second Lieutenant,' was repeated about a hundred times, then changed to 'Good morning, Lieutenant Colonel' again for 15-20 minutes, then 'You are the greatest man in the world,' changed to 'You are the nicest man in the world.'

Out of boredom, I started to repeat back, in front of the enclosure for the central heating, where the voices appeared to be the strongest: 'You are the nicest women in the world ...'
(also in German) For a moment there was silence. I was relieved; at least I knew I was not mad. Then a burst of laughter followed – they were laughing. And strangely enough, I heard the laughter not only through the 'system' but also from outside, the corridor, from the direction of the center of the prison. Then they went on with their monotonous text.

When food was distributed, they came with different pots, and the sergeant watched carefully that every prisoner should get the type of food prescribed for him. Once or twice, in 1947-48, when I was in a cell with the German Sonderfuhrer V.S., and he received a heavy provision, while I was hungry on my 'obschee' (general) ration, we made a deal and exchanged our 'kasha' (porridges). The guard immediately reported it to his sergeant.

In 1947, not long after my separation from Lt. V.d.W., I started to make some experiments, to test whether drugs were administered in my food or not. I took my food, but later disposed of it unseen to the guards. I lived for 3-4 days on 'kipiatok' (hot water, for drinking as "tea"), and bread. No changes followed. Then I did not eat my bread. Again no changes in the daily routine. Finally I decided not to drink the 'hot water' given for tea. From not consuming enough water, I became very sick. I felt the same symptoms as a person dying from thirst.

Every little noise was painful, the smell of chloride running from the tap was painful. In the night it felt as if the whole brick building would be rocking. That night I was called to take the 'douche.' Under the hot 'douche,' the colder steamy air blown in by the ventilation smelled like salt. Back in the cell, my pillows smelled like salt; it was clear to me that I was suffering from an inflammation of the nerves.

The same night, while I was lying awake, I heard, in addition to the usual 'texts' and 'sounds' in the cell, a different Hungarian voice saying 'Your girlfriend is expecting you, your parents are well.' I had not heard about them since I left Budapest on December 4, 1944, before the battle for and in the city started. My parents were still hiding Jewish people and a 'partisan organizer' so they were in a very dangerous position. The emotional shock of hearing it set my mind rolling. I could not stop hearing loud voices from my head, inside, and seeing pictures when I closed my eyes. For that moment, it was clear that I had lost control of my hearing and my mind. It was going on and on. One of my friends came into mind. I heard him telling me stories, with his usual, typical intonation. It was evident that I had hallucinations, and I could not control them.

I could not sleep for four days, and on the fourth day I could not go to the door of my cell to receive my food. I lost my balance; the whole world was moving, rolling around me.

I realized that I had made a big error by letting my nerves dry out with dehydration, and after this experience, I drank plenty of water. I think it took years until my ears got healed. A few days after my sick period started was when I was put together with two Germans (Sonderfuhrer V.S. and General K), and for a while it was extremely difficult to listen or speak to them. I could hear their voices only through a maze of loud shouts, as if they would speak to me in a noisy pub, and when I wanted to answer, a lot of voices shouted their remarks before I could formulate my own sentences.

The improvement in my condition was slow. It took perhaps one or two years. During this 'recovery' period, my food was changed from a richer, more abundant food to the meager 'obschee' (general) ration.

When the food was changed, the guard in charge asked the sergeant why it was done and the sergeant answered in Russian, 'He has to heal his ears.'

I later found out that if I didn't accept my food and went on a 'hunger strike,' the 'speaking' or 'text' would be cut off, replaced by an 'automatic' tac-tac-tac sound, pounding periodically on the ears.

The effects were

1. initially a feeling of extreme cold in the head and everywhere in the body
2. nausea
3. sea sickness
4. convulsive gastric and bowel movements, with excretion of water if they were already empty
5. swollen feet from lessened heart movement.

I came to the conclusion in those years that the words, the texts sometimes played from records, were partly used as a means to influence our thinking, mostly as a method of changing the physiological effects of the 'rays,' or whatever the thing was that we were subjected to in the cells. In the 'hot' periods, there were a lot of parallel running texts and words. One time I could count about ten of them. In the 'cold' periods they were fewer. So that was another factor in the physiological effect of the 'rays' or 'sounds.'

The 'sounds' were different from the speech or noises perceived the usual way by our ears. They were perceived as additions to the sounds of the usual world. They sounded as if my own ear ringing would speak to me. The motors running around the prison gave materiality to sounds, as if they would speak. It seems the texts broke the monotonous stream of ultrasonic sound band and changed the physiological effects of it. A periodic interruption caused nausea, an uninterrupted, unchanging tune probably slowed the movement of the heart, by paralysing (cold, icy feeling) the vegetative nervous system.

Meanwhile I learned to read and understand Russian.

The Sound Mix, and a Friend

After I became experienced in living with the sounds, I learned that behind the 'system,' on the other side of it, there were living people, and I could just as well listen to their 'unofficial' conversations, as to the conversation of the guards in the corridor. Conversation of the guards was strictly forbidden, unless it was staged to provide special information, but sometimes still occurred.

One staged example was that the guards several times repeated in front of our door in January 1946 (#111 Lefortovo Prison) that 'the diplomats did not allow the persecution of the English spies' (and we were understood to be 'English spies') for five years after the end of the war. Then I did not understand the sentence because I did not understand Russian, but later I understood it.
(The 'official' persecution started in 1950 and I was 'convicted' of being a British spy in August 1950)

I realized I was able to hear pieces of conversation during the brief silence the same time the guards were changed. There was no other 'text' and the personnel behind the 'sound system' had the same schedule as the guards.

Once, in the middle of Vladimir Prison, after my conviction, in the night I listened to some news broadcasts from Radio Budapest. Another night I listened to an American jazz singer.

One afternoon I heard a performance of the opera 'Rigoletto.' The Jewish doctor who was sitting in the cell opposite me was on the same 'sounds,' as he was even singing the 'Donna e mobile' aria.

I think those types of 'switches' were not allowed because one time one of the broadcasts was interrupted after someone was heard to remark in Russian 'He's coming.'

The 'sound mix' was very often individually oriented.

In the first week of our imprisonment in Lubyanka, I tried to console my friend, the Dutch lieutenant. 'It does not matter that we are sitting in jail. After the war is over, Churchill will get us out.'

Later I was exposed several times to the text 'Churchill saved you.' Although by 1948, 1950, 1952 my hopes for being saved by Churchill were rather dim, I did not mind to listen to the text. I was lying on my bed, just doing nothing, when I heard the voice of a person, through the 'siren' say 'Meaningless teasing' in Russian and the whole 'text' abruptly came to an end. It was probably the supervisor. They never repeated it.

I had several experiences, proving that they could add to the 'usual' band of 'sound waves' some exceptional 'sounds,' giving the sensation of words and ideas at a very high pitch, so that the person 'hearing' it would hardly realize that he was hearing something externally originated, and not getting his own ideas.

Before one of these experiences, in about April 1946, I went on a hunger strike. At this time I was with 2 Germans, General K and Sonderfuhrer V.S. They persecuted me. I was much younger and stronger so I refrained from using physical force against them, but I wanted to be rid of them. On the third day of my hunger strike, I was led to the 'Commissar,' a young captain whom I told my story, asking for a transfer to another cell. He was friendly, promised me a dictionary from the prison's library, told me that if by Christmas I would not be home, he himself would come in my cell to break the window, and advised me to tell the Germans a certain vulgar phrase (to 'kiss my ass'). It was nice to receive some sympathy, but I never intended to use repugnant, obscene or dirty language.

At this stage of my confinement I was thinking a lot in German, probably under the influence of the German 'text' I received 24 hours a day. To my surprise, a few minutes after my return to the cell, I 'heard' sounds telling me the exact vulgar phrase the Commissar had mentioned – only it was in Hungarian. Although my ears were in pretty poor condition at the time, this was so different from my usual 'text' that I never doubted its external origin.

In February 1950, after my 'official' arrest in January 1950, ordered by General Abakumov - who was shot four years later - I was transferred for a 'hearing' to the Lubyanka Prison from the Lefortovo. It was a change. In the Lubyanka I had to wait 48 hours before my hearing by Lt. Simonov, who worked as interpreter with Major Shidorov (Sidorov?).

The day before the evening of the hearing, I was walking up and down in the windowless little cell, 'hearing' and 'thinking' of 'Laszlo Papp,' a rather common name in Hungary.

Finally, when I was at the hearing, Lt. Simonov gave me a photo of a Hungarian 1st lieutenant and asked me whether I knew the face or not. He explained that under the regulations, he was supposed to give two photos so I should imagine there was also another one, of someone I did not know. On the back of it was written (in Hungarian) 'Laszlo Papp.'

I knew the person, but I did not realize that the picture, idealized and showing him without glasses, was his picture. He was also helping the same person – our common friend 'Albert,' who was officially in charge of our group – and he was in the same jail. It was clear they succeeded in directing my attention and they wanted to refresh my memory before the hearing with the 'sound emissions' that repeated the name, but they had no luck.
I knew too many 'Laszlo Papps.'

Effects

All the prisoners whom I met reacted with ringing of the ears from the 'sirens' and the same basic physiological

248

responses. In the 'special' department of the prisons, in the small cells for solitary confinement, for two people, the 'sound treatment' was more intensive than in the 'general' sections, with cells for 6 to 18 prisoners, where I was transferred on April 5, 1954, after almost 9.5 years in the 'special' section.

When I was later released from jail (in Hungary) on September 25, 1956, I started to put together everything I experienced and did some investigation and research in the matter. Already in the Soviet jails, I was convinced that the feeling of sounds, the physiological effects on me and fellow prisoners were caused by ultrasonic sounds. I recalled the trial of British engineers in 1928, who complained later that they were 'physiologically dried out' and suffered from 'desert sickness' (thirst). I remembered the Gotha siren, the ultrasonic siren used by the Gestapo.

In the Russian scientific literature available from the library, there was more written about 'ultrasonic sound emissions' in agriculture, industrial cleaning, etc. than other subjects. In the 1950s, they produced a washing machine, for household use, in which the water was vibrated by ultrasonic sounds. I found out that in a cement factory in Tatabánya (Hungary), they received Russian equipment for the cleaning of the cement from the dust. They were unable to use it, due to the detrimental effect of the ultrasonic sounds on the health of the workers.

The production of ultrasonic sirens was simple and inexpensive. Later I learned that the instrument used in Russian jails was called 'Yagoda Siren.' Yagoda was the successor as chief of the Russian political police (Cheka, later NKVD), of the Polish Dzerzhinsky, the original organizer of the institution. Yagoda had ordered experiments with the ultrasonic siren. He had then made its use institutional.

The siren operates on the following principles: The human skull vibrates with ultrasonic sounds of certain

249

wavelengths. The ear bones of the human ear vibrate with ultrasonic sounds of different wavelengths. By knowing the ranges of the different ultrasonic bands, it is quite easy to create the 'feeling' of sounds from within the head, by causing an interference between the human skull and ear bones. One type of sound perceptions was created by blocking the continuity of one of the 'wave bands.' The hidden ones were probably created by the issuance of ultrasonic sounds, creating impressions of sounds at a pitch unusually high.

Human beings are not used to hearing human voices at the pitch of a bird's song. One or two words will go unnoticed by the listener, but he will not realize that he is hearing human speech. I had no technical means or human guinea pigs available as Yagoda had, so I had to stop in my research at this point, and I cannot explain the actual physiological phenomena caused by refinements in application of the principle. The physical condition of the prisoners, the type of food and eventual drugs mixed in the food would certainly also have an effect on the type of reaction.

The 'Yagoda Siren' is unknown to the western world. Properly adjusted, it can be used in many areas of our human activities. It could be efficiently used in the treatment of mentally sick persons in psychiatric hospitals. It could be adapted for various purposes. In the hands of marketing organizations or individual firms it could influence the behaviour of the shopping public. In the military, it could facilitate training.

The positive aspects of its use are not alarming (we did not lose too much by waiting with its introduction). The introduction and proper use of it is a matter of years or decades away. But the alarming question is whether it is used by the Communist authorities in fields beyond the purposes of control, brain washing, and controlling prisoners.

I saw on several occasions in the Lefortovo Prison in the years of 1947 to 1950 some empty stalls, next to the impregnably fenced little courts where the prisoners took their daily 'walks' of 20 minutes, a piece of portable equipment, similar to a record player, supervised by a junior officer of the NKGB. Was it a portable 'Yagoda Siren,' emitting some special text, directed toward a prisoner 'walking' in the next stall? I cannot answer the question, as I could not check by subsequent experimentation the level of intensity required to operate the siren efficiently outdoors.

The more urgent problem is to find out whether the siren is used by Communist countries outside their political prisons and eventually on the territories of other countries. It is common knowledge in Communist dominated countries that the hotel rooms provided for foreign visitors are 'bugged.' What we don't know is that in addition to the 'passive' bugging, simple listening devices, are there any 'active' devices, 'Yagoda Sirens' added or not. Are portable 'Yagoda Sirens' used for subversive purposes? We may find out that the 'sirens' are used to instigate civil disobedience, or even waves of mob violence. The fighting army may be the target for destructive propaganda by 'unheard voices,' the existence of which is overlooked at the present. Visiting politicians may be subjected to the 'sounds,' causing inexplicable 'lapses' in their behaviour. Was Roosevelt in Yalta not affected by the Yagoda Siren?

It is the duty of the authorities to safeguard the mental independence of their citizens from the 'mental pollution' created by the furtive use of the ultrasonic siren. First of all, detecting devices, 'audio graphs,' have to be constructed. The purity of the air around us has to be ascertained. People visiting Communist countries should be informed about the Yagoda Siren. Military personnel should be properly trained and equipped with detecting devices. The instrument to be fought has been in existence for over 40 years. It is amazing that the public knows so little about it and that the authorities have not thought of eliminating the eventual destructive and subversive use of it." *

* *"The Yagoda Siren," Dr. Karoly William Schandl, 1961 (memoirs).*

CHAPTER 28
EXCERPTS FROM
TEREZIA SCHANDL'S MEMOIRS

EXCERPTS FROM THE PRIVATE MEMOIRS OF TEREZIA
SCHANDL, 1962: (Translated from Hungarian)

"War and Siege

It was a beautiful spring day. The garden was in full bloom, and the air was filled with the refreshing scent of spring flowers. I sat outside on the open veranda of our villa on Kelenhegyi Street - I was very fond of our family house. Still, I couldn't enjoy the beautiful day wholeheartedly as we had been hearing disturbing news concerning an impending war between the Germans and the Russians. I tried to appreciate the calmness of the garden, and said a quiet prayer. All of a sudden, the sky darkened and a strong wind tore at the slender, young trees, tearing off the leaves. Such sudden and strong wind was unusual in our garden, as the house had a southern exposure and it was protected from wind by the slope of Gellert Hill.

My heart felt heavy as I watched the destruction of the thunderstorm, the swirling leaves as they were scattered and carried by the wind towards unknown destinations. As I looked at the disappearing young leaves, my heart felt heavy. Perhaps the torn trees represented our family, and the scattered leaves were its members who, in the future, would be scattered all over the world. Would the storm of the coming war reach Hungary, and was it the sign of things to come?

The events that followed came fast. Persecution of Jews – innocent people whose only 'crime' was that their ancestors were Jewish. Even those who were practicing Catholics and took communion daily were not spared. In accordance with the 'law,' they were Jews.

During those difficult times I had been active in volunteer work, heading up **5 charitable organizations:**

Association of Villages (Faluszövetség)

Charitable Association of Women in Buda (Budai Jótékony Nőegylet)

Lisieux Saint Teréz Residence and Food bank (Lisieuxi Szent Teréz Menza és Kollégium)

Bokreta Street Home for Working Women (Bokréta Utcai Munkásnők Otthona)

Retirement Home for Women Civil Servants (Tisztviselő telepi Urinők Otthona).

I did my best to help the less fortunate during those difficult and trying times.

One morning, someone wearing a yellow star was looking for me. I recognized the young woman – she was one of the hairdressers from my hair salon. Her name was Ilus. She fell to her knees and begged me, sobbing, to help her. Her husband was taken to the front lines by the Nazis for forced labor. I lifted her up, tore off the hated yellow star from her coat, put it in my pocket, and eventually burned it. I promised to help her if she swore to keep her identity a secret. When she did, I chose her a new name and told her that she could stay in our house until I got her papers with her new identity.

I found a suitable escape story in my notebook for Ilus, and for the time being, I had her hide in our home. Budapest in those days was a haven for Erdelyi (Transylvanian) refugees.

Thousands fled Erdely and came to Budapest. They traveled by train, by wagon, some even walked. I had a girlfriend in Budapest whose entire family lived in various regions in Erdely. She and her relatives who arrived in Budapest told me numerous stories of their escape, describing in detail the routes they took, etc. I wrote down these stories in a notebook, including the escape routes, and used the stories later for the persons I obtained false papers for. They were each given a true escape story (as if it was their own) with the false papers, so as to lend authenticity to their new identity.

The Finnish Embassy was our next door neighbor. One of the entrances to their garden was next to our villa's entrance. At the same entrance, around the clock, stood Hungarian police guards who were assigned to the embassy. During cold days in the winter, I sent them hot drinks to warm up and during the hot summer days, I used to send them cool drinks. As the men were not protected from the elements, I also gave them permission to stand in our garage during rainy days, from where they could still see the entrance to the embassy. As we had a good relationship with the guards, they brought me the files (lists) of the new Transylvanian refugees from the police station.

Ilus stayed with us for a few days as a maid. Because she wanted to be useful around the house during her stay, she eagerly answered the door every time the bell rang. Unfortunately, I had several girlfriends who frequented the hair salon were Ilus had worked, and there was a strong possibility that she may be recognized by one of them. I became worried for her and our safety. Thus, after I obtained her false papers, when one of the charitable organizations needed a new servant, she was moved there (with full salary and benefits), as 'Juliska.' She kept her promise and did not reveal her identity for 2 weeks after the war ended. Her story had a happy ending. Her husband came home after the war, and later they became parents of two adorable children. They came to visit us with their children. Ilus's husband, who was a tailor by profession, later became the head tailor for one of the factories in Budapest.

Ilus was only one of the many I helped. The reason I mention her name is that she was one of the few who actually thanked me after the war. With the winds of change after the Soviet occupation of Hungary, as our family became one of the 'undesirables,' some people were afraid to be seen in our company. I didn't really mind it; I felt that it was my duty as a good Catholic to help those in need.

Two refugees we sheltered – the English 'Dan' (name changed) *and our son's good friend and schoolmate, 'Tommy'* (name changed) – *stayed in our son's apartment. Tommy was born and raised as a religious Catholic and attended Catholic schools, but was considered to be a Jew by the 'authorities,' as one of his grandparents was born as a Jew. He was given the yellow star and was told to report to the collector the next day as he would be transported out of Hungary with others. He met my son at the Basilica to say goodbye. My son took off his star, put it in his pocket and brought Tommy home to his apartment, which was the second floor of our villa. He kept it a secret from us (his apartment had a separate entrance). But a change in his behavior aroused my suspicions.*

As a mother, I became concerned, and spied on him one time when he was leaving the dining room. He was making his way to his apartment, which had a separate entrance, clutching food in one hand. All of a sudden it all became clear; he was hiding someone, and taking food for the person. Next time we had dinner, I gave our butler the evening off, and prepared a large plate with piping hot food. While our son was eating in the dining room, I took the plate of food to him and said 'take it to your guest.' He smiled gratefully, and disappeared with the plate. The guest turned out to be Tommy, who later often came down to eat with us – at first in secret, then dressed as a Paulist father. We also took him downstairs to the bunker (dressed as a Paulist father) with us during the air raids.

As our son and the butler had to report for duty in the army, it was a blessing that we had a young man in the house.

255

Tommy was a great help in every way, and we were very grateful to have him.

There were many casualties in our neighborhood. Unfortunately, a poor elderly retired nurse, who was also staying at our house at the time, was hit by shrapnel(?) while she was in her room. It took off half of her head and her brain matter was all over the wall. It was hopeless, we could not save her. We put her remains in a wooden box and carried her to the designated temporary burial ground located nearby, on Orlay Street. Later, the individual bodies were transported to the cemetery for a proper burial.

A few days before Christmas, the air-raid sirens became more frequent. We used our large laundry room located on the first floor (basement), as a bunker. Children were sent to the nearby Paulist fathers, to hide in their bunker, which was 25m underground. Tommy and Dan came down to the bunker during the air raids. They were both dressed as Paulist priests – we obtained frocks for them from the Paulist fathers. Sometimes their sash was tied wrong and we worried about being discovered and reported to the Nazis.

We had a special arrangement with the Paulist fathers. We pretended that we had donated the use of the entire second floor of our house to the out of town Paulist Catholic priests – so that we could hide Jewish refugees in our house.

Three days before Christmas, I received a telephone call from the secretary of the Bokreta Street home (run by nuns). She told me that I should leave the city while I can and hide, because the Arrow Cross took away Sister Sara as they found a Jewish boy in the guard's booth. It was common practice of the Arrow Cross to 'comb' the premises daily. When the boy 'confessed' to them to being a Jew, they took the head of the home, Sister Sara, to the banks of the Danube and shot her in the back of the head. The Arrow Cross then wrote down the names and addresses of the board members and said that they would come back the next day for all of us. Fortunately, the other 'refugees' we were hiding in the Bokreta home were not discovered, as no one, not even the nuns, nor the members of the board knew that they had false papers. So, they were safe. Of course, I could not leave Budapest. My family and those we were hiding in our villa were depending on me.

God must have heard my prayers, because the same day, the Russians reached the 10th district of Budapest, and the Arrow Cross had no opportunity or time to come back for me to Buda. For their own safety, I never told the other members of the board that I was hiding refugees in the homes. The country was full of refugees, but mine were all well provided with false papers.

The battle could be already heard from nearby. We had to spend nights on the main floor. Our house was hit 126 times during the battle. Our son's apartment was in ruins (but was later rebuilt by us). The ceiling of our living room caved in. Fortunately, the main floor of the house was protected by the hill and it was only hit by shrapnel.

The fighting intensified on Christmas day. The Hungarian army was retreating from the Russian army, leaving some of their men behind to 'hold the fort.' When our villa was reached by the retreating army, we had to give up our house to the 25 Hungarian soldiers (except for the two rooms where we all stayed), and provide food for them. As the Russians continued to advance, the Hungarian soldiers, not wanting to be captured by the Russian army, all moved out and dispersed.

Afterwards, we were trying to clean the rooms and get rid of the debris that had accumulated during the numerous hits on the house. In one of the rooms we discovered a large number of guns hidden under a blanket. Evidently, they were left there by the Hungarian soldiers. Because hiding guns, vodka, or any other alcohol was punishable by death (by the Russians), we had to get rid of the guns before the Russians came with their sniffing dogs. At night, we (Dan, Tommy and my husband) secretly carried the guns and dropped them into a large bomb crater located at the

257

entrance of the Finnish Embassy and ca. 10m from the ground floor entrance of our house. Early the next morning, the Russians came to search the house with their dog and found nothing.

The dog, however, did find the guns in the crater.

After the War: Difficult Years

Life became more and more unbearable. They 'nationalized' everything (the government seized everything without legal justification). We could not get a job or work anywhere, as the members of our family were considered 'class aliens' (osztályidegen). But we had to live somehow. Our family had only one hope; that was, to escape from this middle-class hater Communist country.

My widowed sister Victoria lived in the country, in Veresegyhaza, managing her farm. She had two sons, one of whom, Bandi, left Hungary in late 1938 and emigrated to Brazil, and the younger one, Gabor, who escaped to Austria after 1948, because the AVO was looking for him. The reason the AVO was after him was that he was managing his family's mill in Veresegyhaza. He was a hard-working boy with a university degree (in agriculture). A friend of his forewarned him that he was on the AVO list, which meant that he was to be arrested in the near future. Gabor escaped from Hungary – and of course, the mill was immediately 'nationalized.' Gabor did well in Austria, designing shoes. He encouraged his mother to come and live with him. Unbeknownst to his mother he made arrangements with an Austrian man to marry her, so she would be able to leave the country. One day my sister came to us, very indignant. 'An Austrian man came to visit me, and imagine, he proposed after a week, and asked me to go with him to Austria.' Because the man was a stranger, she naturally declined. Ten days later, after he was gone, my sister received a letter from her son, informing her that he was sending an Austrian to her with whom he had made

258

some arrangements. She should marry him (in name only), so she could leave the country legally. Unfortunately, my sister Vicky received his letter too late; the man had already returned to Austria, as his visa expired (the mail was too slow in Hungary). So, my poor sister remained in Hungary.

Her son also sent us a message that if we were able to get out of Hungary, he would be able to help us. We were faced with the problem of getting to Vienna. But how? I went to the passport office and asked for a passport.

In the meantime, I met at one of my relatives' homes a woman called Mrs. Bellak. Mrs. Bellak's husband was an academic, so we had no reason to suspect that she was one of the AVO informers. When she heard of our problems of wanting to go to Vienna, she laughed and said that 'nothing is easier than that.' When I mentioned to her that we had already gone to the passport office, she said that it was too bad, because she knew of a much easier and more certain way of getting out of Hungary. She said that we could meet with some Russians officers in a chateau in the Dunantul district ('Dunantul' is the name given to the entire area west of the Danube), and they would drive us to the Russian occupied zone of Vienna. She mentioned the name of a man from Rakosszentmihaly who would be willing to take us to the chateau – which was located in the Csorna area. She asked us for 1000 forint.

While we were still waiting for the approval from the passport office, I contacted a good friend of ours who used be one of the directors at the OKH, and lived in Rakosszentmihaly, to find out more about our would-be guide. His quick answer was, that under no circumstances should we trust that man.
'He has a reputation as a liar and of being untrustworthy.'

I informed Mrs. Bellak that we were not willing to go with the man. She was not lost for words, and promptly recommended someone from Sopron, whose friend had a daughter studying in Vienna and visited her every month. She stated that he could get us visiting permits from Sopron (near the Austrian-Hungarian border), so we could come and go to and from Vienna even every month. As we had a relative who lived in Sopron and was the managing director of the Eszterházy (prince) estate – we were comfortable with this idea. We thought that if we could not obtain the passport though the passport office, we would try this.

I made several trips to the passport office. One day, we had a visitor – the head of the passport office. He said that there would be no problem receiving our passport, if we paid him 20,000 forint. I promised him the money, as soon as we received the passports. He promised to bring them himself. We did not mention this to Mrs. Bellak. One day, she appeared at our house with a man called Sandor Rozsa ('Rozsa Sandor' in Hungarian). He was the man who was supposed to take us to Sopron, then come with us to the passport office there, where we would receive a special permit that would allow us to cross the border. They both asked us to go with them immediately to a lawyer whose office was on Apponyi square (tér), who would verify that indeed he had this type of permit and it allowed him to visit his daughter in Vienna, on a monthly basis. We went with them to see the lawyer – who verified what they had said, and also that he obtained the permit through Sandor Rozsa.

In the meantime, we were waiting to hear from the head of the passport office in Budapest but we soon read in the papers that he was arrested. This was the end of our attempt to obtain passports by official means.

Mrs. Bellak was an almost daily visitor at our house, asking us, what we were waiting for, as leaving the country was becoming more difficult with each passing day. The pressure was building from all sides; on one side, it was Mrs. Bellak and Sandor Rozsa, on the other, our inability to make a living. We had to decide soon ...

We were on very good terms with the Pálos (Paulist) fathers. They too had problems, similar to ours. Three of the

Paulist fathers wanted to leave the country. So, the head of the Paulist Order, Father Jeno, asked me if Sandor Rozsa could meet with him. After the meeting, as Sandor Rozsa gained Father Jeno's trust, we also felt more confident in trusting him in trying the previously discussed course. We decided that two of my relatives would leave with Father Tihamer, and my husband and myself would follow two days later with two other Paulist fathers.

Finally, it was the date of our departure, September 1, 1950. We said goodbye to my cousin. She broke into tears. 'Don't go, it is a set-up. They will imprison you.' Sandor Rozsa, in order to gain our trust, brought his wife and daughter to help us with packing. Finally, we were ready. As I sat on the train at the railway station, I saw from my window 2-3 men who came to say goodbye to Sandor Rozsa. Later, when I recalled the scene, I thought that I recognized one of the men – perhaps I had seen him at the passport office, or at the police station. The train finally pulled out, and soon we were passing the well known and often traveled countryside. We transferred at Gyor to the train that took us to Sopron, our destination.

When we arrived, I looked around at the station, as I wanted to say goodbye to Sandor Rozsa's wife and daughter. But they were nowhere to be seen, only Sandor Rozsa accompanied us. He was walking very fast – I could barely keep up with him. He was in a great hurry, and took my husband's small black briefcase as to 'help' him. We were practically running with him for 10 minutes, when I realized that he was trying to run away from us. I asked him why he was running - and the next minute we were surrounded by several men from the AVO. We were prisoners. It was a trap set by Sandor Rozsa, who had disappeared, together with the black briefcase.

We were taken to AVO headquarters for questioning. When I told them that the reason we came to Sopron was to obtain a permit in order to travel to Vienna, we were lined up, facing the wall, with our hands up. They took all our possessions, my jewelry, leaving only my wedding band. We were then put on

261

an open truck and taken to Csorna. There we were unloaded, taken to a barn, and told to sit down on the floor, facing the wall. We were not permitted to stand up or lie down. We were questioned again.

We were in the barn for 3 days, then put on a truck again, and were transported to the Gyor prison. Upon our arrival in Gyor(during the night), my husband and I were separated and I was taken to a cell, where I was to stay during the entire duration of the 'investigation.' The cell was dark and silent. I was assigned a narrow bed that was already occupied by someone. There were 2 straw mattresses on the floor, shared among five women.

To my surprise, there were some familiar faces in the room. Irenke, a frail young blonde woman, was one of them. She was trying to leave Hungary with her baby boy to join her husband in Argentina. At her first attempt, she hired an Austrian man who was transporting people across the border in a covered truck. There were 14 other people hiding on the truck when she got on with her baby. The other passengers were uneasy, and voiced their concern about being discovered by the guards and carted off by the AVO if the baby cried. They wanted her to leave. One man became so agitated that he grabbed the baby from the woman's arms and threw him out of the moving truck. The driver in the front, unaware of what was going on in the back, kept driving. Irenke jumped off the moving truck after her baby – who was fortunately unhurt. She was stranded in the countryside near Tatabanya. Finally, a farmer who was passing by saw her on the road, and offered her a ride to the nearest train station. She had no other choice, but to return to Budapest with her child. She tried to obtain a passport again at the passport office, but was told never to come back, as she would not be granted one. A 'friend' came to her aid, convincing her to somehow make her way to Pozsony (it was a Czech occupied territory near the Austrian border) and go to the cemetery, where the cemetery guard would take her across the border. When she arrived there, to her relief, she found a dozen or so others in the group. The guard then escorted the entire group - not across the border, but straight to the local police station. That was how she became a prisoner. She was transported to Gyor with the others. They took away her baby, who was then forwarded to his grandmother in Budapest. That was 6 months earlier, and she was still waiting for her 'case' to be heard in court.

Another acquaintance in the room was Jolanka, widow of the colonel who used to be in charge of the city of Tata. As her husband was an officer of the former Hungarian army, he was a 'class alien' (osztályidegen) and therefore, she did not receive a pension. After her husband's death, she stayed in the city, and was running a small chicken farm to make ends meet. Her housekeeper stayed with her and helped her. One day, the AVO came to search the house for papers that may have been left by her husband. As they didn't find any, they searched the pantry, and found a few dozen eggs she had put away, ready to be hatched. She was arrested immediately and charged with 'hording food.'

Jolanka was a great opera fan, and we used to whisper songs from various operas to each other.

Mrs. Berczy was another nice woman in my room. She was the owner of a very large needlework and embroidery store on Koronaherceg street. The store was 'nationalized' (taken away) and she was left without means to support herself. As her children lived in England, she tried to join them. Just as many others, she was tricked by someone, and was arrested at the Austrian border while trying to cross.

Among us was also a very sweet nun. Each evening we gathered around her bed to pray. She was brought to the prison on trumped-up charges. Her popularity and influence on the children in the village was not looked upon kindly by the Communists. They needed an excuse to remove her from the village. Thus, when some children set fire to a large haystack, the officials accused the nun of telling the children to do it. They arrested her and brought her to the Gyor prison.

Other women in my cell were of Jewish faith and had escaped the hands of the Nazis. They tried to leave Hungary with their family to join other members of their family in England. They chose the same route as Irenke – the cemetery in Pozsony, with the same guard – and they too were betrayed by the guard, and arrested. One of the five occupants of the two straw mattresses was a poor elderly sick Jewish woman in her 70s (she had breast cancer). I was very sorry for her and traded sleeping places with her. I didn't want to see her sleeping on the floor. That didn't bode well with some Arrow Cross women who were also in our cell, and from then on, I got dirty looks from them.

Two large buckets stood in two corners of our cell, substituting for a toilet, as we were not permitted to leave the room and use the regular toilets. The buckets were emptied twice a day by two of the prisoners. Unfortunately, the water we used for getting washed was also emptied in the buckets. When they were filled, we had nowhere to go – we suffered a great deal from such discomfort.

If the weather permitted, we were taken for a daily walk in the courtyard of the prison. Of course, talking was not permitted. Not far from our cell was the cell that housed the gypsies. They too were 'under investigation.'

I met seven other families in the prison who had been the victims of Mrs. Bellak.

When my prison guards found out what class I belonged to, they decided that I would have to do the most arduous work in the prison. Next day, I was assigned to the laundry room to hand wash the overalls of prisoners (men) who worked in the cement factory. The other women working in the laundry room were all gypsies. Because one had to stand in water on a cold cement floor all day long while washing the clothes, the women were given workman's boots to wear. All, except me. I had to stand in the water with bare feet while washing the clothes. We could not use soap for washing, only a hard brush to get rid of the cement.

The reason for using the hard brush was that the cement was extremely difficult to remove. As soon as it was immersed in water, the cement on the clothes hardened, and could only be removed by rigorous brushing under water. I was assigned 17 overalls for the day's work. From the corner of my eye, I saw the guards gathering and watching me to see if I would break.

I started singing in a very loud voice a popular country song: 'Ritka buza, ritka árpa, ritka rozs...' One of the guards came over to ask me why I was singing. 'Because the work goes faster,' I said. They all looked disappointed that I wasn't crying. I finished the work fast, and was taken back to my cell. That was the first and last time I had to do laundry duty. I was never asked to do it again.

Finally, we had our 'hearing' in court. It was a ready made decision. We were each sentenced to 2 years, because the court 'assumed' that our reason for traveling to Sopron was not to acquire a permit to cross the border (as we said), but to 'unlawfully leave the country.'

Later I learned that our house in Budapest had already been confiscated, and (ironically), had been occupied by the passport office. So, that was the reason that we had to be imprisoned – with the help of Mrs. Bellak.
They wanted our house!

After the hearing, I kissed my husband, whom I had not seen since our arrest, and on the same evening, I was transported to another prison, which was in the town of Balassagyarmat.

One day, an officer came to the prison asking us who would like to be transferred to another prison where extra seamstresses were needed. I volunteered, because I was becoming weaker by the day on the food rations. The other prison was in a small town, Kalocsa. It was a definite improvement over the other prison. The food was somewhat better, and we had the luxury of having a toilet instead of the usual bucket.

In the new cell, the room supervisor (also a prisoner) was Countess Eszterházy. Her husband was already in Austria. He had sent one of his people, a forest engineer, to help his wife and their two children across the border. They started by foot. However, the smaller boy couldn't continue the long journey, and they had to stop for a rest in the cabin of the forest ranger. The cabin was occupied by a group of AVO men who promptly arrested them. She was sentenced to four years.

In the Kalocsa prison, I fell into the same routine as before. We all said our evening prayers together, and after, I told my cellmates stories, so they would sleep better.

During our daily walks, we could see the steeple of the church of the Jesuit fathers nearby. I always quietly said my prayers during the walks.

There was an elderly woman, over 70 years old, among us. She and her husband owned a large apartment. Her husband was an avid hunter and owned some very expensive hunting rifles. When the new Communist government ordered everyone in the country to turn in their weapons, he pretended to his wife that he did. After her husband died, she had to rent out one of the rooms (in accordance with the law). She rented it to a quiet police woman. The 'quiet woman' searched her place while she was not at home one day, and found the guns her husband had hidden behind the paneling of the front hall. She reported it and the poor woman was arrested and was sentenced to 10 years. Her son, who was considered as an 'accomplice,' was sentenced to 12 years. She took it very hard, and cried a lot and was inconsolable.

One day a messenger pigeon flew on her windowsill, holding in its beak a page which someone had sent her from a prayer book. It dropped the page. She retrieved the paper through the bars. On the page was a prayer about the sufferings of the innocent and about the strength of faith. This had a huge impact on the woman. She was so elated with this 'message' that she never cried again. By the way, this is a true story, and the

266

message brought by the pigeon was witnessed by the other women in the cell ...

The months were passing very slowly. I seldom heard from my husband. The last message I received, 6 months before our release, was that he had to be taken to hospital and underwent surgery with a hernia on both sides. I was very worried about him. Finally, August 31 was our release date. When I arrived at the western train terminal in Budapest at 9 a.m. I quickly called my sister-in-law, who said that my husband had already arrived there the previous day. I took the nearest tram to the inner city church, to give thanks to God that we had both survived those two terrible years.

Long and difficult years followed the war, and I still did not hear from my son. But I always trusted in the Virgin Mary that she somewhere, somehow was protecting him. Every Christmas Eve, I set a plate on his empty place, waiting for him to come home. My prayers were answered. After 11 years, we learned that he was alive! During those long years, I never lost faith and truly believed that he was alive – and was waiting for him to come home.

*Earlier, at the end of the war, I had received a sign that our son was alive. The siege of Buda lasted 55 days. During that time our house was hit 126 times. The second floor where my son's apartment had been was in ruins. The ceiling had fallen in and everything, including the heavy furniture, was in shambles, with the exception of a porcelain statue of the Virgin Mary holding the Baby Jesus – a gift we had given to our son one Christmas. Among all the rubble, the statue stood unharmed. I considered this to be a sign by the Virgin Mary, who thus let me know that our son was alive."**

* Private Memoirs of Terezia Schandl, 1962
('Tommy' and 'Dan' are not their real names as their names have been omitted from this book)

AUTHOR'S NOTE

Sword of The Turul tells the incredible true story of my father, Karoly William Schandl, and his activities and experiences during and after the Second World War. He was unjustly imprisoned by the Soviet Union from 1944 until 1956, and was one of only a few dozen prisoners assigned an identification number in the entire Soviet penal system. The Soviets assigned prisoners numbers when they considered them "high profile," and wished to keep them hidden from the rest of the world, by not referring to them by name. For the entire 11 years he was imprisoned in Lubyanka, Lefortovo, and Vladimir prisons, his parents had no word of him, and the Soviets denied having seen him, just as they denied seeing the Dutchman and the very famous Swedish diplomat while they were imprisoned.

The events described in this book happened.

The Timeline from page 271 until page 275 is completely authentic, though some names have been changed. "Dan" was not the name of the Hungarian born British agent that my father's anti-Nazi resistance group sprung from prison, where he was held as a POW, yet he, as a person, was very real, and I have endeavored to accurately describe what he did during and after that time. He *did* attend meetings of my father's anti-Nazi Hungarian resistance group, including one recorded by the Cave Church (Sziklatemplom) in November 1944, he *was* in hiding in my father's apartment from autumn 1944 to February 1945, and he *did* lie about the dates, etc. in his book of memoirs – which was based on his filed reports.

Karoly Schandl was officially arrested by the Red Army on December 8, 1944 (see scanned document on page 8). "Dan" claimed that he stayed at the Schandl villa only from around December 8 onwards and that Karoly was there in December and throughout January. This has been proven to be untrue. Had Dan arrived after December 4, he would never have met Karoly, as he was already in the hands of the Red Army! In addition, Dan made no mention of Karoly's disappearance - which occurred while Dan was staying at his apartment - nor did he acknowledge meeting the Dutchman. He also failed to mention that Karoly's

British led anti-Nazi resistance group sprung him from prison, and that a number of those resistance members were subsequently arrested by the Soviets and imprisoned by the NKVD and SMERSH – in the Soviet Union.

Karoly did indeed report to a British intelligence agent whose code name was "Albert," but his real name was not George. "Albert" was presumably killed by the NKVD/SMERSH around late 1944. He was an idealistic young Hungarian lawyer who was a school friend of my father's. He had also belonged to the Catholic Piarist School Boy Scouts, as did Karoly and all the others in that anti-Nazi resistance group. A number of them were of Jewish origin.

"Albert" reported to "Jack." Jack, the Polish friend from the Boy Scouts who recruited the members of the group for British intelligence, was real. He was an ISLD agent and had a few aliases.

"Tommy" was real, though his name has been changed. Everything written about him is accurate. He was my father's Jewish school friend whom he hid in his apartment at 16-18 Kelenhegyi Street ("Dan" later hid there, too, while Tommy was still there). Tommy stayed at the Schandl villa from June 1944, until the war was over. He ended up in Australia, where he was killed in a car crash in 1959.

Sam and Nick are composites, in order to protect identities. The friends did, after all, have a pact which I did not intend to break by writing this book. *It should be mentioned, however, that "Sam" did have an OSS contact – who later became CIA.*

The Dutchman and the Swedish Diplomat were real individuals. According to my father, Karoly - the Dutchman worked for the Diplomat. Both were imprisoned by the Soviets. Neither one survived.

Father Vezer and the priests mentioned in Terezia's memoirs were also real and their real names have been used. Father Horvath, however, is a composite of all the wonderful fathers of the Cave Church with whom the Schandls were in contact.

It is a great tragedy that "Albert," the Dutchman, the

Diplomat, "Tommy," Sam's brother, and the Head of the Cave Church – Father Vezer – were all casualties of this horrific time.

Other characters based on real persons were Mark, the Polish officer Karoly met in a Soviet prison; Mrs. Kovacs, the retired nurse who was killed during the bombing; Ferenc, the friend who was too afraid to be Karoly's friend after he returned from the Soviet prisons; Anna, with whom Karoly stayed prior to escaping Hungary; Mrs. Kis and her son, who hid their suitcase of documents at the Schandl villa; Esther, the Jewish hairdresser Terezia helped; and Joseph, the boy the Arrow Cross found in the guard's booth at the Bokreta Home for Working Women.

Sister Sara was the real name of the courageous sister in charge of the Bokreta Home. She was shot in the back of the head by the Arrow Cross, on the banks of the Danube River, three days before Christmas in 1944.

All of the people Karoly met in the Soviet prisons were real. The excerpts from Karoly and Terezia's memoirs are actual excerpts.

Mrs. Bellak and Sandor Rose (Sandor Rozsa) were the names of the AVO informers/agents who arranged the arrest of Karoly Senior and Terezia Schandl, when they tried to flee Hungary in 1950. Their names have not been changed, though it is not certain that Sandor Rose (Rozsa) gave the Schandls his real name, as that is also the name of a highwayman in Hungarian history. *A detailed account of these two AVOs' tactics can be found in the excerpts from Terezia's memoirs (Chapter 28).*

Finally, it should be mentioned that there are presently three international historians who are in possession of Karoly Schandl's memoirs - and those memoirs contain the real names of the major players in this true story (i.e. "Dan," the Dutchman, the Diplomat, "Albert," "Jack," and one of the group members who was imprisoned at the same time as Karoly).

The Roman Catholic Church also has a copy, for the fathers and brothers of the Cave Church (Sziklatemplom) were indeed among the unsung heroes of that time.

Catherine (Kati) Eva Schandl

TIMELINE

July 20, 1912 – Karoly Schandl is born in Budapest, Hungary.

1921 – Karoly Schandl Sr., his father, becomes Hungarian State Secretary of Agriculture and calls for land reforms in Parliament.

1928 – Karoly Schandl Sr. leaves his post as State Secretary of Agriculture, as he has been appointed President of the National Credit Cooperative (OKH). He remains a lifetime Member of the Upper House.

May 1930 – Karoly graduates from Catholic Piarist High School, Budapest, Hungary.

1932 – A group of Hungarian Piarist Boy Scouts, including Karoly, attend Jamboree in Poland, where they make friends.

1935 – Karoly graduates from Petrus Pazmany University, Budapest Hungary, with a Law degree.

1934-1935 – Karoly spends a year as a postgraduate student at École Libre des Sciences Politiques, Paris, France.

1936-1937 – Karoly spends a year as a postgraduate economics researcher at Cambridge University, U.K (where one of his supervisors is John Maynard Keynes). He later returns to Hungary and becomes a lawyer.

1939 – "Jack," one of the Polish friends the Piarist Boy Scouts made at the jamboree, escapes war-torn Poland for Hungary, where his old friends shelter him. He later becomes ISLD, and recruits his Boy Scout friends for anti-Nazi resistance activities. The group is later led by "Albert," a Hungarian lawyer who is Karoly's friend. "Albert" continues to report to "Jack."

March 19, 1944 – Germans occupy Hungary.

May 1944 – As a reservist Second Lieutenant, Karoly is mobilized to serve as "Tactical Adjutant" with the H.Q. of Hungarian Defense Air Forces.

June 1944 – Karoly brings home Jewish friend "Tommy," whom he hides in his apartment.

Autumn 1944 – Karoly's anti-Nazi resistance group springs British agent "Dan" from prison and he is then sent to Karoly's apartment in the Schandl villa (Gellert Hill). He stays there until February 1945. The Cave Church is providing priest's frocks.

October 16, 1944 – Germany puts Arrow Cross in power.

November 1944 – Karoly's anti-Nazi resistance group has secret meeting in the Cave Church (Sziklatemplom). "Dan" attends.

December 4, 1944 – At the request of "Albert," now an agent of the British Intelligence Service, Karoly accompanies a Dutch Lieutenant over the fighting lines to the Soviet troops. The Russians are supposed to forward the Dutch Lieutenant to the I.S., and him to the allegedly newly formed anti-Nazi Hungarian government. The Russian NKVD arrest both men and hand them over to SMERSH.

December 22, 1944 – Sister Sara and the Jewish boy hiding at the Bokreta Home for Working Women are murdered by the Arrow Cross. The Arrow Cross take the names of all board members and vow to round them up the next day. Terezia Schandl, who has been hiding Jewish refugees at Bokreta and other homes, with false papers, receives the news from the frantic secretary.

December 23, 1944 – As the fighting has intensified, the Arrow Cross does not make it to the Schandl villa to arrest Terezia.
The siege of Budapest has begun.

Late December 1944 – "Albert" is believed to have been murdered by the Soviets (NKVD/SMERSH).

January 15, 1945 – Karoly and Dutch Lieutenant arrive at Lubyanka Prison. They are then transferred to Lefortovo. After a year with Karoly in the same cell in Lefortovo, the Dutch Lieutenant is removed. Karoly later learns of his death in prison.

February 15, 1945 – Swedish Diplomat comes to Schandl villa. Karoly is not at home. The diplomat meets with British Agent "Dan" *(as later reported to Karoly by Terezia).*

1947 – Soviets continue to deny any knowledge of Karoly's whereabouts or the whereabouts of the Dutch Lieutenant.

January 1950 – Still languishing in Soviet prisons, Karoly is "officially" arrested and accused of "contact with an anti-Soviet organization during the war – the British Intelligence Service."

August 1950 – Karoly is convicted to 25 years in prison by a committee, without trial, and is transferred to Vladimir Prison, where he is assigned an identification number. To the outside world, he is still "missing."

September 1, 1950 – Karoly Schandl Sr. and Terezia Schandl, with 2 relatives and 3 Paulist priests, are set up and arrested by the AVO. First taken to Gyor Prison, they are imprisoned for 2 years, for attempting to flee the country.

1951 – The fathers and brothers of the Paulist Order are arrested and imprisoned by order of the Soviets. The Cave Church is sealed. Father Vezer, head of the Cave Church, is sentenced to death.

1952 – Father Vezer is hung.

1952 – Karoly Senior and Terezia are released from prison. The Schandl villa on Gellert Hill and properties and assets have all been seized by the Communists.

1953 – Joseph Stalin dies.

1954 – General Abakumov is executed by a firing squad.

1954 – Karoly is transferred from the "Special Section" to the General Section of Vladimir Prison, Soviet Union.

November 1955 – Karoly is transported to Jaszberény Prison in Hungary to be "rehabilitated."

May 1956 – Karoly is released into the custody of Hungarian Communist authorities, who keep him imprisoned for 4 months.

September 25, 1956 – Karoly is freed, reunited with his parents in Budapest, but immediately goes into hiding.

October 23, 1956 – Hungarian Revolution (against Soviets).

November 4, 1956 – Hungarian uprising is crushed by Soviet tanks. Red Army is again looking for Karoly, who is in hiding.

December 4, 1956 – Karoly flees from Hungary, to Vienna, Austria.

December 10, 1956 – Karoly arrives in London, England.

January to May 1957 – Karoly is employed as a researcher, interpreter in England. He leaves after Whitehall refuses to listen to him about the RAF pilot and Allied anti-Nazi resistance members still imprisoned in the Soviet Union.

May 1957 – Karoly arrives in Canada, where he marries, starts to raise a family, after becoming a Chartered Accountant and university professor.

October 1959 – Karoly's first child is born.

December 1959 – "Tommy" dies in car crash in Australia.

June 1961 – In New York City, Karoly meets with an old

Hungarian friend from his resistance group (who has CIA contacts), as well as a former Soviet prison cellmate.

1961 – Karoly writes "The Yagoda Siren."

1961 – Two clean cut North American men in suits visit Karoly in his home in eastern Canada. After a lengthy discussion, they thank him for his help and inform him that his parents will soon be able to leave Hungary, due to an "exchange." They instruct Karoly to tell them to put in their application to leave. He does. It is accepted by the Communist authorities.

May 1962 –Karoly's second child is born.

1962 – Karoly Sr. and Terezia are permitted to leave Hungary, and arrive in North America.

1962 – Terezia writes her private memoirs.

May 1964 –Karoly's third child is born.

1972 – Karoly Senior dies.

1973 – Terezia dies.

1990 – Karoly William Schandl dies, at age 77.

1991 – Soviets finally withdraw all troops from Hungary. Communism has fallen.

1998 – Cave Church is re-opened.

Early 2005 – Dan's documented lies are discovered.

2005 – Karoly's memoirs and recollections are given to international historians, as well as the Paulist Order in Hungary.

Printed in Great Britain
by Amazon